Snake Island
Born of Shadows Book 5

J.R. Erickson

Copyright © 2018 J.R. Erickson

All rights reserved.

This is a work of fiction. Names, characters, places, and incidents either are the products of the author's imagination or are used fictitiously. Any resemblance to actual persons, living or dead, businesses, companies, events, or locales is entirely coincidental.

ISBN-10: 1726294803
ISBN-13: 978-1726294805

DEDICATION

For Matt – who always said yes to the next adventure. I'll see you again.

ACKNOWLEDGMENTS

Thank you to all of my family and friends who have been my avid beta readers, and to my wonderful husband who has supported my writing. Thank you to Rena Hoberman, my cover designer, and to my Born of Shadows fans who have read the series and offered feedback along the way. Thank you to various editors and proofreaders. It never ceases to amaze me how there's still a typo or two after five drafts.

CHAPTER 1

Abby recoiled from Ethel's dark laughter. She swiped the air and a wall of ice rose up between them. Ethel took a step toward her, flicking her fingers at the ice. It exploded at the same moment that Abby jumped backwards through the open window. Her back hit the roof and she slid, scrambling with her hands to grab hold of something to stop her fall. Slamming her feet into the shingles, she envisioned thousands of tiny ice filaments reaching from her body into the roof. As her head and shoulders slid off the edge, her back grew cold and she ground to a halt.

Ethel's head poked through the window and Abby felt a shudder of magic move through her body. A wave of fire coursed through her. She clenched her eyes against the pain as the heat slithered through muscle and bone. It melted the ice holding her in place, but she stayed rooted to the spot, held by whatever spell Ethel had cast over her. Abby could not blink her eyes or open her mouth to scream. Ethel lifted her hands and drew them back toward her. Abby's body floated, paralyzed, back through the open window and settled onto the floor.

In her mind, Abby screamed. She begged for Ethel to spare her child, but no sound emerged as the dark witch dropped to her knees beside her. She slid her black hood down and her long silver hair appeared electric, floating in the air and snapping with tiny bursts of light. When she touched Abby's belly, a jolt of current stunned her. She felt her teeth snap closed and her body twitched. Within her, Vidya shifted and rolled away from the sensation. The movement of her daughter was excruciating, like her baby would suddenly rip through the tender flesh of her abdomen.

A grotesque smile spread over Ethel's face as she hovered her palms above Abby's body. Abby's unborn daughter squirming within her. Ethel jerked her head up as something crashed through the window. A spread of white and brown speckled wings and sharp black-tipped talons appeared as a hawk soared into the room sinking its clawed feet into Ethel's hair.

She shrieked and fell back, trying to grab the bird as it raked its claws against her scalp. A stream of blood poured down Ethel's forehead. Abby felt the inertia lift from her body as Ethel struggled with the bird. Rolling sideways, Abby stood, wincing from the pain in her stomach and struggled to the window, climbing back onto the steep roof. She clutched at the eave above the baby's window and moved left. Pulling hard on the ledge, she scrambled up to the next level of roof.

"Sebastian," Abby screamed. The sound pierced the quiet. Abby climbed higher. She reached the widow's walk.

From the forest, she saw Oliver emerge, racing toward the house.

"Abby, what is it? What's happened?" Sebastian yelled back. He was in the house, moving towards the nursery and Abby suddenly had a horrible vision of Ethel killing him the instant he opened the door.

"No," she screamed. "Don't go in the nursery, Sebastian."

Oliver leapt onto the lowest level of roof, reaching her in three quick jumps and hopping over the rail where Abby stood, shaking.

"It's Ethel." Abby gestured frantically to the bay window that jutted from the baby's room.

Oliver turned as the curtains in the nursery billowed out and a figure jumped onto the roof. Abby backed into the iron rail, convinced another of the L'Obscurite emerged, until she saw Sebastian's familiar dark curls.

Sebastian spun towards Oliver. He spotted them both and grabbed the eave, jumping onto the widow's walk. When he reached her, he pushed the hair from her face and frantically searched her body.

"Are you hurt? I saw blood. Is it the baby?" he asked.

"Ethel? Did you see Ethel?" Abby demanded, shaking her head back and forth.

Sebastian glanced behind him.

"The L'Obscurite witch? She was here?"

Abby pointed toward the window.

"She was in Vidya's room. The doll..."

Ezra stuck her head from the nursery window.

"Is everyone okay? There's blood all over the floor in here."

Sebastian pulled Abby away, his eyes traveling over her.

"It's not mine. It's Ethel's, a hawk attacked her. Is she gone?"

"There!" Oliver shouted, pointing.

At the edge of their forest, a flash of dark slipped toward the shadow of trees - Ethel. They all saw her, but Sebastian acted first. He slammed his fist into the open palm of his hand. The house beneath them shook as a deafening tearing sound filled the air. Several trees ripped from their trunks and fell sideways. The boughs shook, and a plume of leaves burst into the air as the trees plummeted. Abby heard a high scream and knew that Ethel had been struck.

Oliver jumped to the roof and slid down the eaves, landing gracefully on the ground. He ran toward the woods. Sebastian helped Abby back into the house.

"Stay here," he told her, but she didn't listen and followed close on his heels.

Ethel lay trapped beneath a thick maple tree. It had caught her in the back and forced her into a crouching position. Her hands disappeared into ferns and dirt as the weight bore down.

Oliver had squatted in front of her.

"I've put a paralysis charm on her, but it won't last long. We need something stronger. Abby, send Lydie through the mirror. There are magic shackles in the dungeon at Ula. We need something that can block her element."

Lydie had already come in behind them.

"Got it," she said and sprinted back toward the house.

"How did you get in?" Sebastian fumed at the witch. Her dark hair shielded most of her face, but Abby thought she saw a twitch.

Abby bent to the ground, placed her hand above the soil and pulled water from the earth. She held it close to her mouth and whispered her intentions that this water bind Ethel's water to Abby. She had never tried the magic before, but feared that Ethel might come free of the paralysis charm at any moment. She sprinkled the water on the woman's head, and shivered as the power of the other witch traveled into her own body.

Abby surveyed the trees that Sebastian had toppled. They rested in an almost perfect triangle, creating a little cage. Had Ethel not been struck, the trees might have trapped her anyway.

Moments later, Julian burst into the clearing holding a long white link of chain. Faustine followed close behind. As Oliver and Sebastian lifted the tree, Julian and Faustine wound the chain around the witch. At her ankles and wrists, Faustine secured glistening black balls.

"Those stop the flow of magic from the chain," Julian explained as Abby and Sebastian watched them curiously.

Julian lifted the witch and her eyes looked venomous in her frozen face. He carried her back to the house where Lydie and Ezra stood. Julian pulled a black shroud from his cloak and pushed it over her head. Ezra grimaced.

"Is that really necessary?"

Julian glanced at her and nodded.

"I can't control what she does with her mind. It's better if she can't communicate her location."

"Where are you taking her?" Oliver asked.

Julian held a finger to his lips and pointed into the woods. Only Sebastian nodded as if he knew exactly where Julian meant. Abby realized that Julian intended to take Ethel to the underground tunnel that she and

Sebastian had escaped through months before when Kanti attacked them.

"The less of us, the better," Faustine told them. "I intend to examine her with the Crystal of Sight, and I prefer fewer energies in the space."

"I'm going," Sebastian cut in before anyone else could speak up.

"Sebastian, Faustine and I, then," Julian said. "Oliver follow us so that you know where we're at and then come back to watch the house."

"I know where it's at," Abby said.

"Good enough," Julian replied.

The three walked off. Abby watched as they disappeared into the forest. Although the woman was restrained and Julian and Faustine were superior witches, her stomach knotted with fear.

****

Sebastian pulled back the tarp and opened the door into the cellar. Faustine walked down first, creating a ball of light that banished the shadows. Ethel wriggled in Julian's arms, but the chains were heavy, and she had no access to her power. He set her in the corner and she slumped against the dirt wall.

"How did you get in?" Sebastian spat.

Ethel pressed her lips in a thin, ugly smile.

"Don't bother," Julian muttered. "We have ways to help her talk, but for now, let Faustine look into her mind."

Ethel's eyes darkened, but she did not look afraid.

Faustine took a silk pouch from his cloak and pulled out the crystal. He positioned it over his third eye and then whirled his hand in a sweeping motion. Four wooden chairs appeared in the room. Julian moved forward and lifted Ethel onto a chair. Faustine settled into a chair facing the witch.

Faustine watched Ethel for several minutes. He sighed and removed the crystal.

"She's not alone. An additional four L'Obscurite have come to Trager. They're renting a house near town."

Ethel remained expressionless.

"Why did they come?" Sebastian asked. "Revenge? Just to screw with us?"

Faustine pressed his lips in a line and looked like he'd rather not say.

"What is it?" Sebastian barked.

"They wanted Abby's baby. They intended to take Abby and steal her baby after the birth."

Sebastian made a strangled sound and Julian stepped closer to her, rage flashing in his eyes.

"They would have killed everyone if it came to that," Faustine continued.

"Sebastian," Julian cautioned.

Sebastian had felt the power within him growing and trying to burst into the room. He took a deep breath and blew it out. They were underground. He didn't want to collapse the ceiling, and bury them all.

"I'm going to check on Abby," he murmured, knowing if he continued to watch Ethel, he'd be unable to quell his fury.

"Send the women to Ula." Julian stopped Sebastian before he left.

He nodded and ran up the stairs, sprinting back to the house and watching the woods. He spun when a branch snapped behind him, but it was only a squirrel.

****

"Oh Lydie, you don't need to do that," Abby said, finding Lydie in the nursery scrubbing the red stains from the carpet.

Lydie glanced up, her curls falling into her face. She brushed them away, irritated.

"It's okay. I want to. The sight of blood gives me the heebie jeebies. There's a spell for this, but I can't seem to remember it."

"That's what blood does to a person," Ezra interrupted, walking in behind them. "Here let me."

Lydie scooted out of the way and Ezra leaned over the blood. She rubbed her palms together and spoke.

"Mother earth we seek you here
In this room so young and pure
Cleanse this space, take darkness too
Let this be our gift from you
Mote it be."

The blood vanished and a burst of sunlight seemed to spill through the window.

"Wow, thanks," Abby murmured, leaning against the wall. As the chaos of the moment settled, Abby felt her body grow heavy.

"You should lie down, Abby," Ezra told her. "We'll wake you if anything happens."

Abby rubbed her eyes and yawned. She couldn't imagine trying to sleep and yet her feet felt as if someone had poured wet sand into her socks. She moved heavily toward the door.

"Okay, just for a few minutes."

She went to her bedroom and collapsed, not bothering to change or pull back the covers.

****

Oliver met Sebastian on the porch.

"Find out anything?" Oliver asked, sensing Sebastian's distress.

"Ethel and four other L'Obscurite are in town. They intend to kidnap Abby to steal our baby after her birth and to kill everyone else."

"What?" Oliver spat. "That freaking psycho thinks she's going to kill us?"

"Who's going to kill us?" Ezra asked, walking onto the porch. "Ethel?"

"Ezra, we need you, Lydie, and Abby to go through the mirror to Ula," Sebastian told her.

"Because we're women?" she asked, narrowing her eyes at Sebastian.

"Abby is pregnant and Lydie is thirteen," Sebastian snapped. "You're welcome to stay if you'd prefer to fight."

"I think you should go, Ezra," Oliver told her. "Not because you're a woman, but because I'll be distracted if you're here and I need to focus."

"Abby just laid down, she's exhausted. We'll go when she wakes up," Ezra muttered stalking back into the house.

"That will be a fun conversation later," Oliver grumbled.

"Better a tough conversation than a funeral," Sebastian murmured. He noticed Oliver's surprised expression. "Sorry, that was uncalled for. I'm shocked this just happened. How did Ethel find us?"

Oliver gazed at the forest and then shrugged.

"She's a witch, a nasty one. I'm sure she has a dozen ways to find out things, most of which involve manipulating and hurting others."

Sebastian grimaced.

"I'm starting to understand the purpose of covens. We've lived here a few months and already been attacked by Vepars, a spirit and now a dark witch. What's next? Zombies?"

Oliver shuddered.

"Don't even say that. I still have nightmares about those dead things from the lair."

Sebastian frowned remembering the stench of the charnel ground. Just as he had that day, Sebastian had tapped into some hidden source of power to trap Ethel. Where had it come from? And how did he learn to control it?

"Wicked trick with the trees," Oliver added, as if reading Sebastian's thoughts. "She would have escaped if you hadn't done that."

Sebastian grunted.

"Now if only I could figure out how to do it again and this time, it's Victor I'd be trapping."

****

Victor paced the underground room, ready to claw at the walls, the floor, his own eyes if it would stop the burning in his veins. Alva held the amulet, turning it in his sharp bony fingers, touching the snake's pulsing red heart.

"Truly a dilemma we have here, young Victor," Alva murmured, his eyes glowing in the jewel's sparkle. "You failed to cross over, to seal the power within you." Alva clicked his tongue.

Victor's skin crawled, his hands shook, his eyes felt dry and itchy. He couldn't stop trembling and it enraged him, the weakness, the failure.

Was there also a twinge of guilt? He had forsaken the guerrilla witches, Abby, the Coven of Ula… If he had risen to power, none of it would have mattered. He would have met his destiny and left behind the witch's burden - harm none. But now, living in both worlds, the shame pervaded his magic. Conjuring a puff of air nearly crippled him.

"She wanted me to fail," Victor whispered, pointing a trembling hand at the amulet.

Alva sneered.

"She will free us."

"But if we lose Clyde, we lose everything…" Victor mumbled.

Alva snapped dark eyes toward the ceiling as if he could see beyond the confines of the dungeon.

"Don't speak his name. You will call him to us."

Victor started to respond, but already a subtle shift had begun. Alva's features changed. His eyes grew darker, sharper. They trained on Victor and held him in their pointed glare.

Victor swallowed and tried to look away, but he remained transfixed watching Clyde who watched him.

"There is still time," Clyde crooned, as if speaking to a small child. "And a gift has arrived. A coven of superior power and their leader already weakened."

Victor listened, almost afraid to hear the answer.

Clyde, in Alva's body, held out his palm. An orb of light glowed in his hand and Victor moved closer. He saw Julian carrying a bound, but otherwise still, Ethel. Sebastian and Faustine followed him into the woods. The scene dissolved, but another rose in its place. Maze and Sabre, two of the L'Obscurite that Victor had met months earlier, roamed the streets of Trager. They stood out in their long black cloaks, elbowing through the crowds with little regard for the tourists who gawked as they passed.

Clyde closed his hand.

"Do you understand what you must do?" Clyde asked, curling back his lips to reveal Alva's dark tongue.

Victor nodded.

"Night is your ally, use it," Clyde whispered.

CHAPTER 2

Abby woke to a flutter against her cheek. In the realm between dreams and waking, she saw a blood covered hawk - his wings beating against her face. She gasped and pulled away from the bird, opening her eyes to find not a hawk, but Sebastian sitting on the edge of the bed.

"I'm sorry to wake you. You looked so peaceful," he told her, leaning down to kiss her head.

"Did something happen with Ethel?" Abby asked, pushing up to her elbows.

"No, but we want you, Lydie, and Ezra to go back to Ula."

Abby squinted at him, not fully awake.

"And leave you here alone with her? No."

Sebastian took her hand.

"Ethel has back-up in town and you're the target, more specifically our baby."

"What?" Abby put her hand over her belly.

"Just go to Ula, honey. We'll…"

"You're staying here to fight them?" she shook her head no. "They're dark witches and you're outnumbered."

"It's okay," Sebastian assured her. "Julian, Oliver and Faustine are already making a plan. Plus, we have Ethel. The L'Obscurite won't do anything to jeopardize Ethel."

"But what can you do?" Abby asked, fear edging in. "Kill them? What will possibly make them stop? They'll just come back again."

"No," Sebastian disagreed. "Faustine has been around for a long time. He'll know magic that will get rid of them for good. I'm sure of it."

****

"It feels wrong, being here," Ezra complained later that evening as she smoothed a sheet onto a bed in the healing room. "They're sitting ducks. If Ethel knew where Abby's house was, so do the other L'Obscurite."

Helena smiled and handed her a spray bottle of lavender to spritz on the bed.

"Faustine is brilliant and Julian is fierce. Oliver has been hunting and tracking for years, and what Sebastian lacks in magic, he makes up for in passion. Have faith, Ezra. Dark magic is convoluted. It is powerful, yes, but it is not aided by Mother Nature and she is the greatest witch of all."

Ezra finished the bed and started on the next.

"Still, I should be there. More of us should be there. Is it always this way? The women stay home making beds and the men go fight?"

Helena chuckled.

"I've seen plenty of fights, and I promise that Oliver has made many a bed in his time. No doubt Julian and Faustine are planning to set a trap for the L'Obscurite, which work better with fewer witches to keep track of. It wasn't an insult, Ezra, only a precaution."

Lydie wandered into the Healing Room looking agitated.

"What is it Lydie?" Helena asked.

"I'm worried about Oliver. I mean, I'm worried about all of them, but Oliver especially. I..." she cried and Helena pulled her close.

Over Lydie's head, Ezra looked equally emotional. Though it was not sadness in her face, but anger.

"Elda's mind is open to Faustine. She knows moment by moment what is happening. If they need us, we have only to step through the mirror and we'll be there. Don't be afraid, dear," Helena told Lydie.

"I'm going to sit with Elda in the library," Ezra announced. "I want to be ready if it comes to that."

****

"I could have consummated the ritual," the Vepar Fritz hissed. "And I thought he had to do this alone."

Fritz paced around the lair, his hulking form blotting out the door.

Alva had already begun to shift, dropping to all fours. His spine arched and he bared his teeth. Wide leathery wings burst from his back. He groaned and roared as his human body lost its shape and the skin-walker emerged.

Fritz fidgeted and stole glances at his master, hissing and salivating, grumbling under his breath. He needed to feed. It had been months since their last sacrifice and each day he lost power.

"Change," Alva shrieked in the strange animal voice that the skin-walker possessed.

The other vepars in the room, less vocal than Fritz, immediately dropped to the ground and started to shift. Fritz wanted to complain, but the black hatred in Alva's eyes deterred him. He fell to the floor in a ball of writhing, screeching pain. The transformation that turned him from man to monster felt like hot knives ripping apart his flesh. After the ripping another sensation emerged, his skin grew taught - stretching wider, further. Wings exploded from his back and claws from his hands and feet. His eyes bulged and his jaw snapped as his face grew long and wolfish.

Fritz had followed Alva blindly for decades and then Tobias after him, but this new master, Victor, smelled of the stink of prey. He wanted to rip his head from his neck each time he walked into a room. And now tonight they would do his bidding. They would help him rise to power so that Fritz could again bow to a new master.

He snapped at another of the skin walkers that stepped close to him.

"Go," Alva snarled.

They shuffled from the room, awkward, a huge pack of winged animals vying for space in the tunnels beneath the earth. When the cave yawned, they took to the sky. Fritz spread his wings and soared higher, wind whipping his sore body. They followed Alva who arced over Trager City and then dove toward a patch of woods that lined Lake Michigan. The darkness offered them shelter. They landed in the trees, their bodies huge and heavy, causing branches to snap and night animals to scurry in terror.

Fritz followed the lift of Alva's long snout. He too sniffed at the air finding the scent. The reek of witches was horrible and delicious. He could barely hold still as his hunger took hold.

Tucked deep in the woods, a house blazed with lights. A witch stepped through the doorway. He walked to the edge of the porch and lifted a cigarette to his lips, lighting it with the tip of his finger. He took a long drag and blew the smoke into the night. Fritz watched the smoke form into a mouth with long sharp fangs. Fritz grinned. Perhaps the witch foretold his own future through the figures in the smoke.

Alva nodded toward Fritz.

"Mine," Fritz grunted taking flight. He swooped through the trees, relishing the look of terror on the witch's face as he spotted the monster crashing through the forest toward him.

Before the man could scream, Fritz sunk his sharp talons into his shoulders and plucked him from the porch. He pulled up and rose into the sky as the witch's howl echoed through the trees.

As the other skin-walkers descended upon the house where the L'Obscurite waited for their leader to return, Alva took flight. As he flew, the rumblings of his hunger panged him. The night smelled of witches, their powerful blood drifting on the currents air. He dropped lower, hovering, and then felt the blackness edge into his vision as Clyde entered him.

Clyde swooped through the trees knowing he would find the back door to the cellar open and waiting - Ethel unprotected inside. They had abandoned that post for only a moment, but it would be long enough.

****

Despite her nerves, Abby slept. In her dreams she ran from phantoms, ducking through doorways and down stairs only to see the shadow ever looming behind her. She woke, sweaty and twisted in her covers only to fall back asleep.

The next dream had an edge of clarity, of realness.

Abby stood in the woods outside her home. On the porch behind her, she could see Oliver sitting with his bow and arrow. Julian paced along the beach. She drifted toward the trap door and down the stairs. Ethel sat shackled in a chair, her eyes trained on the dark tunnel opening deeper into the woods. Abby and Sebastian had fled down that tunnel. Abby wondered if one of the witches had blocked the other side.

A low heavy breath came through the tunnel, a panting sound. Something large seemed to be moving toward Ethel. It scraped against the floor and walls. Abby saw two shining yellow eyes. Ethel saw them too and tried to wriggle in her chair, but the chains stunted her movements. Abby sensed the power within Ethel, her desperation to escape, to defend herself, but again the chains, bewitched, kept her magic as captive as the woman herself. A long face, dark with matted hair, moved from the tunnel. Pointed fangs poked from its muzzle, and the eyes, human, trained on Ethel hungrily.

Ethel's scream pierced the quiet.

Abby sat up gasping for breath. She held the blankets balled in her fists. Disoriented from sleep, she half fell from the bed in her haste to get to the door. She stumbled down the spiral staircase, still struggling to catch her breath. She found Elda dozing in the library, a cold cup of tea on the table beside her. Faustine had promised to stay connected telepathically to Elda so they could send messages if needed.

Abby glanced at the tall mirror, shining in fire light, and almost stepped through, knowing in an instant, she could be back at her home in Trager.

She turned to Elda instead and shook her. "Elda?"

Elda's eyes snapped open, and she sat up.

"What is it? Abby?" she looked around the room, alarmed.

"I had a dream. You need to contact Faustine."

Elda nodded and rubbed her eyes. "Yes. Tell me."

"A skin-walker attacked Ethel in the tunnel."

"Just now?"

Abby nodded. "It was real."

Elda closed her eyes and Abby studied her face, trying to discern the emotion that passed, but she remained stoic.

Elda blinked and looked at her.

"They know," she whispered. "Ethel is gone."

****

"We heard her scream," Oliver explained in the library at Ula. He, Sebastian, Faustine and Julian had crossed back through the mirror after Ethel vanished.

"It was a skin-walker," Abby repeated.

"But how did it break her chains?" Elda asked, rubbing the crease between her eyebrows.

"It didn't," Faustine said. "It took her, chains and all."

"By the time we got to the cellar, she was gone," Sebastian said. "Her scream was the only clue that something had happened."

"Why wasn't anyone with her?" Abby asked.

"Faustine walked in the house to use the bathroom and I wandered away from the tunnel because I heard something in the woods. They must have been watching and waiting," Sebastian admitted.

Abby glanced at Faustine, surprised he would bother with a bathroom at such a critical moment.

"Why did the skin-walkers go after her?"

"Vepars feed on witches, Abby. Their blood makes them powerful," Julian reminded her, as if she'd regressed to a child who knew nothing of the witches' enemies.

"I know that," she told him, keeping her voice even. "I mean, why did they go into that tunnel to attack her? Why didn't they attack any of you? If they're just looking to feed, they had a whole house full of witches fifty feet away."

"I agree with you, Abby," Elda noted. "Vepars want new witches. Ethel would not be an easy sacrifice. They must have had a purpose and, yes, how did they find her?"

Faustine moved towards Abby.

"I fear they found her the same way you found them, Abby. Through your mind."

Abby frowned and Sebastian wrapped a protective arm around her.

"They have access to Kanti's power. It makes sense they also have access to her knowledge. I believe she sent you that dream to alert you they took Ethel. I also think Clyde, who is still an entity, at least in consciousness, can access Kanti's mind as well. Maybe not all the time, but perhaps…" Elda trailed off.

"That's quite a leap," Julian interrupted.

"Maybe not," Elda murmured. "Abby drank the blood of the Vepars' ritual. I feel confident now it was Clyde's blood and that perhaps as we move closer to his transition back to power, his awareness grows, his connections to all of his kin deepen."

Abby shook her head, wanting to argue, but kept her mouth shut.

"Then nowhere is safe," she muttered.

"How do we block it?" Sebastian asked.

"There are ways to create a barrier between Abby and Kanti," Faustine responded. "That's our next step."

"And more importantly, how did a skin-walker access our property. You've done a hundred spells!" Sebastian demanded.

Julian nodded, thinking out loud.

"I almost hate to consider this, but perhaps the link is the key here. Blood is stronger than almost any magic. We can shield against your enemies, but we're fighting your ancestors, your blood. That connection may override the magic."

"Ugh," Sebastian threw up his hands and stomped to the window.

"What spells protect against blood? There must be some," Abby added.

"There are," Elda insisted. "We have rarely used them, but I will start my research tonight."

"What about Ethel?" Oliver interrupted.

"I fear she is beyond our help," Faustine told him.

****

Galla stepped through the mirror, her long silver cloak shimmering in the firelight. Elda stood to greet her, and they embraced.

"The doorway is open for only another ten minutes," Galla reminded her.

"Yes, I know," Elda murmured, already pulling the long silver hair from the pouch. "We were lucky to find it on Julian's cloak. I can only hope you might give us some insight into what occurred."

Galla went to the window.

"Could we open this, Elda? A bit of wind will speed the process."

Elda gestured to the high library window, and it flew open.

Galla leaned forward and Elda fought the urge to hold the witch's shoulders. It was a dizzying drop to the Lake Superior rocks below. Elda had never been especially fond of heights.

Galla's face pinched with pain and she recoiled, flinging the hair away. The wind caught the single silver strand, and it rushed out disappearing into the dark horizon.

"Oh," she reached a hand forward as if she might draw it back, but her shoulders had sagged and she sank slowly to her knees.

Elda knew Galla not only received impressions about the fate of witches, she often experienced a direct connection to the physical pain they endured.

"What is it, Galla? Please tell me. We have only four minutes left." Elda sunk to the floor next to her friend.

Galla took Elda's hands in her own, looking at her with haunted eyes.

"He burned Ethel, Elda. He burned them all."

"All?" Elda asked, not understanding.

"Her coven. All who came with her to the north. I felt her calling out to them. She watched them die."

A cold trickle of sweat slid between Elda's shoulder blades and she convulsed, feeling sick to her stomach. She needed to help Galla, weakened by her vision, but felt rooted to the floor.

"Elda?" Faustine asked from the doorway. He had only peeked inside, but hurried to the witches when he saw them.

"What is it?"

Elda gestured at Galla.

"Help her back to the mirror, Faustine. I will explain after she is safely through."

Galla leaned heavily on Faustine as he lifted her and they walked across the room. A chilled breeze blew in from Lake Superior and sent a sheaf of papers on the desk rustling.

"Galla?" he asked, trying to read her face, but her lips remained pressed tight.

She offered him a nod before stepping through the mirror. Seconds later he watched the reflection change as the doorway to Sorciére closed for another week.

He returned to Elda and helped her shakily to her feet.

"What has happened, dear? What did Galla tell you?"

"He burned them, Faustine. Victor burned Ethel and the other L'Obscurite."

CHAPTER 3

The gray light of pre-dawn forecast rain. The earth, already damp with dew, leaked a pungent odor of scorched earth. Abby saw the blackened ground and briefly closed her eyes. Sebastian's hand grazed her shoulder, and then he and Julian moved closer to the burned ring, a near-perfect circle of blackened forest.

She had expected to see the bodies of the L'Obscurite, but no evidence of them remained. Perhaps the charred earth was worse somehow. Julian squatted and touched something Abby could not see. Her stomach rolled, and she swayed on her feet, feeling the world tilting beneath her.

"Whoa." Sebastian grabbed her and held her steady.

"Just a little dizzy."

"You shouldn't have come," Julian stated matter-of-fact. He had also mentioned it before they left the house and twice on the drive, but Abby had insisted.

"I'm okay," she assured Sebastian. "Really."

He released her, but stayed close, watching Julian move around the space, bending close to the earth and then shuffling to another area to examine things that Abby could not see.

Abby had almost died in the exact spot only weeks before as had Sebastian, Julian, and practically everyone she cared for. That memory hurt, but the scene before her caused a bubbling rage. Ethel had intended to kill her, to steal her baby, and yet Abby could not deny the absolute horror of that charred ground. The wind in the trees seemed to hold their cries of anguish. Abby wanted to stuff her hands over her ears.

A century ago, Dafne, Abby's ancestor, had watched her friends, her coven, burn in those woods. How many witches had perished in the Ebony Woods? How many of her own blood?

"It has to end," she whispered.

"What?" Sebastian asked, leaning close.

Abby walked to Julian.

"Did you find anything?"

He shook his head. "There's nothing left to find."

Abby retreated from the circle, wandering toward the trees. Beyond the raw, burned space, the forest was dense and fragrant. She took a deep breath of the dank foliage. It was not only scorched earth lingering in the space, but smells of burned flesh and hair. It was subtle, but hung like the tepid mist slipping off of Lake Michigan. She pushed her face into a thicket of glossy leaves and inhaled. As she pulled away, she spotted a single silver hair caught on a branch. She pulled it away and thought of Ethel - the dark witch with her long silvery hair and empty eyes. In some sick way, Ethel had gotten her revenge after all. She had helped Clyde rise again.

****

"This is our fault," Oliver barked, shaking his head in disgust.

He stood with Faustine, Julian and Elda in the library.

Faustine stared out the window, his back to the group. The dark lake stretched beyond the castle, illuminated by the moon.

"You're right. We weren't expecting a skin-walker. It was her coven we waited for. All of the magic we set up was intended to detect witches. It never even crossed my mind that Vepars would appear," Julian said.

"A skin-walker no less," Elda added, forcing a cup of tea into Oliver's hands though he tried to wave it away. "Drink it, Oliver. It will help you relax."

"Is this really a good time to relax?" he asked, nearly spilling the cup as he threw up one hand in exasperation.

"We wanted them to get in. We intended to trap them all in the cellar. The skin-walker took us by surprise. We left the backside open so that the L'Obscurite could enter and attempt to rescue Ethel," Faustine said, still not looking at them.

"Then we'd swoop in and slam the door and lock it. Ha," Oliver laughed and set his tea on the fireplace mantle. "Sounds like a plan that a group of thirteen-year-olds come up with to catch a stray dog."

Julian sighed. "You were there with us, Oliver. You had plenty of opportunities to disagree with the plan or offer your own."

Oliver looked angry and defeated. He sank into a chair and leaned his head back.

"I know," he sighed. "Except in retrospect, I feel like a complete idiot."

"The important thing is that everyone is okay," Elda murmured, going to Faustine and putting a hand on his shoulder. Still, he did not turn.

"Everyone is not okay," Oliver argued. "Ethel and those other

L'Obscurite are dead. Burned alive for Christ's sake! Elda if you try to hand me that rock, I swear I'll throw it through the window."

Elda paused, returning the hunk of black tourmaline to the desk.

"Oliver is right," Faustine sighed. "We lost sight of the real issue, Victor and Clyde. We played right into their hands. Abby sacrificed her own life to prevent Victor from rising. Now we turned around and gave him a coven to murder in our place."

"It was going to happen anyway," Julian argued. "Victor had to sacrifice a group of witches. Clyde couldn't transition otherwise. Do you honestly think they wouldn't have found some other unsuspecting coven to attack? Or worse, tried for us a second time?"

"That's not worse," Oliver said. "We were ready. We might have finished this once and for all."

"But we didn't," Faustine murmured. "The fates have something else in store for us."

Elda pulled on Faustine and eventually he allowed her to guide him to a chair. He sat down and gazed toward the fire. Though summer had arrived, fires burned year-round in the drafty castle.

"You believe Victor has taken the place of Tobias?" Elda asked.

"Worse." Julian intoned. "For a period, Clyde and Victor are one. Clyde is restored, and he has full access to his power and Victor's as well."

"Do we have any idea how long?" she continued.

"Not really, though what happened with Dafne here at Ula when she arrived in 1908 lasted only a couple weeks. That doesn't mean that Clyde's reign had ended, only that he stopped terrorizing us," Julian muttered. His eyes grew stormy as they always did when he recalled the violent encounter that took the life of his beloved wife, Miranda.

"Let's assume that Clyde has no more than a month to do his worst and then some balance is restored and Victor takes back his body," Faustine thought out loud. "Are we better off trying to destroy Victor while Clyde has full control or would our chances improve if we wait?"

"We can't wait," Oliver interrupted. "Kanti has power too, and she directly opposes Clyde regaining power. She wants to be free, which means Abby, her mother, and the baby are in danger."

"I still don't understand why the Vepars would help Kanti…" Elda mentioned, searching their faces as if one of them could offer a suitable explanation.

"Vepars aren't the type to dutifully serve a master," Julian scoffed. "They'll shift their allegiance to whoever gets them what they want."

"Clyde can't have absolute power over the Vepars in his lineage because he draws some of that power from Kanti," Faustine offered. "She figured out how to tap into that channel. And I agree with Julian. She offered them something."

"She helped them transform," Oliver said suddenly, looking up. "None of us ever saw a skin-walker before. They couldn't change. Somehow she helped them transition."

"Maybe," Julian started. "But Sebastian saw drawings of the skin-walkers in Victor's room in Australia. They're obviously a product of his imaginings."

"What if he envisioned them, but never accessed enough power to create them? What if Kanti has been holding back all this time? Just because he used magic to trap her doesn't mean she wasn't fighting back from beyond the grave, preventing him from full access to her power," said Oliver, standing and pacing the room.

"I agree with you, Oliver," Faustine told him. "Perhaps it is a combination of Kanti growing stronger and Clyde growing weaker."

"Which would be wonderful if both were not our enemies," Elda murmured.

"Nora, the witch from Montana, said the amulet and dagger were both stolen from Serpent House. We have to destroy those items and anything else he created that gives him power," Julian said. "The truth is that they are linked. If we destroy Clyde, we eliminate Kanti as well."

"Which is what she wants," Faustine added.

"Can't we just kill Clyde?" Oliver asked. "I mean how does he continue to exist? Is he inhabiting those objects?"

Faustine wrinkled his brow and shook his head.

"Yes and no. I believe Clyde's body still exists. He was a hybrid, not a witch. He could not survive merely through bewitched objects. But is that body alive? I cannot say."

"Would Meghan know?" Julian wondered aloud. "I keep coming back to her. It was no accident we chose the Sky Mothers to help us destroy the curse. Clyde's deadly plans were born there. She still waits for him to return."

"But she's locked in a world of her own creation. We can't get in even if we wanted to, which I can tell you right now, I don't," Oliver said.

"Binda could speak with her at the pond," Julian continued, ignoring Oliver's arguments.

"You gave her a false amulet," Elda reminded him. "No doubt she's angry now."

Julian nodded.

"I need time to meditate on this, but Meghan is a resource for us, a reluctant one perhaps, but valuable nevertheless."

****

"I'll be a half hour, tops," Sebastian told her, grabbing his wallet from the counter.

"I'm fine, Sebastian. I promise, take your time. And don't forget the gelato! Sea salt caramel or Blondie Fudge Swirl," Abby told him, standing on tip-toe to kiss him goodbye.

He kissed her back, his hard abdomen pressing against her equally hard and huge stomach.

"I fear this baby is coming between us," he whispered, his eyes twinkling.

She laughed and pushed him away.

"Wait until she's laying in the center of our bed crying at 2am. You'll miss this beach ball body."

"I will miss it," he agreed. "But not for the quiet. I'll miss my gorgeous pregnant wife. You know you're stunning, right? I have to remind myself not to ravish you in your fragile state."

Abby grinned and shook her head appreciating Sebastian's ability to lighten the mood.

After their trek through the Ebony Woods, a cloud of despair had settled over her. Sebastian had insisted on cheering her up with a foot rub and a promise to get gelato and make lasagna for dinner. They couldn't escape the darkness surrounding them, but for a little while they could close the shades and imagine sunny skies.

"No ravishing until you get back with the gelato," she ordered.

"Yes, my Witchy Goddess. I am your loyal servant." He bowed out the door and Abby watched him drive away, experiencing the first pang of fear creeping back in.

She busied herself cleaning the kitchen, throwing out old food and searching for the box of raspberry leaf tea that Helena had tucked in some impossible to find location. Brewing a cup of tea, she scanned the kitchen for dust. A few Baboon fur balls floated beneath the refrigerator so she pulled on her rubber gloves, settling onto the floor for a good scrubbing. In the last several weeks, she found the urge to clean insatiable. She had never been an especially tidy person, a tiny act of rebellion against her perfectionist mother. Helena said she was nesting, which she found to be hilarious considering the penchant for birds to hover around their house at all hours of the day and night.

Abby mopped the dust and hairballs from the floor. A chill whispered along her neck and she shivered, rubbing her arms. The day had grown hot, the temperature at least seventy-five degrees, but the kitchen suddenly felt like a freezer.

"Sweaters in summer. Probably another funky pregnancy thing," she said out loud. Abby hoisted herself up and walked toward the living room, sure that Sebastian had discarded a hooded sweatshirt the previous evening.

She spotted it draped over the back of the sofa. As she reached to put it on, a spasm ripped through her abdomen. It wrenched like fire across her torso and she stumbled forward grabbing at anything to break her fall. She caught the back of the couch and braced her hands for support as a searing pain cut through her.

"Arghh!!!!" her scream tore through the quiet house.

The bulb in the lamp on the table next to her exploded.

The agony did not subside. It rose to a crescendo and held the peak. She hunched forward and dropped into a squat, resting her head on the back of the couch and closing her eyes. She grabbed a throw pillow and stuffed it into her mouth.

Pressure, like hands wrapped around her womb, squeezing, caused a terrible cramping that raged into her thighs. A pipe burst in the house. She heard the explosion and the sound of gushing water.

"What's happening?" she shrieked, dropping onto all fours.

The baby jerked in her belly as if trying to escape from something.

Abby crashed onto her back. Her head smacked on the wood floor, but the sensation barely registered. The tearing in her belly overwhelmed every other sensation. She watched the mound beneath her white shirt. It wriggled and shifted in a wave of motion that made Abby fear the baby would rip clear from her stomach and flop onto the floor at her side.

She pressed her hands into her rolling flesh and focused.

"Sshhh...shh..., it's okay," she whispered and even though it did not feel okay, she forced her energy to grow slow and thick and calm. Less like a turbulent sea, more like a placid river, barely moving, sleepy in its creek-bed.

The baby jerked again and Abby hissed as she watched her daughter shift to the other side of her body.

An enormous pressure invaded her. Abby thought her womb would rupture. She gasped and called upon her element, seeking the great body of water that lay just outside her home. The pressure eased and something dark slipped out of her. She sensed it more than saw it, a presence, a cold, slippery blackness that lifted away - Kanti. The room turned from cold to ice. The chill bit with such force that Abby's eyes ached. She continued to slow her breath, hands on the stiffness in her belly, chasing away the demon that had invaded her womb. She felt violated.

After several more pain-free breaths, Abby rolled to her side. She touched the floor, fearing a smear of blood or a puddle of water that would signal early labor. Nothing. The dry, smooth wood met her searching hands.

She shifted onto hands and knees and then slowly, like she had gained a hundred pounds since walking into the room, she climbed to her feet. The floor swam and tilted. Shutting her eyes, Abby shuffled to the front of the couch, and collapsed, resting her head in her hands.

She wanted to get out. To run from her own home and find Sebastian or Oliver or Helena. Yet her body would not obey her and anyway, where could she run to that Kanti could not follow?

CHAPTER 4

"I think she's trying to possess the baby," Abby sobbed.

She lay on the bed beneath their huge comforter. The crying had started when Sebastian returned, likely due to relief, and had continued for an hour.

It was not the pain that terrified her, but fear for her child.

"No." Sebastian shook his head, squeezing a pillow between his hands. "No, she can't, she won't. You're protected, you're blocked. Faustine assured me, nothing can get to Vidya."

He paced around the room, slapping the pillow against his leg, staring at every surface as if the answer might be sitting there just waiting for him to spot it. He glanced at her and then down at the pillow, throwing it on the ground. She watched his slow intake of breath as if seeking calm for her sake.

"She's angry with us. We let Clyde rise again. After it ended, I knew Kanti was lashing out to punish us," Abby told him.

Sebastian sat on the edge of the bed and pulled her towards him. She snuggled into his side and cried.

"We'll go to Ula," he murmured. "It's safer. We need the power of the other witches if something goes wrong."

"I'm scared, Sebastian. The pain. The baby was in pain. I felt her trying to get away."

Sebastian frowned and closed his eyes. His face looked drawn. Abby watched him trying to hold it together for her sake.

"Ula," he said.

****

"I should have been there," Helena fretted, shaking her head back and forth as she gently prodded Abby's belly. "I'm so sorry, honey."

Abby offered a weak smile, wincing as Helena touched a sore spot. Tenderness stretched across the mound of her stomach. Her hips ached as did her ribs and low back. She wanted to be surrounded with ice packs or soaking in a scalding tub. Both opposing sensations sounded better than her current discomfort.

"It wasn't your fault, Helena," Sebastian insisted. "I wasn't even there for Pete's sakes. I went into town to get ice cream of all things."

"Stop it, both of you," Abby murmured, closing her eyes at another tender push from Helena. "Kanti wasn't in the room. You couldn't have stopped her, somehow, she was in my body. I can't explain it. It was like she was attacking Vidya in my womb."

Helena inhaled a sharp breath. Sebastian's face contorted into a Halloween mask of rage and pain, and Abby regretted her words. She thought he might punch the stone wall and tried to think of a distraction. Helena picked up a bottle of lavender and spritzed it in his direction.

He frowned and swatted the mist away.

"Inhale it, you fool," she told him. "It will help you come down a few notches."

He took a deep breath and perched on the edge of Abby's bed.

Elda walked into the healing room carrying a tray of tea.

"Bridget sent refreshments. And I spoke with Galla. She's coming through the mirror in an hour to do a banishing spell for Abby," she explained.

"A banishing spell?" Abby asked, not bothering to take a cup of tea. She wasn't ready to sit up.

"Galla has a special ability to move into the experiences of others. It makes her vulnerable to psychic attack. She has a tool to block such things and has graciously offered to perform that magic on you."

Abby nodded, grateful, and also scared.

"It won't hurt the baby?"

"Of course not," Elda promised.

****

"I'm sorry I missed your wedding, Abby," Galla, the witch from the Coven of Sorciére, told her, as she spread a huge silvery blanket on the floor. "Although on second thought, maybe I'm not sorry."

Abby forced a smile, but after her experience that afternoon, laughter was scarce.

"It seems like a lifetime ago," Abby admitted.

"It was," Galla murmured, smoothing the creases from the blanket and beckoning Abby to lie down in its center. "Elda told me you died and came back. Do you remember?"

Abby moved onto the blanket and laid down, blinking up at the high stone ceiling. They were performing the ritual in one of Faustine's towers to enhance Galla's air element.

"No," Abby admitted. "I haven't wanted to think about it. I feel sick to my stomach when I remember that night."

Galla laid a cool, dry hand on Abby's forehead.

"I understand. Let's shift then. I don't want to muddy the spell with high emotion. Close your eyes, Abby."

Abby did as she was told. The blanket felt alive beneath her, the fabric undulated and shivered. The movement caused goosebumps along her arms and neck. Even her scalp tingled.

"Good, she's responding to you. I named this blanket Venus many, many years ago when she was given to me as a gift. I can only use her with witches of the divine feminine. Venus does not respond well to the masculine or perhaps they do not respond well to her."

Galla lifted the edges of the blanket and folded them over Abby. The fabric descended upon her, light, airy, more like a cool vapor than a tangible object. As the blanket settled over her face, she inhaled a charge like static electricity. For an instant, it transported her to a world of bursting stars raining streaks of light in every direction.

Darkness enveloped her a second time, and she settled into it, deeper, as if swimming in an ocean of black. And then Kanti's face loomed before her. A face filled with terror and tears. A face with a story to tell.

Abby stood at the edge of the forest as Kanti sang to the flames. In the wooden pyre, her baby, her tiny daughter, cried. The man, Clyde, the monster, danced and spun. He threw his hands into the air. His face looked wolfish. He was not a man at all. He was a demon in a man's body. When he heard Kanti's song, his dancing slowed, his body stopped and he turned on her, his face ugly with hatred and desire. He lunged and she darted into the woods, desperate to save her child and lead him away. As she ran, her belly ached with emptiness. Her womb called out for Nadie, the daughter she'd left behind. Her sore breasts filled with milk and made the running harder, slower, but still she ran. She leapt over down trees, splashed through a stream. He gained on her.

Kanti whispered a silent prayer that her child be protected. Before she went in search of Clyde, she had visited Agnes, the old woman in the forest. Kanti gave Agnes the last of her money, begged that she follow the smoke, find the baby and whisk her away. Clyde would never find her. The old woman was a ghost. She lived in the shadows of other people's stories. With Kanti's gold, stolen from Clyde, Agnes and Nadie would disappear. Kanti's child would never know her true name, nor her mother, her father, her blood, but she would be free. It was too late to undo his magic. Kanti had interrupted the ritual, but not soon enough. She saw the drop of blood where Clyde had pricked Nadie with his golden dagger. She saw the amulet around his neck. Even as she ran, Kanti felt pulled toward the amulet, a magnetism existed now. He had created a link to her and he could always hunt her and draw upon her magic. Kanti had known when she started out on that night that only her death would pull her power back from him, but she must die at her own hand.

Kanti raced through the trees and when the hole in the earth appeared, she dove into it. It was a lair, a series of tunnels, pitch black, but she'd been in them before. She wound through them, all the while hearing him behind her. He transformed. He screeched like an animal and his sound filled the caverns.

Kanti burst from the underground tunnels onto the cliff-side. She ran to the edge and jumped.

In her own body, beneath Galla's shimmering blanket, Abby gasped. She waited for Kanti to plunge to her death, but a black creature swooped from the sky. Sharp talons snatched her from the air.

"Noooooo," Kanti screamed and tried to break away. She had to die on her own. If Clyde killed her, he would own her forever. She fought against the claws holding her like a steel trap. Their sharp points pushed into her skin, only a nudge and they would puncture her. He flew her over the lake. Her only solace was that Nadie had been left behind. Clyde had not turned back to retrieve their daughter. No doubt he believed her safe for a while more, tucked in her wooden box crying for her mother.

An island appeared beneath them, and the winged beast dropped lower. He released her and Kanti fell. She hit the sandy earth with a thud, the air knocked from her lungs. She lay gasping, crying and stood when she heard the hiss of a snake. "Wischalowe," she whispered, the name Rowtag, the shaman gave to such serpents as these. The first snake struck her naked calf, his fangs sinking deep and holding. The next attacked her arm and then another bit her hand. Kanti kicked them off, but already the venom weakened her. She fell to her knees, knowing she must die in the lake, she must get there first and drown so that Clyde could not forever own her soul. Again, she stood and stumbled toward the water, desperate to let the lake claim her. Her feet sunk into the sand, her legs so heavy. She fell and crawled toward the water, but a crippling numbness spread through her toes, out to her fingertips. Kanti slumped forward in the sand. The snakes slithered around her. She whispered her child's name a final time "Nadie," before death came for her.

And then Galla lifted the blanket from Abby's face. She blinked at the suddenly bright sunlight filtering through the high tower windows.

Abby clutched her belly and rolled to her side. Her sobs echoed in the tower room.

"What happened, Abby?" Galla asked, kneeling beside her.

Abby shook her head and tried to release the grief and horror of Kanti's final moments.

"Kanti," she choked out. "Kanti showed me the end. Her death."

Galla nodded.

"I should have prepared you for that possibility," Galla admitted. "When we break the connection, sometimes there is a final surge to pull you in. She is gone now. Gone from your mind. You will have no more dreams from Kanti."

Abby nodded and tried to pull her knees to her chest as if she were a child, but her own child prevented the movement. She settled for an awkward crossed-legs pose and leaned forward, putting her head in her hands, and strangely mourning the loss of Kanti. She cried for her death, for her daughter, Nadie, left in the forest, and even for the emptiness in Abby's own heart now that the spirit had left her.

Galla rubbed her back.

"Sometimes it's hard letting go," she said. "But it must happen. Spirits are not meant to be in our heads or our hearts. You might grow to love them, but they are no longer of this world. They must move on. You are helping her to move on."

"How does it work?" Abby asked, touching the blanket and marveling at Galla's words. She didn't love Kanti. Right? Kanti wanted her to die. Kanti's release from the world depended on Abby's death, her mother's death and her child's death. Yet Galla's words resonated in some deep part of her.

Galla smiled.

"I love the curiosity of new witches. After a lifetime in a world of science, you're always searching for the levers and gears tucked inside the machine. It's a mystery. Magic that has traveled thousands of years. It is gifted to witches with minds who are quite open, dangerously so. It is our protection from psychic invasion. And now it shall protect you."

****

"Lovely to meet you, Adora," Galla told her, taking her hands and squeezing. She had hoped to meet the witch before she left Ula and as luck would have it, found her in the library.

Adora smiled self-consciously. Though she felt better, meeting new witches distressed her. Her hair, once long and obsidian, was slowly growing back as a dusting of yellowish fuzz, which she covered in a variety of Helena's scarves. Her skin looked sallow and her teeth felt loose and grimy.

"You as well, Galla," Adora said, forcing a confidence she didn't feel. "I recall seeing you at an All Hallow's Ball or two over the years, though I must admit my memory is slow to return."

"I'm not surprised," Galla replied, sitting on a chair close to Adora. "You went through a terrible ordeal."

Adora nodded, not allowing the memories to gurgle up from the mountain of rock she'd pushed them beneath.

"I hope to ask you a few questions about your experience, Adora. But I understand if you're not ready to talk about it."

Adora could see pain behind Galla's eyes. It hurt to remember, but she would not deny the witch any answers she needed.

"Please, go ahead. I'll tell you what I can."

"One of our Sorciére witches vanished with Dafne. Her name was Indra. We know the spirit Kanti possessed Dafne, but not what became of Indra. I sensed..." Galla paused and swallowed. "I sensed that she died."

Adora sighed and bunched her hands in her robe to quell their shaking.

"There was another witch in the lair. I never saw her, but I heard Tobias and Alva speak of someone who wasted away under Kanti's possession. I believe Kanti possessed her first. Perhaps they were saving Dafne because she offered direct access to Abby and the witches of Ula."

Galla pursed her lips and nodded.

"We suspected as much, but I hoped for confirmation. This may be the most I'll ever know."

"I'm sorry I can't help you more, Galla. It's all quite hazy. The only contact I had with others happened during the possessions, and I only experienced consciousness for fleeting moments."

Galla stood and leaned forward, placing something in Adora's hand.

"You will recover, Adora. I can see it," she told her before moving toward the fireplace. She offered a small wave and then stepped through the glass.

Adora looked in her palm and saw a small yellow stone. It was an omen stone, given to those whose fortune would soon change. Adora had never received one before. She pressed it against her heart and closed her eyes.

****

"I believe we have a good grasp on this curse, especially considering Abby's dream of Kanti's baby in the pyre. It's clear Clyde was attempting to curse the child, and Kanti was trying to stop it," Elda said, stoking the fire.

After Galla returned to Sorciére, they had gathered on the stone patio and Abby had divulged her vision of Kanti's death.

"Which didn't work," Sebastian cut in. "I mean, right? We're in the throes of it right now."

"Maybe it did work," Elda disagreed. "Clyde only has access to a new body every one-hundred years. I doubt that was his intention. Perhaps Kanti's interference caused the gap. It ultimately saved her child and her children's children. Generations would pass before he would have access to another in the bloodline."

"I think so, too. Kanti wanted to protect her child," Abby added. "In the beginning I felt her hatred of their child, but then it shifted. She loved her daughter. She died saving her."

"What about all the women who have died in your family, Abby? And how about Dafne? Kanti didn't come to your house to make friends," Helena reminded them, setting aside her knitting needles and standing up. She stretched her arms overhead. "It would be quite a stretch to say she's on our side."

"I didn't say she was on our side," Abby told them, taking a cookie when

Bridget held out a tray.

"Lemon blueberry," Bridget hummed.

"But I still believe it was Clyde who placed the curse," she finished.

"Obviously he did," Julian agreed. "He was the one who would benefit. But Kanti is equally dangerous, especially where you're concerned, Abby."

Abby nodded, chewing, and unconsciously placed a protective hand over her belly. Sebastian put his hand over hers.

"Kanti's also using the Vepars," Oliver cut in.

"Tobias and Alva seem to think she's helping them. As if they all have the same goal," Julian agreed.

"Which would be?" Sebastian asked.

"To end Clyde," he stated.

"But why would the Vepars end Clyde?" Helena argued. "He created them, he's their source of power."

"No," Elda shook her head. "He's the one siphoning the power, remember? All the death, the magic objects, the rituals. All those things support Clyde. According to the information Faustine has read in that Egyptian spell book, Tobias and Alva are bodies for Clyde so he can enter the world."

"Does he know Kanti is working with the Vepars? Why doesn't he just possess them and put a stop to it?" Helena wondered out loud.

"Because his consciousness and his energy are with Victor. This is the only time each century where Clyde's focus is elsewhere. Which is why she is choosing this time to make her move," Julian explained.

Abby pushed her hands through her hair and shifted in the metal patio chair. Her pregnancy had reached an uncomfortable stage. She felt large and cumbersome.

"Put your feet up here, honey. I'll give them a little rub." Helena patted the stool in front of Abby and she obliged, lifting her bare feet and leaning her head back on the chair. Helena paused and closed her eyes, frowning.

"What is it?" Elda asked, sensing her change in demeanor.

"This baby will come early," Helena murmured, holding Abby's heels.

Abby sat up and Sebastian's face darkened.

"How early?" he asked.

Helena frowned and shook her head.

"During this moon cycle," she said.

"The new moon was over a week ago," Oliver offered.

"What does that mean, Helena? Soon?" Abby asked, sacred.

"Could your vision change?" Elda asked. "Or is this a future already happening?

"We can't stop it," Helena sighed, releasing Abby's feet. "But we can prepare. I'll come to your house every day to check on her."

"Is she okay?" Abby asked, touching her stomach and wondering if

Kanti had hurt.

"I think she's just fine," Helena reassured them, "but she's coming into the world earlier than planned."

"Two months earlier," Abby objected. "How can that be okay?"

"She's growing fast. Magic in her blood, your special blood," Helena continued as if watching a movie only she could see. "This little girl is strong."

CHAPTER 5

"I thought you were buying a birthing tub," Abby laughed. She found Sebastian and Oliver in a little alcove of wildflowers close to the house. Sun shone through the canopy of trees overhead.

They stood in the center of a huge basin built from boulders. It looked like the kind of nature jacuzzi a spa in Montana would advertise. Sebastian pressed a silver lining inside, and when Oliver touched the material it took on a shimmering glow.

"Only the best for the future little Hull," Oliver laughed. "It looks thin, Abby, but it will feel like satin pillows once you're in here."

Sebastian grinned.

"Our baby can come into the world under the stars," Sebastian grinned, gesturing towards the opening in the trees overhead. "And later we'll have a hot tub made of rock. Who wouldn't love that?"

"Oh, I love it," she promised him. "It's your backs I'm worried about."

Oliver cocked an eyebrow at her.

"You think we carried these? I'm an earth element, Abby."

She laughed.

"Good point."

"Lydie's bringing some enchanted lights from Ula, and judging from all of Helena's totes, she plans to stay here for a year after the baby's born," Oliver told her.

Abby grinned and Vidya shifted within her.

As she watched Sebastian and Oliver build the birthing pool, a shiver of fear ran down her spine. The birth was becoming real in a way that left her unable to think of little else. She didn't have much experience with birth. Her mother had never shared her own birthing story and Aunt Sydney had never had children. It relegated her knowledge to movies and random blips on the internet. When she found out she was pregnant with Vidya, she knew there would be no hospitals and epidurals involved. Though she imagined magic offered far more powerful numbing agents if need be. Except she didn't want to be numb. It was strange to admit, but she wanted no barriers when Vidya came to into the world; she desired perfect clarity.

****

"Did your mom ever tell you about your birth?" Abby asked Sebastian as he rubbed coconut oil onto her feet and legs that evening.

She sat next to the fireplace in their bedroom, her feet propped on a large ottoman and her head leaning on one of Helena's warm rice pillows.

Sebastian glanced up. The fire light added an orange glimmer to his blue eyes.

"I was born in my parents' bed," he said, continuing to rub. "My mom told me I must have gotten lost on my way out because she spent two days in labor."

"Two days?" Abby shrunk away from the thought.

"Not active labor," he promised. "For the first twenty-four hours, the contractions were easy, she said. Her partera, or midwife, was a woman from Mexico named Elena. My mom had met her at an art gallery while she was pregnant. Apparently, my mom asked her that same day to be her midwife."

Abby laughed. "And she didn't even know her?"

"Nope." Sebastian shook his head. "She was a good judge of character. My dad always joked that she dreamed her midwife into being. She worried about having a hospital birth because she hadn't found a midwife and she was already five months along."

"Why didn't she want a hospital birth?"

Sebastian shifted next to her chair.

"Here, scoot forward and I'll rub your shoulders too," he said. "She didn't believe birth should happen in a place where people were sick and dying. She believed in modern medicine for broken bones and major disease, but thought it had no other place in our lives. I have to admit, I share her feelings. I haven't been to a doctor in more than a decade."

Abby groaned as he pushed into a knot beneath her right shoulder-blade.

"Oh, right there. Yes. Ouch, but no, keep going." Abby laughed. "My mom used to take me to the doctor a lot. Vaccinations, flu shots, runny nose, you name it and we were in the emergency room. She worried a lot about illness. Now that I know what happened between her and the Lourdes, I'm starting to understand the paranoia. Fortunately, her neurosis didn't rub off on me and I agree with your mom. Why introduce a newborn baby into a place filled with disease? I've tried to imagine giving birth in a hospital and it seems so…"

"Sterile?"

"Yeah and disconnected. Vidya coming into the world is its own kind of magic."

"It is," he agreed.

"I guess it's easier to justify a home birth when you have magic," Abby continued, wondering if she'd be heading to the hospital if she were not a witch.

"I think everyone has to follow their inner knowing. If it doesn't feel right, don't do it. Life is much simpler that way."

He opened her robe and rested his large hands on her belly.

The baby shifted beneath his touch.

Sebastian smiled and smoothed his hands back and forth.

"We're talking about you in there," he told her belly.

The baby did a huge roll and Abby gasped, squeezing her eyes closed.

Sebastian stared at her belly with mingled horror and amazement.

"That hurt, didn't it?" he asked, guiltily.

"It didn't feel good," she told him, "but I'm getting used to it. I think she's preparing for her journey into the world."

"I like that, her journey. She needs a theme song to prep her for her adventure. Life is a highway and I'm gonna drive it all night long," he crooned, leaning close to her belly.

"Wait, wait," Abby interrupted. "How about Free Falling? Let's make this birth as easy as possible."

****

Abby cried out and fumbled in the darkness.

"I'm here. Are you okay?" Sebastian's voice came to her. He flipped on the light and their bedroom materialized.

Abby winced and touched her belly as a cramp pulled her muscles taught.

"It's a contraction," she told him, straining to see the glowing neon numbers of their bedside clock.

He blew a big breath out.

"Okay. It's two-fifteen in the morning. Let me grab my phone and we'll time them. I downloaded an app a few days ago."

Abby smiled and leaned back on her pillows. The contraction had passed quickly, but she tensed with anticipation for the ones to come.

"I can do this," she whispered to the empty room. "Everything will be good, great even."

Sebastian returned and held out his phone. "Click the blue button when another one starts. I'm going to the library to tell Helena with a shell."

Abby grabbed his arm.

"We don't need to wake her yet. Remember she said it's liable to take hours and we'll have plenty of warning from the contractions."

He leaned forward and kissed her cheek.

"I appreciate your relaxed attitude. It's good for you, but I want her to know, anyway."

Abby watched him plod from the room, naked except his underwear. On his head one black curl stuck straight in the air and she almost laughed. Nothing was funnier than a sleepy man on a mission in his skivvies.

She peered at the clock, but over ten minutes passed without another contraction. When it hit, Abby had nearly fallen back asleep. The spasm jolted her awake.

Sebastian returned looking more alert.

"Coffee's started and Helena is on her way," he announced.

"Sebastian." She threw a pillow at him. "Don't you..." but she had to stop talking as the contraction caused her muscles to seize and a ball of pressure to appear in her low spine. She squirmed on the bed. "Don't you remember that Helena said to go back to bed when the contractions started," she huffed out.

He smiled.

"I'm sure you'll be sleeping through those," he joked. "I'm ready to be awake, though."

Abby shrugged, not wanting to agree that he was right.

"You realize that this may be our last night of peaceful sleep for quite some time," she reminded him.

He sat on the bed next to her, taking her hand.

"I'd hardly call it peaceful. Plus, who wants to sleep when you have a baby you can stare at instead?"

Abby touched her belly, having almost forgotten about the contractions, but a glance at Sebastian's phone told her another would start in four minutes.

"What did Helena say?" she asked.

Sebastian smiled at her wryly.

"That we should go back to bed and rest up for your big performance. She's coming through the mirror to get the house ready."

Abby took a deep breath and closed her eyes, not surprised this time when the muscles in her uterus pulled tight.

"Does it hurt?" Sebastian asked.

Abby opened one eye and looked at him.

"Not exactly. It's just...uncomfortable."

The contraction lasted for less than two minutes. Abby sighed and rested her head back when a light knock sounded on the door.

"Well, a very early morning to you," Helena bubbled, looking wide awake and excited. She shooed Sebastian from the edge of the bed and sat down. "I'll do a quick check of your heart rate and blood pressure and baby's heart and then leave you to rest."

"I'm not sure I'll be getting much more sleep," Abby admitted as Helena blew on the cold stethoscope before placing it against Abby's skin.

"You'll be surprised, honey. Those contractions take a lot out of you.

Even ten minutes between will help with your energy," she explained, wrapping a cuff around Abby's upper arm.

"That's a good idea," Abby admitted, yawning. She was tired.

"Sebastian, I think you better get some more shut-eye as well," Helena started, but he shook his head before she finished.

"Nope. Put me to work Helena. I'll just toss and turn and keep Abby awake if I'm in here."

****

Abby slipped out of her robe and climbed into the large tub. The warm water rose over her, easing the pain as a contraction surged through her. Oliver had been right, the floor of the tub felt like clouds wrapped in silk. She settled against the edge and looked up through the trees at the starlit sky above. Lydie had strung white twinkling lights from the branches. It was terribly romantic and Abby allowed her mind a moment of reverie before another fist of pain arose within her.

Abby had been having contractions for eighteen hours. The last two hours they had changed. When Sebastian asked what they felt like, Abby told him she wondered if someone were grounding spices against her spine with the dull end of a hammer. He didn't ask again.

He sat in a chair at the edge of the tub and wrapped his arms around her, settling his head on her shoulder.

"You're amazing," he whispered.

She nodded, but didn't speak as another contraction drew the muscles of her abdomen tight.

All the witches of Ula had come to her house. Bridget was cooking and stocking the freezer with pre-made meals. Elda and Lydie were performing spells of welcoming, nurturing and setting up little bits of magic to soothe nighttime cries. They bewitched the washing machine to call out to soiled clothes and blankets so they'd float to the laundry room and self-wash. Faustine, Oliver and Julian had spread across Abby and Sebastian's property standing vigil. Faustine had come equipped to fortify their house against invasive energy. Even a human could not stumble upon the place. Divergent shields would send wanderers passing by and deflect enemies. If Kanti knew of Abby's birth, then Clyde would know as well, though they hoped that Galla's blanket had blocked her access.

Helena brought Abby a plate of fresh fruit and a glass of water.

"Here, honey. We've got pineapple, mango, strawberries. Have a little something to eat. We want to make sure you're refreshed when the time comes."

"Thank you," Abby told her, touching her hand. She took a few strawberries and a piece of mango and settled back into the water.

The time between contractions had reduced to less than four minutes.

She popped the fruit in her mouth and pushed away from the edge of the tub, moving in a circle. It helped to move. Breathe and move, breathe and move. Another contraction squeezed, and she rushed to the side of the tub gripping the rock ledge and closing her eyes. She imagined a lotus flower blooming on the surface of a pond. She had read about visualization in a baby book. As the lotus petals folded back, her muscles loosened and relaxed. She sagged against the side of the tub where Sebastian stood, ready. He didn't ask what he could get for her, but offered a sip of water and wiped her sweating face with a cool, damp rag.

As another contraction overwhelmed her, she cried out. She grabbed a towel and bit down. A vice-like pressure wound through her middle and a wave of nausea rolled over her. As the pain peaked she whimpered and bit back a desire to scream.

"You're doin great, mama," Helena murmured. She stood next to Sebastian and reached for Abby's wrist, holding her pulse.

"I need to push," Abby said, suddenly wanting to bear down as an enormous pressure moved against her pelvis. Helena might have spoken, but Abby didn't hear her. She pushed and cried out. For twenty minutes the pushing continued. Abby descended into her body so deeply it was as if she were outside of it. The external world ceased to exist and a primal urge to deliver her baby engulfed her. Abby released a guttural cry.

"Nice, slow pushes now, honey. Let the skin stretch on its own," Helena urged her.

Abby blew out a long ragged breath trying to lengthen the push.

"Reach down, Abby. Feel for Vidya," Helena urged.

Abby stretched her arms into the water, gasping as her fingers brushed the soft crown of her daughter's head.

Sebastian climbed into the tub.

"I feel her," Abby shrieked, locking eyes with Sebastian. He breathed loudly through his nose and looked rapidly back and forth between Abby and Helena. Abby laughed and Helena laughed with her and then Sebastian started to laugh, but Abby saw tears pouring down his cheeks.

Helena climbed onto the edge of the stone tub.

"Another push, mama. There, that's good. Guide her out."

Vidya slipped into the water. Together Abby and Sebastian lifted their slippery infant. Her cries echoed through the forest. Abby held her against her chest and cried with her baby. Somewhere in the night, Abby heard the witches of Ula clapping and hooting. They too had heard Vidya enter the world.

CHAPTER 6

Though Vidya had come into the world two months before her due date, she was a healthy seven pounds with a tuft of golden hair and piercing blue eyes. Helena had set up Abby and Sebastian's bedroom with everything they needed and she would sleep in the room adjacent and check on them frequently.

It was nearing dawn when Abby and Sebastian lay in bed and marveled at their tiny creation. Her pale blue eyelids were capped with wisps of black lashes. Abby touched her fingers and hands, curled in as she slept on Abby's chest. Sebastian stroked the back of their baby's little head, watching both Vidya and Abby with an expression of complete wonder. They were both exhausted - beyond exhausted - but those first moments alone with each other and their new baby gave them a boost.

"You were amazing, Abby. I don't know what I expected, but I had no idea," Sebastian whispered, shaking his head from side to side as if he still couldn't quite believe it.

Abby smiled and strained forward to kiss the top of the baby's head. Helena had helped guide her to Abby's breast shortly after the birth and she'd latched easily, though Abby's nipples were now sore and raw.

"Me too," Abby agreed. "I felt primal, like an animal."

"You looked primal." Sebastian smiled, tracing Abby's collarbone with his finger. "Like an amazon warrior goddess. I've always respected women, but now I revere you."

"I'm feeling very unwarrior-like," she yawned. "I'm so tired and seepy."

"Sleepy or seepy?"

"Sleepy and seepy," she laughed.

"Well let me take this little beauty and you knock off for a few hours," he told her, sitting up in the bed. He gently lifted Vidya from Abby's chest and held her against his own.

Abby blew him a kiss.

"Thank you, Sebastian. I love you so much."

"I love you." He leaned over and kissed the top of her head.

Abby closed her eyes and drifted away.

****

Sebastian held the baby against his bare chest, savoring the warm puffs of her breath on his skin. He sat in the gliding chair that Abby's mom had bought for the nursery. Downstairs he could hear the bustle of the other witches. Bridget cooking, Helena cleaning and Lydie likely adding little bits of magic to every household item with the pretense of making their lives easier. He'd agree if he hadn't gone to get his shoes the day before and been attacked by the vacuum. He heard steady footfalls on the widow's walk above him. Most likely Julian scanning the skies for signs of skin-walkers as Oliver and Faustine did the same at ground level.

"The entire world is keeping you safe," Sebastian whispered into the top of Vidya's head. She was so soft, her skin like flower petals, and his hands seemed huge and clumsy. He'd always considered himself a graceful, gentle man, but his baby daughter turned him into a bumbling ogre. She released a tiny sigh followed by a mewl, more like a kitten than a baby.

He leaned back in the chair and rocked, closing his eyes and noticing the heaviness in every limb of his body. Like Abby, he was exhausted, but also determined to be present for a little longer. The Ula witches waited downstairs for their chance to whisk Vidya into their arms and shower her with kisses. Sebastian wanted a little more time alone with his baby girl. The force of her arrival called for some time in quiet reflection. As he listened to the steady drum of her breath and followed the rapid beating of her heart against his chest, he imagined his parents and Claire in the room with them. He could almost sense them hovering in the space.

"Isn't she beautiful?" he asked them. Only silence followed until a tiny sparrow flew to the window and pecked on the glass. Another arrived just after. Several minutes later, more than ten birds sat on the eave outside the window. Sebastian studied their tiny black eyes. "They're here for you," he told Vidya.

Abby had told him that birds were drawn to their child.

The door pushed in and Helena peeked around the corner.

"Am I interrupting?" she asked.

Sebastian shook his head.

"No, just admiring our bird welcoming committee," he told her, nodding his head toward the window.

Helena smiled and walked to the glass.

"This is nothing," she laughed. "You should see the front porch. Crows, seagulls, blue jays, cardinals, sparrows. It's like a bird sanctuary out there."

"Really?" he asked, glancing at his baby as if she somehow called out to the birds.

"Yep, she's a force all right. Ready for a nice rest? Or are you getting some daddy time under your belt?"

Sebastian yawned and took another breath of her infant smell.

"I'm ready. I'm getting that up-all-night stoned feeling, better nod off before I start wanting to pound coffee instead."

Helena grinned and put her arms out.

"Ooh now I get to snuggle that sweet little nugget," she cooed, taking the baby from his arms.

Helena whispered and giggled to the baby as she carried her down the stairs. He returned to the bed and crawled in next to Abby, watching her. A long curl fell across her forehead and rested on the pillow. Her face, lined with exhaustion a short while earlier, was seamless in sleep. He closed his eyes and allowed the sound of her breath to carry him away.

****

"This week had been a blur," Sebastian told Abby, carrying a breakfast tray.

"For moi?" she asked, eyeing the piping hot coffee and equally tantalizing cinnamon roll slathered in frosting.

"Yes, it is mi amour," he settled the tray over her lap on the bed and slid in next to her. "I've safely deposited Vidya with Auntie Helena and you get to drink your coffee without worrying you'll slop it on our baby's head."

Abby laughed. "Oh, the things you take for granted." She took a sip and closed her eyes, allowing the steady thrum of caffeine into her blood. "The week has flown though," Abby agreed, "when it wasn't crawling like a sloth that is."

Sebastian smiled. "Yeah, a few of those late night wake-ups seemed to span hours and when I looked at the clock, fifteen minutes would have passed."

Abby picked up a cinnamon roll and inhaled.

"Your recipe?" she asked.

"Yep, I trusted Bridget with my Infinitely Tubular Cinnamon Rolls."

"Is that their formal name?" Abby asked, taking a gooey delicious bite.

"Claire called them that," he admitted. "I figured I should make it official."

"Well they definitely live up to their name."

Sebastian took a coffee and leaned back against a pillow.

"How can our lives change so much in a week? I feel like the same person and yet totally different."

Abby nodded.

"Me too. Though the whole witch revelation obliterated any ideas I had about the slow progression of reality. What's weird is that it doesn't sink in. One minute you're Abby and the next you're a witch and a minute after that you're a wife and then a mother..." She trailed off trying to make sense of all the new roles in her life.

"A son and a brother, then an orphan with no family. A man and then a hybrid, a husband, a father." Sebastian frowned into his coffee as he spoke. "Where's the lightning bolt? Shouldn't the transition be a little more pronounced?"

Abby squeezed his hand.

"Vidya's arrival had the lightning bolt. I don't think I'd wish for anything more intense."

"True enough," he said, his eyes wide at the memory. "I'd do it again in a heartbeat. The energy that night was like..." he searched for a word. "Magnetic. Obviously, you were there on a whole other level."

Abby touched her belly, already nearly gone. Some vigorous massage from Helena and her body's own contractions had shrunk her womb back to a non-baby holding size in the hours after the birth. A bit of belly remained, and it made Abby sad to think of it gone, all evidence that her child had lived within her, rooted and been nurtured there, would vanish.

"I'd do it again too," she told him, feeling strangely shy at the implications.

He paused with his coffee halfway to his lips.

"Really?" He asked, a smile of delight spreading across his face. "As in a second time? Two babies?"

"Not anytime soon, cowboy," she laughed, handing him a cinnamon roll. "But yeah, right?"

He nodded, chewing his cinnamon roll slowly and staring at her with mingled wonder and terror.

"Yeah. Hell yeah. Now it seems strange that I've never even thought about it," he confessed.

"To be honest, I haven't either. Not to mention, we've had other stuff on our minds. But seeing Helena and the other Ula witches this week, I've thought why aren't there more babies in everyone's lives? I mean, have you ever experienced so much joy? And presence?"

He cocked his head to the side.

"No, I haven't. But I have to admit, I've never been so scared either. I probably shouldn't say that, being your protector and all. Sometimes when I hold Vidya, I want us to move to another planet where she can never get hurt."

Abby chewed her fingernail and then stuffed her hand beneath the comforter.

"I know, me too. I'm scared for her and for us. But we will survive this curse and when we're all free, that's when we'll talk about another baby."

Sebastian smiled and lifted the tray from Abby's lap. He climbed over her, letting his curls brush her forehead, cheeks, her lips. When he kissed her, Abby rose to meet him. They kissed for a long time, holding and touching, without allowing their desire to carry them away. It was too soon to make love, but Abby already felt her passion regenerating her.

****

Lydie lifted the baby from her bassinet and carried her downstairs. She cradled her head trying to mimic Helena who held the baby as if she'd been cradling babies for two hundred years. She probably had been. Lydie had never seen a baby at Ula. She was the last baby born at the castle and Lydie wasn't so sure another one ever would be.

She sat in a chair by the window and the baby did not stir. Lydie examined her splotchy face and tiny misshapen head. Beautiful would not have been her first description for the baby, but she was special, so fragile and soft. Lydie found herself intrigued by this new addition to the Ula clan. Would she be a young witch? Would Lydie become her babysitter? Or mentor perhaps?

Lydie lifted one of her tiny hands and the fingers curled around her own. She smiled at the baby's grip.

"She's a champion sleeper," Oliver laughed. Lydie looked up, startled. She hadn't heard him come in. Oliver had been outside shooting his bow in the woods.

"Yeah, Abby just finished nursing her. I figured I'd better grab her while she was in a food coma or she'd scream like a banshee," Lydie told him.

"Nah. I bet you have mysterious baby soothing magic you're not even aware of."

Lydie secretly hoped so, but didn't tell him that.

"Where's Ezra been? I feel like I haven't seen her in a while..."

"She's back in Chicago, rebuilding her life and all that. Dante and Marcus found an old building for sale. They're trying to set up a community garden, health clinic and yoga studio in the building and then live on the top floor. She's busy to say the least. And to be honest, she's salty with me for sending her back to Ula when the L'Obscurite were here."

"And you're not joining her?" Lydie asked, trying to sound like she didn't care, but hearing the strain in her words. She blushed.

"Lydie, I'm not going anywhere. Okay? My home is up here with you guys and if I ever decide to go somewhere, I'll be asking you to join me."

"Don't you want a life like Abby and Sebastian with a house and a baby?"

Oliver shrugged.

"Depends on the day, but that life would include you, Lyds."

"Does Ezra want you to move to Chicago?"

He smiled and brushed a hand through his ruffled blond hair.

"Giving me the third degree?" he asked.

"It just seems like we haven't talked lately."

"Ezra's happy on her own. Even if I was willing to move, which I'm not, she wouldn't pressure me to do it. Witches don't have to live in little nuclear families. In fact, they usually don't."

"I guess it's hard for me because I think I want that someday. I want what my parents had and what Abby and Sebastian have." She ran her fingers through the baby's hair. It was so soft, like strands of fine silk.

Oliver watched the baby and nodded.

"I get it, Lydie. Maybe sometime I will want that too, but you'll come with me. And we'll do it just like this." He gestured to the house around them. "We'll have a mirror so we can hop back and forth to Ula whenever we want. We'll make it the best of both worlds."

****

"I feel very guilty," Bridget confided to Helena.

They stood, elbows touching, in the Vault. Bridget had spent days creating an elaborate family tree and time-line for the curse.

"This is amazing, Bridget. You have a gift." Helena traced her fingers over each name and date drawn in elegant black calligraphy. It looked more like a piece of art than an investigative tool.

"I saw a doll in my tea leaves, in the steam rising from my soup, in the clouds…" she trailed off. "The same doll that the L'Obscurite put in Abby's nursery."

Helena turned and looked her in the eyes.

"How can you possibly divine an unfamiliar symbol, Bridget? You're not a seer."

"But had I taken the omens to y'all, somebody might have known."

"You told Julian. You did your best," Helena promised. "Everyone was preoccupied and, unfortunately, the L'Obscurite seemed like the least of our worries."

"Except they weren't," Bridget continued, growing flustered.

When Bridget became stressed, her southern accent grew more pronounced and Helena smiled.

"What are y'all grinning about like a mad dog? I'm tryin' to have a serious conversation."

"I know you are, love. I'm sorry," Helena told her, wrapping her in a hug. "I hear you my friend. I swear that I do. But there's no peace in the past. We can't change it. I believe you did what you could. The next time a symbol appears, shout it from the rooftops. Do what you need to set things right in your heart, but let it go. Okay? It's time to let it go."

Aepa, Helena's Siberian Husky, nosed the door open and walked in, lying at Helena's feet.

Bridget nodded and shifted back to the long scroll that held the time-line.

"Since we're on the subject, I might as well admit I've been having troublesome dreams," Bridget confessed, sighing.

Helena leaned down to run her hands along Aepa's silken back. She glanced up at Bridget's admission.

"About what, honey?"

"Sebastian."

Helena frowned.

"Tell me."

Bridget picked at the edge of the scroll until Helena moved it out of her grasp.

"It's the same dream each time, several nights in a row now. He is sitting on a beach flipping a coin over and over. Next to him sits a snake, unless he flips the coin and it lands on heads, then the snake becomes a bird. When the coin lands on tails, the bird returns to snake form."

"That's the entire dream?" Helena asked, chewing her lower lip.

Bridget nodded.

"What do you feel, Bridget? Do you have a sense of something when the dream is over?"

Bridget nodded and blew out a long breath.

"That the wheel of fate is spinning his destiny."

CHAPTER 7

"Well it's about time you came to visit your Grandma," Becky cooed, lifting Vidya from Abby's arms.

Her daughter blinked her pale blue eyes at Becky's puckered mouth.

"I want to eat you up," she continued, and Sebastian gave Abby a grimace that made her snort with laughter.

"Sorry, mom," she told her, following Becky into the house. "But you could have come to visit us."

"Hmph," she grunted. "After your wedding when we were abandoned by all the hosts. That poor woman Adora had to row us back, and she looked near to death, the poor thing. Cancer?"

Abby rolled her eyes at Sebastian who set about the kitchen making a pot of coffee. They'd driven down early that morning after another long night of Vidya wake-ups and couldn't get enough coffee to wipe the sleep from their eyes.

"Not cancer. But yes, she's ill. I'm happy she drove you," Abby amended.

"Row, Abigail. I said row. Though your dad did most of it, bless his heart. Lord knows any muscle he had has gone to rot beneath the donuts and lasagna."

Abby had only learned of her parents' fate after her near-death in the Ebony Woods. Despite her anger towards Victor, she had been grateful that he'd left her parents behind.

"Where is dad?" Abby asked, having expected him to be there waiting for the baby to arrive.

"Picking up sandwiches and signs," Becky told her, settling into a chair and balancing Vidya on her knees. "What a gorgeous little princess you are! And wait until you see the pretty little dresses your Grandma bought for you."

She turned to Abby, excited.

"You know those Polly dolls I got for you ages ago? They have a children's clothing line! I bought the lot. They're in your room upstairs, just gorgeous. Intricate little pearls sewed to the collars," she sighed dreamily.

Sebastian walked in with steaming mugs of coffee.

"Thank you," Abby sighed, sinking back into the couch with the mug pressed between her hands. She took a long sip and closed her eyes, savoring the rich flavor.

"Are you breastfeeding?" her mother asked sharply.

Abby left her eyes closed and weighed the possibility that if she didn't answer her mother would forget that she asked. Sebastian saved the day.

"This is beautiful, Becky. Is it pine?" Sebastian ran his hand along a hutch filled with tiny floral saucers.

"Oh yes, isn't it lovely? It's an antique. It belonged to my mother, but it's been sitting in our basement for years. Jim brought it up to stage the house."

"Stage?" Abby asked sitting up straight.

"Yes, dear. If you ever called me, you would know we're listing the house this week."

"Listing it for sale?"

Becky nodded, waving one of Vidya's little hands back and forth.

"Yes, Grandma and Grandpa want to live closer to their new little grandbaby. Don't they?"

Vidya gurgled and Abby widened her eyes at Sebastian. He shrugged, but Abby saw the slight downturn of his mouth.

"Closer where?" Abby asked.

"Sydney's old house. It hasn't sold. We're not even getting any showings. Plus, your dad and I need a new start. He doesn't have to work anymore so why not move north? Lots of retirees do it."

Abby frowned. She had mixed feelings about the news. She loved Sydney's house, but the thought of her mother popping in unannounced, daily, made her want to run screaming from the room.

"Are you sure that's a good idea, mom? Dad loves his work. And you always said living on a lake would be tedious. Plus, winters up there get brutal."

Becky narrowed her eyes at Abby, but her stony demeanor melted when Vidya grabbed for her finger.

"I'm a different woman now, Abby. A lot has changed and this old house feels stuffy. Why shouldn't we live on the lake? Your dad thought he'd buy a pontoon boat. We can all have picnics on the water."

Abby bit back the laughter threatening. Every visit to Sydney's, for as long as she could remember, her mother complained about the bugs, the tourists and the boats. Most of all the boats.

"That's great mom," she lied.

Sebastian continued to examine the hutch though he darted a glance at Abby. She knew he had similar thoughts to her own. It was one thing to have a magic mirror that Oliver or Lydie might pop out of on a moment's notice and quite another to have her ever-critical mother standing on the doorstep. However, her mother's watchful eye was the least of her issue with the move. It wasn't safe in Trager City, especially for anyone in Abby's family. Clyde had risen, and it was only a matter of time before he would attack.

****

"I met with Horace and he had some theories about the artifacts that washed onto the Serpent's House shore all those years ago," Faustine explained.

Julian set aside the journal he'd been reading.

"Who is Horace?"

"A witch from Egypt. We met at an All Hallow's Ball decades ago. I thought it prudent to call upon his expertise regarding the Egyptian text."

"I see," Julian said.

"Horace told me about a group of witches in Egypt who devoted their lives, very long lives might I add, to creating immortality. They bewitched several objects that could contain a piece of the soul and, more importantly, could channel the life essence of those who still lived to enhance the energy of a witch whose life essence had waned. So long as they siphoned only a small amount of spirit from many, they claimed to be doing no harm. According to Horace, they justified their actions by insisting the world needed true elders who had seen and heard all, and could give a complete account of the history of the world."

"How noble," Julian said dryly. "And all they had to do was steal a tiny piece of someone's soul."

"Eventually the covens of Egypt formed an alliance against them. They raided the covens of these witches and took their magical objects and books. The witches survived for a period, but without new life to add to these artifacts, they gradually died. I have a theory that several of those items made it to a boat in the Americas and that boat capsized on Lake Michigan. Thus, the Serpent House intercepted some strange artifacts indeed."

"How could Clyde have known their power?"

"The books that washed up likely contained that information. Remember, you said Nora's grandfather was studying the items from Egypt. He must have created a rough translation from the texts that revealed the hidden nature of those items, which Eugene confided to Clyde."

"Ah, the misguided trust among siblings," Julian sighed.

"I told my brothers everything," Faustine admitted, looking wistful.

"You had a brother, Faustine?" Julian asked, surprised at Faustine's revelation.

"Six, in fact."

"Six?" Julian asked, amazed. "Any sisters?"

"Two," Faustine added. "Of the six of us, four were witches. Ula originally started as a family coven. Until Napoleon invaded Croatia and our little world dissolved around us..."

He trailed off and Julian started to ask more, then thought better of it.

"Why didn't the covens in Egypt destroy the artifacts? Why keep them?"

"Apparently, they claimed to have done just that, destroyed all the immortality artifacts. However, over the centuries, Horace says several of them have popped up in various locations."

"So, they kept them," Julian shook his head angrily. "I'm starting to question the purity of witches. Once upon a time, I thought we were the divine answer to evil in the world. Now I'm beginning to wonder."

"Everyone is fallible. It's not enough to do good work in the world, we must also plant those seeds in our own heart. If we plant seeds of hate then hate will grow, if we plant seeds of love then perhaps we can cover the earth in trees blossoming with kindness."

Julian smiled, pleased in spite of himself. It was rare to see Faustine sharing in such matters, he appreciated the witch's desire to jump into the fray rather than standing neutrally on the sidelines as he'd done so often in their life.

"One thing has become clear. Clyde got his hands on those items."

"By murdering his brother," Julian said, disgusted.

"Yes, though he likely murdered his brother to strengthen the dagger in particular. Horace told me that a transfer of power into the items occurs if death is inflicted by the item or in its presence."

"Did he kill his brother simply to strengthen the dagger? Why not kill a stranger or a witch at Serpent House?"

"It's not only energy attained by the killing, but also the attributes of the murdered," Faustine explained. "Clyde wanted access to Eugene's special powers, whatever they might have been."

"And now he has Victor," Julian grumbled, crumpling the paper in his hand and then quickly smoothing it back out and setting it on the desk.

"Did you tell Horace what we're up against?"

Faustine shook his head.

"It seemed prudent to keep this amongst ourselves," Faustine replied.

"We could use the help," Julian added.

"We have a lot at stake here. I fear the repercussions if other covens get involved. Abby and her new child are already at risk."

Julian nodded, though he did not look convinced.

"We need to know about the third item," Julian concluded. "Which means we need to return to Australia."

"I agree. Clyde's mother will be the best resource, though I'm not confidant she will speak honestly."

"Take the Crystal of Sight," Faustine encouraged. "The magic surrounding her may muddy the images, but I'm sure it will pick up something."

****

"Guess what, Lyds?" Oliver announced, after exploding through the mirror in Abby's house and nearly causing Sebastian to drop his freshly poured cup of coffee.

"You're lucky I wasn't holding the baby," Sebastian snapped, stalking out of the kitchen.

Lydie sat on the kitchen counter drinking chocolate milk.

"Sleep deprivation," she told Oliver. "He's refusing magic. He's taking this natural parenting thing quite seriously."

Oliver grinned.

"We're going to Australia!" he bellowed, striking a pose with his hip jutted to the side and one finger in the air.

"Are we disco dancing in Australia?" Lydie laughed.

"We can do whatever you want in Australia. Well so long as it includes grilling Meghan, the mother of our worst enemy, for information."

"We're going? Me too this time?"

"Yes, you too. When Julian suggested he and I go, I insisted that we needed you this time. He was on board. It will be a short trip, but an awesome one."

"Is Ezra coming?" Lydie asked, a slight blush rising up her neck.

"Nope. I won't ask her. It will just be us, like old times."

Lydie grinned and jumped down from the counter.

"When are we leaving?"

"First thing in the morning so better head to Ula and pack your stuff. I'm going to fill Abby in. Probably best if I avoid Sebastian if he's stomping around in a sleepless rage."

"She's on the porch with Vidya," Lydie told him.

****

"He's been allowing it," Faustine blurted, interrupting Elda who nearly dumped a cup of tea down her robe.

She carefully set it back on the saucer.

"Who's been allowing what, dear?"

"Clyde!" Faustine held up the yellowing journal. "The number three denotes a powerful opportunity in the realms of all magic, and especially in this dark magic. Horace told me this magic uses three objects. We know of two. What we didn't realize is that three also applies to this century. We are in the third century of this curse, the third time it claims another heir. Clyde has been aligning everyone, using their desires to boost his own secret needs. If Kanti kills the bloodline, she defeats his enemies, and she channels all the power into a single child. The third child born to the curse."

"But how could that help Clyde?"

"The same way his own child helped him, but this time, he intends to complete the ritual."

"And sacrifice Vidya?"

Faustine nodded solemnly, the enthusiasm at his discovery already gone.

"If he sacrifices Vidya, he will not only have all of the power he has amassed, his body will be rejuvenated as well."

Elda set her shaking hands in her lap and looked toward the window. A distant blue sky greeted her, but she felt a storm coming.

CHAPTER 8

Abby held Vidya wrapped in a bundle of blankets. The baby looked up at her mother and offered the tiniest smile.

"Was that a smile? Are you my happy baby? Huh, little sweet pea?"

"I hate to interrupt the baby talk," Oliver teased walking through the sliding glass doors.

Abby turned and smiled.

"Feel free to join the baby talk, she's used to me, Helena and Sebastian all doing it simultaneously."

"She's a multi-tasker then?"

"More like a multi-listener."

"How are you feeling?" he asked, pulling a chair closer to Abby's.

"Good actually. The first 48 hours were rough. I'll spare you the details, but us women have some wickedly cool and rather freaky bodies."

"Oh, I already knew that." He winked at her. "I hear Sebastian's casting for Oscar the Grouch."

Abby laughed.

"He'll be more like Big Bird once he gets a few cups of coffee down. Vidya woke up a lot last night, and he insists on taking her after she eats. He doesn't want me to become overwhelmed. The funny thing is I feel really good. This special blood of mine seems to make me more resilient. I try to tell him to go back to bed, but he doesn't want to miss a second of her life, and I understand. When I'm sleeping, I miss her."

Oliver leaned over to look at Vidya. She had fallen asleep.

"It's hard to believe she's been living inside you. Very science fiction if you ask me," he told her, making a ghoulish face.

Abby swatted at him. "Cut the small talk. What's going on? I get the impression you're not here to inquire about my health?" she asked.

"We're going back to Australia to talk to Meghan. Just me, Lydie, and Julian this time."

Abby nodded.

"I figured it would come to that. I almost wondered if we shouldn't have pressured Binda while we were there to get more information."

"After Sebastian got out of the dream wood, I think we were all ready to get on a plane for home," Oliver said. "I feel more confident going back without him. Better if we have nothing she wants - hybrid and all that."

"Hybrid," she said, looking at her daughter with the uncomfortable thought Vidya too could be a hybrid. She wondered why that put her on edge.

"Why do you look like someone just pinched your baby?" Oliver asked. Abby glanced up at him.

"The hybrid thing, I guess. It reminds me of Clyde, but then again Liam is a hybrid, isn't he, and he's not part of that lineage."

"Let's hope not. I've talked with Julian about it. He's heard of hybrids. They're not isolated to Clyde and it seems like Clyde was never a hybrid at all. He only exhibited powers after he murdered Eugene and stole those items from Serpent House."

"Sounds like a good question for Meghan," Abby said. "Maybe she and Binda created the story of Clyde as a hybrid. It brought him a step closer to being a witch and made future Sky Mothers more likely to accept him."

Oliver nodded.

"I wouldn't doubt it. They were deceptive, although I bet Binda was just a pawn in whatever sick game Meghan was playing."

"Do you think so?" Abby asked, kissing Vidya's head. "I'm not sure Meghan was malicious back then. She probably wanted to protect her son and feared if she told Binda the truth, the woman would turn on her."

"As any sane person would," Oliver pointed out.

Abby shrugged.

"I feel differently now." She looked down at Vidya. "I can't imagine abandoning my child. Maybe it's crazy. And surely Meghan is partially at fault for everything that transpired after Clyde escaped. But I can understand her motivation."

Oliver gazed out at the lake, not answering right away. Abby wondered if he envisioned his own future children, and if he'd be willing to make such sacrifices.

"My mother would have done the same," he admitted. "Even now she writes several times a year. She's not angry that I took off. I don't like to admit it, but I'm sure she'd do just about anything to get me back."

Abby studied his face, the slight downturn of his mouth.

"Why don't you go see her, Oliver? What's holding you back."

He laughed, short and harsh, and shook his head.

"Oh, you know, Vepars, Victor, Clyde - hundred nameless faceless enemies that might follow me there. I won't put them at risk so I can sleep easy at night."

"How about so they can sleep easy? You said yourself, she'd do anything to have you back. Don't you think she'd put herself at risk to hug her son?"

He frowned.

"It's easy to say that when you're a witch, Abby. But consider Sydney. Would you have ever gone to her house if you'd known what you were bringing to her door?"

Abby sucked in a breath and looked away. She could sense that Oliver regretted the words the instant he'd spoken them. After all, he had been the one that killed Sydney.

Abby didn't say more and after several minutes, Oliver quietly left.

****

"You gonna miss me?" Oliver asked Ezra, watching her sift through a box of medicine donated to her clinic.

"I wish people would stop giving us expired meds. I mean seriously, throw this shit away. It's too old for them to take, so they pass it off to the homeless guy. Who cares if his stomach lining rots!"

"Ahem," Oliver said, clearing his throat loudly. He sat on her bed in the new loft. Ezra had thrown away her old furniture, bedding - everything that reminded her of the old loft. Oliver noticed a dark theme in her new room. The soft velvet comforter beneath him was such a dark purple as to be nearly black. The candles on her bureau were all black, and she'd even bought black lace curtains.

She glanced up at him and scowled.

"If you think I'll be sitting here pining for you, then no. But sure, I'll miss those big blue eyes imploring me to wake up in the morning," she told him, returning her gaze to the box.

He laughed.

"Well I'm happy you said my big blue eyes instead of the coffee I make every morning. I would have felt truly irrelevant if that were the case."

"Oh, I'm gonna miss the coffee, for sure," she said. "Kendra thinks espresso is the only coffee worth drinking so I will be forced to make my own."

"Finally," he said triumphantly. "A show of emotion on my behalf."

She laughed and threw an empty bottle of chewable vitamins at him. The plastic bottle bounced off his head.

"You don't mind?" he asked. "I would have asked you, but…"

"Oliver, you don't need my permission to live your life. No, I don't mind. Honestly, I'm behind at the clinic. We've had staff changes. I need to hire another pediatrician. I've been spending way too much time in Michigan."

He watched the tight set of her shoulders and the firmness in her jaw and knew she wasn't being entirely truthful. He stood and went behind her, wrapping his arms around her waist.

"I'll miss you, Ezra." He kissed the back of her neck where the petals of a lotus flower tattoo peeked from her black t-shirt.

She reached a hand back and grabbed his head, turning into him. She sighed as she kissed him, and he understood the things she didn't allow herself to say.

When she pulled back her eyes glistened, but she twisted away quickly. When she glanced at him a moment later, not a tear remained.

****

"What's the occasion?" Abby teased as they pulled out of their driveway.

Sebastian turned onto the road that led to Trager, and glanced at her from the corner of his eye.

"I wanted us to have a night of normal, a date night if you will," he told her, reaching a hand to her knee.

She rubbed her finger over his knuckles.

"I don't think we've ever been on an actual date." She thought back over the previous year and couldn't remember a single time they'd gone out just to have dinner and connect.

"Exactly."

"But how come today? What spurred this sudden desire for normalcy?"

Sebastian kept his eyes trained forward, but Abby saw the downturn of his mouth.

"Are you okay, honey?" she asked, lifting his hand to her lips for a kiss.

He swallowed hard and nodded.

"Yeah. I just wanted some time with you. Just us. I figured with Lydie and Oliver gone, it was good timing."

She smiled and turned toward the window, watching the trees whiz by. The sunny sky revealed ominous dark clouds in the distance.

"I think we're going to have a rainy date," she told him.

He leaned forward and looked up through the windshield.

"You think or you know?" he joked.

She laughed and felt the buzzing of her element gathering.

"I know."

He parked downtown and they walked to a new brewery that had opened earlier that summer.

Abby admired the frosted glass, drawing a little heart on the icy surface. The glass was so full, the beer frothing to the rim, she leaned forward to take her first sip.

"Oh wow, that's good," she said, licking her lips. "It tastes like raspberries."

"Right? That's craft beer for you. I've been so distracted since... well pretty much ever, I didn't realize the world had graduated beyond Bud

Light."

She laughed. "I never even graduated to Bud Light. I've been more of a wine cooler kind of gal myself, but this is delicious."

Sebastian ordered bacon wrapped dates and garlic crusted asparagus for appetizers.

"I feel like I haven't been in public in ages," Abby shifted and pulled her skirt lower over her thigh as if people could see beneath the booth. "I feel oddly exposed."

Sebastian nodded.

"Me too, but let's pretend just for tonight that we're like everyone else in here. We're new parents escaping Babyville for a night on the town. Other than dirty diapers and how to ensure that our baby's a genius, we don't have a care in the world."

Abby laughed.

"Yes, please. I never thought ordinary would be the thing I most missed."

Abby remembered the morning nearly a year earlier when she'd climbed into her car and driven north. She had watched Lansing and her life there fade into the rear-view mirror. In a moment of impulse, she had abandoned her boyfriend Nick, her job and even her cat. It wasn't only dissatisfaction that prompted her departure; she understood now that it was her power desperate to reveal itself. Less than twenty-four hours later, she had discovered the body of Devin in the Ebony Woods. She recalled that tiny bit of red fabric hanging from a branch. What would have happened if she'd disregarded it and walked on by?

"I believe I now fully and completely understand the statement 'be careful what you wish for,'" she said.

Sebastian grunted.

"You know what's crazy? I never wished for anything other than what I had. I loved my parents and Claire. I didn't long for an exciting life."

Abby bit her lip, guiltily. She had. She had yearned for something to make her feel alive.

The waitress delivered their food.

"I'll take another," Abby said, pointing at her glass.

Sebastian cocked an eyebrow at her.

"Better keep up with the lady. I'll take one too," he said, downing the last of his beer.

They drank and ate and avoided the most pressing topics in their lives. For tonight, they were just a husband and wife out on the town.

"Tell me something about your childhood. A secret that no one knows," Abby prodded.

Sebastian screwed up his eyes and then nodded.

"Okay, got one. When I was seven, I drank an entire Margarita that my mom had put in the kitchen sink. I promptly threw it up all over the yellow rug in our bathroom. I stuffed the rug in the trashcan and claimed ignorance when she asked me about it the next day."

Abby laughed, grimacing.

"Poor little guy. Were you afraid you'd get in trouble?"

"Hell yeah," he exclaimed. "I knew I wasn't allowed to drink those, not to mention, my mom loved that rug. She had bought it from a flea market in San Francisco when she was younger. She told me about it every time I used the bathroom."

"In that case I would have lied too."

"Your turn. A childhood secret you intended to take to the grave, but will now reveal to your beloved husband."

"I flushed my dad's keys down the toilet," Abby admitted, covering her eyes and peeking at him between her fingers.

"Okay," he said thoughtfully. "Tell me more."

"I was eleven and my mom was having one of her days. I could always tell because she'd do fidgety things like scrubbing the same spot on the counter ten or fifteen times. My dad had an open house for a new client, a very affluent client, but I didn't want to be home alone with my mom so I grabbed his keys and flushed them down the toilet."

Sebastian tilted his head to the side and offered her a sympathetic look.

"That's kind of sad. Did they go down?"

Abby shook her head.

"They seemed to at first and then when I checked a few minutes later they were back in the toilet bowl so I fished them out with a wire hanger and hid them in my closet. He missed the open house and had to pay the dealership to make him new keys."

"Was he pissed?"

"My dad never got pissed," Abby responded, taking another sip of beer. "My mom was pissed. She lit into him, told him he was irresponsible and if we couldn't pay the mortgage that month it was his own damn fault. I felt terrible and wanted to tell him, but I just couldn't. I'm still embarrassed."

Sebastian watched her with sad eyes and leaned in to kiss her cheek.

"I wish I had known little Abby. I would have come to your room at night so we could sneak out to our tree house in the woods. I would have slain all your dragons with my wooden sword and you could have faced the days with your mom a little easier."

"I would have liked that," she said, wishing that she had found Sebastian twenty years earlier. How different their lives might have been?

When they drove home that evening, they could barely see through the downpour. Outside the city, Sebastian pulled the car down a grassy two-track road.

"Where are we?" she asked, squinting into the rainy darkness.

He plugged his phone into the stereo and turned the volume up as a slow R&B song played.

"Dance with me," he said, stepping from the car.

They were instantly soaked. Abby's sandaled feet sunk into the soggy ground. He pulled her beneath a canopy of trees where the rain still poured, but it offered a partial shield.

He pulled her body against him and they danced, twirling around and around as their soaked bodies clung together. Abby looked into Sebastian's face and thought she saw tears pouring down his cheeks, but perhaps it was only the rain.

CHAPTER 9

"This place is legendary," Lydie announced, jumping out of the Range Rover.

Oliver faced the glass structure of the Sky Mothers Coven. He nodded, but the grandness of the compound had somewhat soured after his last visit.

Matilda floated from the main archway, holding her arms out graciously. Julian hugged her, but with an air of coolness.

"I'm so happy to have you back," Matilda crooned, kissing Julian's cheeks. "And you must be Lydie? A fire witch through and through." She took Lydie's hands and squeezed before moving on to Oliver. She hugged Oliver and his stiff body relaxed into her. He had the ability to calm people, but Matilda's soothing qualities were unmatched. He felt immediately at ease in her embrace.

"Kit has prepared a lobster salad by the pool," Matilda told them, leading them through the breezy hallway that led to the ocean.

Kit smiled and waved when she and Oliver made eye contact. He felt a funky flip in his stomach at the sight of her. Things had developed with Ezra and he dreaded telling Kit if she expected time alone with him.

"Kit, this is Lyds," Oliver told her, eyeing the salad and licking his lips.

Kit stood and offered a hand to Lydie. She had pulled her dreadlocks in a high bun and wore a soft looking white t-shirt over a pair of cut-off black shorts. Oliver saw Lydie studying the markings on Kit's arms and neck.

"Crikey, you're a little beauty, aren't you?" Kit asked, cocking an eyebrow. "And a force to be reckoned with, I dare say. Lovely to meet you."

Lydie blushed and shook Kit's hand.

Oliver had not mentioned Kit to Lydie, but he'd told Kit a great deal about Lydie. Kit had been curious to hear of a witch who exhibited powers so young.

"I like your hair," Lydie told her. "Maybe I should get dreads?" She looked at Oliver.

"Nah," Oliver disagreed. "If you get rid of those curls, Helena and

Bridget will keel over dead."

"Sometimes you gotta do it because no one else wants you to," Kit told Lydie, with a sly wink.

"Oh great. Well let's get your lip pierced and a tattoo while we're at it. Helena will be thrilled," Oliver complained.

Lydie and Kit laughed, but Oliver saw a twinkle in the young witch's eye.

"Helena probably would be thrilled," Kit cut in. "I don't think you're giving her enough credit, Oliver. She's one bad-ass witch. She happens to be sweet and gentle too. I bet you and Helena have a lot in common, Lydie."

Lydie looked thoughtful.

"Bad-ass is not a word I'd use to describe her, but then again, I have seen her fight."

"Ha, fighting is the least of it. She told me a story about an all Hallow's Party where she swam with great white sharks because another witch challenged her to show her water element by lifting a shark out of the water."

"And she did it?" Lydie asked, incredulous.

"She did it. And lifted three at once. They didn't go near her in the water. Apparently, she made them uneasy," Kit laughed.

"Or they weren't hungry," Oliver remarked. He shook his head, grinning. "I could see Helena doing that too and probably trying to pet them while she was at it."

"The point is, Oliver, Helena is no softie. She'd love to see Lydie come home with a hair full of dreads and a barbed wire tattoo around her neck."

Oliver guffawed and Lydie snorted.

"Okay maybe a flower tattoo on your ankle." Kit continued, laughing.

Julian and Matilda had stepped closer to the ocean and were deep in conversation, no doubt about Binda. Oliver wondered if Binda was as enthusiastic about their return as the other witches of the Sky Mothers, unlikely he thought.

"Dig in," Kit told them. "I've been eyeballing this lobster for an hour. I'm starved."

****

"I thought you might stand me up," Ezra said, when the door finally swung open and crashed into the brick wall. A chunk of brick crumbled away and dust flew into the air, obscuring him for a moment.

Victor strode into the room. He looked different, larger somehow and his eyes, which had always been dark had gone black. His lips were red and his teeth white and sharp when he smiled. Ezra felt the first smoky tendrils of fear dropping through the center of her body and settling in her hollow belly. She ignored the sensations.

"Ezra," he said, and she heard a strange sob drifting beneath the hardness in his voice. The sob sounded almost like Victor trapped beneath another voice, a voice she realized now belonged to Clyde.

"Victor? Or is it Clyde I'm speaking with?"

The smile grew wider and Victor's eyes glinted.

"I am so much more than all that," he said, stepping further into the room. He had come alone. No Vepars accompanied him, but Ezra knew they could be hiding in the hall, blocking the entrance to the building. They could be perched on the roof as demons with wings.

"I need to know why, Victor? After all we've built. How could you sacrifice us? How could you destroy everything?"

Victor's familiar eyes seemed to grow darker, deeper in his face. The black holes in their place had no warmth for her, no recognition.

Victor cocked his head to the side.

"My vision was always so much greater," he murmured. "We share that, you know? Victor and I. He saw what the world could be. He tried it your way, the white way, the pure way. But there's no triumph in the witch's world. You muddle along saving a life here and there, growing your magical plants, parading your goodness like a badge of honor." He laughed and shook his head. "What a waste of magic. I showed Victor the only true path to greatness."

"Being your slave? Allowing you to control him? Seems pretty great," Ezra scoffed.

Another flash of Victor, but anger this time.

"He's allowing me, Ezra. He wants to know what I know, feel what I have felt. He welcomed me into his body. He so desperately wanted this union that he was prepared to kill you to invite me in. Not only you, but all your little clan and the witches of Ula too. A thorn in my side those witches have become. But their time for this world is short so I am not troubled that they continue to live."

Ezra felt the anger rising at his words and fought to keep it at bay. Anger would not serve her now.

"I want to speak with Victor. Only Victor."

Clyde opened his hand with a flourish and took a deep bow.

"As you wish."

The transformation was slight and had she not known Victor so well, she might never have noticed it. His eyes were softer, his shoulders slightly sagged and when he leaned against the wall, he had that cool Victor stance that she remembered. It almost made her cry to see him.

"How could you?" she asked, unable to keep the tears at bay. They rolled up and out, flowing over her cheeks hot and angry.

He didn't smile and mock her as Clyde had done.

"He's right," Victor told her evenly. "White magic merely keeps the peace. I want a revolution. Sacrifices are necessary."

"Us? Kendra? Abby and her unborn child? Those sacrifices are worth it? For what? What can you possibly gain?"

Victor shivered and then reached a hand up to his chest. She saw a slight bulge beneath his shirt and realized that he wore the amulet. Was that how Clyde possessed him? Would the possession end if he took it off?

"I would have sacrificed us all," he told her.

"You realize that you've given Clyde power? Not you. He has your power now."

Victor shook his head.

"You don't understand, Ezra. You never understood. I tried to find witches that could create a new world, but you wanted more of the same. All of you."

Ezra felt her power wanting to burst up and out. It was hard to hold the space with him. She had a new respect for Oliver, a Vepar hunter. Every cell of her being detested the man before her. He was no longer a witch and her magic sensed that and struggled to be near him.

"So now you're an animal? A demon that feeds on witches?"

Victor narrowed his eyes, and she saw his fists clenched at his sides. Would it benefit her to make him angry? Could she use that somehow?

"You have no vision, Ezra. When I first met you, I thought we would do amazing things. Did you know the original name I wanted for our coven was The Anarchists? Did I ever tell you that? What good does it do to heal people if our leaders continue to poison them? I've played by the rules and only gotten buried deeper in the mud of this world. Left to their own devices, humanity will be extinct in a few hundred years. Fortunately, by then we'll be stronger, smarter and ready to usher in a new world."

"We?" Ezra asked snidely. "You and a bunch of brain-dead Vepars who will kill each other the minute food gets scarce."

"Not Vepars," he hissed. "Witches. Do you think I'm alone, Ezra? There are so many others. Powerful witches just waiting for a strong leader to show them our power does not have to be contained and channeled into tinctures and novelty magic. There are a dozen sitting in New Orleans right now waiting for their leader to return."

"The L'Obscurite?" Ezra laughed, disgusted. "You're nuts, Victor. I didn't want to believe it, but now that I've seen for myself... You think the L'Obscurite will follow you after you destroyed Ethel and the others. They'll kill you the moment they see you."

Victor pushed away from the wall at her laughter and Ezra felt a rumbling in the old building. The ground beneath her shook and dust rained down from the ceiling.

"Will you kill us both?" she asked, smiling. She no longer felt scared. If

Victor sacrificed himself to kill her, she would happily die. In the few minutes she had spent talking to him, she understood that he had terrible plans. Hundreds, thousands more would die. She was facing the greatest good she could ever do in her lifetime in that moment, but it meant she had to kill the man who changed her life, who opened her to the world of witches, who saved her.

"Every sacrifice strengthens you," he whispered under his breath. Ezra heard Clyde in that voice and saw Victor's expression as he absorbed the words.

She took a deep breath and steadied her own energy that had begun to swirl and rise, preparing to fight. It wasn't time to fight yet. She wanted answers. She had come here for answers.

****

Kit maneuvered the jeep down a rutted trail. For several minutes, Lydie could see nothing but dense brush pressing in and then the canopy opened to reveal an isolated lagoon. A long weather-beaten dock jutted into the water.

"Now that is a sailboat," Oliver announced.

The boat, its black hull shining, took up nearly half the dock.

"It's a Hanse," Kit told them, stepping from the car and admiring the boat. "Her name's Guwara."

"What's a Guwara?" Lydie asked, her eyes following the high silver mast.

"In my native language, Guwara means high wind. That boat," Kit cocked her head toward the vessel. "She makes the wind."

"I bet," Oliver murmured. "You know I was expecting a big old splintered beast from the 1800s."

Kit laughed.

"Guwara is only three years old. Everything about her is contemporary, especially her speed. I love old boats, but I prefer to admire them from afar."

She walked down the dock and jumped onto the deck of the boat.

Oliver and Lydie followed.

"You fish in this boat?" Oliver asked.

"I do everything in this boat," Kit told him. "I sleep here a lot. The water is like the partner I crawl into bed next to every night."

"But you're a fire element," Lydie commented.

"You understand then," Kit said, giving her a wink. "There's balance within me when I sleep on the water. Too much time on dry land and I start to get unruly."

"Two steering wheels?" Oliver asked.

"Twin helms," Kit told him.

Oliver followed Kit's orders and they were soon underway, the vessel slicing through the water in a seamless spray of crystal.

Kit pulled the boat along a sheaf of towering gray cliffs. Tall jagged caves created the illusion of pointed black teeth carved into the cliff.

"Are we going in there?" Lydie asked, pointing a trembling finger at the sparkling water beneath the cave opening.

"Don't worry, mate," Kit told her. "There's plenty of light in there. And once you spot a stingray, you'll forget all about the creepy entrance."

They dropped the anchor, and Kit went below deck to retrieve snorkeling gear.

"This water is so clear," Lydie said, leaning over the rail and staring into the ocean. "Do you think we'll see a shark?"

"I hope not," Oliver told her, looking into the crystalline water. "At least not a hungry one."

"Yeah, my fire element would probably not be super helpful under the water."

"Sure, it is," Kit answered, dropping a pile of flippers and masks at their feet. "Haven't you ever practiced magic underwater?"

Lydie frowned.

"No. I mean I can swim fast and hold my breath for a long time, but I haven't produced a fireball or anything," Lydie admitted.

Kit placed her palms together and as she drew them apart a golden bubble appeared. In its center a rolling orb of fire hung suspended. She dropped the ball of fire over the side of the boat and they watched, mesmerized, as it floated lazily beneath the surface. Kit snapped and the bubble rose up from the water and returned to her, melting into her open hands.

"Once we're in the water, it will be your turn," Kit said, sitting down and squirting oil onto her feet. "Helps the flippers slide on a bit easier," she explained.

Lydie and Oliver followed suit.

CHAPTER 10

Kendra stopped on the ground floor of their new building in Chicago. Construction had begun on the emergency health clinic and a series of men and women wearing everything from hard hats to dreadlocks wandered in and out of the space. The sound of hammers pounding and drills buzzing soothed her as she carried a tray of sprouts to the elevator.

"Top floor?" one man asked her. He was tall and slender with ebony skin and bright, inquisitive eyes.

"Yeah, thanks," she told him, appreciating not having to set the sprouts on the floor to push the button.

"My pleasure, Kendra," he said, winking at her.

She rode the elevator to the guerrilla witches' new loft and allowed the tears to flow. It was a new ritual. Every day she went into the world and worked like a fiend, feeding the homeless, planting gardens and healing with her magic. She refused to think of Victor during those times, but the moment the elevator slid closed she burst into tears. For the elevator ride and for three minutes when she returned to the apartment, she could cry. After that, she dried her eyes and focused on her work.

Still crying, she unlocked the door and stepped into the new loft. Dante and Marcus had painted the walls in bright oranges and yellows. Large cream-colored couches and chaises crowded around wooden coffee tables. Sunlight poured through the floor to ceiling windows between rows of potted plants. The old loft had been Victor's perfect space, simple, aesthetically pleasing and minimalist. They had all agreed that the new loft would foster a sense of home and comfort. Their own little version of beauty as therapy.

Kendra set the sprouts on a drafting table next to a window. She made a cup of tea and grabbed a handful of trail mix before slipping back to the tech room. Dante had insisted they keep all the technology in a separate room in the loft with extra magic to protect it from external invasion. They worried about Victor hacking into the system. They had sold their huge projector screen and replaced it with a simple, albeit large, flat screen. Kendra touched the screen and the Chicago city grid lit before her. A video icon blinked in the lower corner. She pressed it and an image of a rundown room appeared. For an instant, she thought Dante had used the GoPro and toured some abandoned Chicago buildings, and then the camera turned and Kendra gasped, stumbling away from the desk.

Victor had slid into view of the camera. She could see his lips moving, but heard nothing.

"Where's the volume?" she shrieked, searching the keyboard and finally spotting the tiny speaker icon. She clicked it and Victor came to life.

"I have no intention of killing myself, Ezra," Victor said. "I do however intend to kill you."

Victor's eyes looked dark, his lips pressed in a thin vicious line.

"Because that's what Clyde wants, right? You're just his puppet?"

Kendra heard Ezra's voice and realized she was wearing the go-pro. A hollow emptiness entered her stomach.

Victor smiled, but there was no laughter in his expression. He looked mean and worse, indifferent. He didn't care about Ezra. That was plain on his face.

Kendra looked around the room searching for help. She had to do something, but she didn't know where they were. Her cell phone lay discarded on the desk and she snatched it up, opening her contacts and punching Ezra's name. The phone clicked straight to voicemail. She tried Oliver next. It rang three times and also went to voicemail.

"Someone pick up," she shrilled as Abby's voice came through the phone.

"Hello?" Abby sounded unsure as if she'd caught the end of Kendra's cry.

"Abby, it's Kendra. Ezra is meeting with Victor right now. He's going to kill her. He just told her and it's true. I can feel it."

"Whoa, slow down, Kendra, I can barely follow what you're saying. Ezra is with Victor now? How do you know?"

"I'm watching it on our computer. We have a GoPro that streams live to our system here in the loft."

Kendra paused to listen as Victor spoke.

"You're trying to bait me, but you don't realize how much I see now. I can feel the power bubbling within you, Ezra. I can almost taste it. You're letting it build. You believe you can beat me, but you can't. I don't mind though. I rather like seeing you ready to fight. It was the first thing that drew me to you. You were so scrappy, Ezra. Ready to punch your shadow if it didn't stop following you around."

"And now I'm nothing to you?"

"Not nothing. If you were nothing, why would I bother killing you at all? You are energy. You will strengthen us."

Kendra had put Abby on speaker phone so she could hear the exchange occurring on the computer.

"Oh God," Abby moaned. "We need to find her. Have you called her?"

"Yes, straight to voicemail. I don't recognize the room. There's a faded mural on the back wall. It's a brick room, looks old."

"What's the mural?" Abby asked.

"It looks like a ship, maybe an island behind it. I don't know. It's unclear and Victor's blocking it."

"A ship?" Abby asked. "Is there a mermaid on the island, Kendra? Look for a mermaid with long black hair."

Kendra leaned closer to the video, but Victor had blotted most of the island out. Finally, he shifted and she glimpsed a woman in the image.

"Maybe, yes. I don't know." Kendra fought the panic from her voice. "I think so, do you know where it is?"

"There's an old building in Trager. It used to be a speakeasy," Abby told her. "But why would they meet there? I'm going right now."

"No wait!" Kendra bellowed, never having thought the building would be near Abby. She had assumed it was in Chicago. "Where's the baby?"

"She's with Sebastian. I'm already in town. It's not far."

Kendra could hear Abby running.

"No, Abby, no don't go. It's…" But the words died on her lips as Abby ended the call.

****

Abby ran hard. It was easier than she expected. Only her breasts, swollen with milk, ached from the effort. As she rounded the pharmacy, she nearly collided with a group of pre-school kids on a day trip to the ice cream store. They talked animatedly, ice cream dripping down their faces and over their tiny hands. Abby stopped inches from crashing into a little boy holding a sugar cone overflowing with superman ice cream. She sprang into the air at the last second and jumped over the group of gawking children.

"Super Woman!" the little boy shrieked.

Abby didn't look back. She was two blocks from the building and knew from Kendra's tone that Ezra would be lucky to have minutes left.

The building had been condemned decades earlier and a developer had bought it with the intention of tearing it down and building condominiums, but the town had resisted his developments and the structure remained untouched. As Abby ran toward the door, she saw a huge padlock securing it closed. She moved around the building and found a stairway leading to a basement door mostly rotted, its window smashed in. It swung open easily. She took the stairs two at a time racing to the second floor where she knew the mural to be.

Sydney had taken her into the building when she was a teenager. Harold,

Sydney's first husband, had boasted of plans to purchase it and create a three-level shopping center complete with wine tasting and state-of-the-art fitness center. That too had not come to pass, but Abby remembered Sydney showing her a room used during prohibition.

When she reached the closed door that led into the old speakeasy, she paused, listening. She heard nothing. Had he already killed Ezra? Tempted to hesitate another minute, Abby overcame her fear and kicked the door in hard, hoping for an element of surprise. The door bashed against the wall and splintered, sending a wave of dust and wood into the room - the empty room. She walked in, ready for Victor to jump out, but they were nowhere in sight. Abby stared at the dust on the floor. She could see footprints, but had no way to know if they belonged to Victor and Ezra.

"Damn it," she snapped. She pulled her phone out and called Kendra. She should have stayed on the line. How stupid. Kendra could see everything that was happening. She had fourteen missed calls from Kendra. She must not have heard the phone ringing as she ran to the building.

"Abby!" Kendra shrieked as soon as she answered.

"Yes, I'm sorry. I just got here. They're gone."

"I only looked away for a second and they vanished. He must have taken her. The screen is black."

"Damn it," Abby muttered, wondering if she should run back outside and try to follow him.

"He's going to kill her," Kendra sobbed.

"I'm going to do my best to stop him, Kendra, but I've got to call Sebastian."

"Where's Oliver? Can Oliver help too?" Kendra asked.

"He and Julian went to Australia."

Kendra groaned and Abby heard her breathing heavily as if having a panic attack.

"Are you okay, Kendra? What can I do? Are Dante or Marcus there?"

"No, no. Call Sebastian. I'll be fine. Help Ezra."

"I will," Abby promised and hung up the phone.

****

Ezra watched the splinters of the door fly into the room. Unable to move, to scream for the help she so desperately needed, she watched Abby stare at the scattered prints in the dust. The venom oozed through her slowly, but it was not the venom that had paralyzed her. Victor had magic she didn't understand. One moment she'd been ready to attack and the next she started to fall, limp, but he caught her. Without a word or a gesture, she watched her own body vanish and then his as he shuffled them against the wall.

Could Abby hear their breath? Sense them in the room? Abby took out her phone and called Kendra. Ezra could hear her through the phone, felt Victor's hands tighten across her waist.

Ezra tried to draw upon her element, but she had no power. It wasn't only the venom. She felt the amulet pulsing against her back and all of her energy seemed to pour towards that space. Clyde was drawing it from her. She had to warn Abby, had to scream, but her tongue lay thick on the floor of her mouth. Her eyelids drooped and she forced them back open. Once they closed she wouldn't be able to open them again. Abby grew fuzzy and indistinct. The light through the window seemed to dim. She counted the seconds, made it to three before the poison overwhelmed her and she lost consciousness.

****

"Honey, don't freak out, but I need you to pass Vidya off to Helena and meet me in town," Abby told Sebastian the phone.

"Hey babe," he exclaimed. Abby could hear Helena talking in the background. "Helena is giving Vidya a baby massage and she loves it!"

"Sebastian. Listen to me. This is urgent. I need you to come into town."

"Hold on." Abby heard him moving away from the sound of Helena's voice. "What's happening? Are you okay?"

"I'm okay. But Victor took Ezra. They had a meeting in Trager and he kidnapped her."

"Shit," Sebastian cursed. "I'm coming right now."

"Meet me at the library," she told him.

Abby walked back and forth in the parking lot until Sebastian squealed in, spraying gravel into the street. He jumped out and Abby saw a bag slung over his arm that she knew contained pouches of Julian's Vepar powder and the knife that Oliver had given Sebastian for Christmas.

"Tell me," Sebastian said, striding to Abby and hugging her.

Abby explained quickly.

"You're sure they were here in Trager?" he asked.

Abby nodded.

"I went to the room. I could feel the energy. They were there."

"Where would he take her?"

Abby threw up her hands, frustrated. "I have no idea. I think we need to search the woods. He obviously can't have her in the open."

"Yeah, but why wouldn't he just throw her in the trunk and drive back to whatever lair he's living in now?"

"That's what I'm afraid of," she admitted. "But we have to look."

"Okay. I agree, but we're not splitting apart and we need to be careful."

They crossed the street and moved through the Ebony Woods slowly weaving toward the beach and then doubling back. For three hours they searched until finally deciding that he must have left Trager with Ezra.

****

Ezra woke to coppery tasting liquid filling her mouth. She sputtered and nearly gagged, but a hand clamped over her lips prevented her from spitting it out. She swallowed and opened her eyes to find Victor, hooded, and crouched above her. He held an old bottle filled with dark red liquid in his hand and a golden dagger in the other. Ezra saw a dragon's head emerging from the handle end of the dagger. Its jeweled eye watched her as if alive.

She tried to twist away from Victor, but her arms and legs had been staked to the ground. She also felt heavy, drugged, and she knew that Victor now contained the Vepar venom in his teeth. He had truly become one of them. As she craned sideways, she saw others. Maybe four or five hooded figures. They wore black, their faces mostly shielded. Night had fallen, but the full moon had passed days earlier and the sliver of waning moon barely lit the sky. A single torch burned from a post that had been thrust into the ground.

"Please, Victor," Ezra croaked. Her throat hurt and her eyes felt heavy. She fought to stay conscious and to make eye contact with her former friend, but he ignored her. The grass and leaves had been cleared away. Victor held a long stick and drew designs in the dirt that Ezra could not see.

Victor crouched close to her body, dagger in hand. He guided the blade as if led by a source outside his body. His face had changed. It looked long and pale, his features sharper, his lips the dark red of blood. As she stared at him another face began to emerge-the face of a monster trapped in a human body. As the dragon's eyes glowed, Victor plunged the blade into Ezra's chest. It burned as it sliced through her skin. She felt enormous pressure as if she'd been caught by an undertow and was being pulled out to sea. The blood in her body flowed toward the dagger, but Ezra had lost touch with the physical sensations. Victor's face had vanished, and she swam in a sea of stars. It didn't hurt. Nothing at all hurt and, she wished she could tell Kendra and Oliver that it was okay. She wished too that she could help Victor to see that he was lost in a dream, a nightmare really, but she knew in that moment that someday he would know. They would all know. She surrendered to death.

****

Kit was right. The water in the caves sparkled and undulated with life. Bright green algae coated the rock walls that stretched down and down, finally ending at a sandy bottom strewn with huge boulders. A stingray with a black stripe down its back swam directly beneath Lydie and she waved wildly at Oliver. He opened his eyes wide beneath his goggles and offered her a thumbs up before swimming further into the cave.

Plugging her snorkel with her tongue, she dove towards the bottom. She swam along the boulders, allowing her fingers to graze their slimy surfaces before darting back to the surface and releasing the water from her snorkel like a whale emptying his blow hole. She could not see Kit or Oliver, but she didn't care. Lydie dove under again, this time staying down longer, exploring crevices tucked into the cliff where it met the ocean floor. A dark shape slipped through a fissure in the rock. It was a crack just large enough for Lydie to squeeze through. She had breath for another few minutes at least.

She wriggled into the opening, searching for the fish, or perhaps eel, that eluded her. The water grew darker as Lydie swam further in. A pinpoint of light streamed in from deeper in the cave. Searching the floor and cave walls, she saw no sign of the creature. She rose toward the light, but when she poked her head up, only a narrow hole in the rock allowed light in, and she had to press her face close to the rock ceiling to get a breath before diving back under. She gazed around a final time for the dark creature and then seeing nothing, retreated the way she came in.

Except as she swam, only solid rock greeted her. She turned back, but could not find the glitter of light. Darkness pressed in from every direction. Panic started to seize her. She fumbled the snorkel back into her mouth, but when she pushed toward the water's surface her head smacked against the slimy cave ceiling. Not even a puff of air existed between the rock and the water.

Beneath her, shadows started to dart back and forth. Thoughts of blood hungry sharks assailed her as she turned in a circle, searching for a sliver of light. One of the shadows drifted up to her. The girl, dead, stared through blood-filled eyes, her tattooed arms reaching for Lydie.

CHAPTER 11

"Lyds? Lydie?" Oliver's voice sounded watery and distant. Lydie tried to call out to him, but could not find her lips, her tongue.

A sensation of being roughly lifted and carried registered in a vague, far off part of her brain, but Lydie felt heavy. She drifted back down and down. The water had grown warmer, it swallowed her whole. Soon she would be like the dead girl. They would haunt the ocean together.

A sharp crack cut through the cottony thickness in Lydie's brain. She opened her eyes and searing light pierced her head. Flinging an arm over her face, she rolled onto her side. Her face pressed against a feathery pillow.

"Oliver?" she croaked, her throat raw.

"Drink."

Someone pressed a cool glass to her lips, and she gulped, keeping her eyes closed. She opened them gradually, allowing the light to filter in. Achingly she rolled onto her back.

Oliver sat on the edge of her bed and Julian stood in the sunlit doorway of the yurt.

"You scared the crap out of me, Lydie," Oliver murmured, pushing a damp curl away from her face. "I tried to find you, I…" he stopped and looked away, unable to go on.

Guilt coursed through Lydie. Why had she swum into that cave?

"Kit feels terrible," Oliver continued. "She reckons it's her fault she didn't make sure we stayed together. I do too, Lydie. I'm so sorry."

Julian watched him from the doorway and from his sour expression, Lydie knew he blamed Oliver as well.

Lydie shook her head. "I shouldn't have gone in. I saw a fish or…" she left the truth hanging in the air, strangely embarrassed to admit that she thought she saw a ghost in the water.

"No, it wasn't your fault. It was mine, all mine," he continued.

"Did I die?" Lydie asked.

Oliver shook his head, but Julian spoke.

"No. You passed out and floated up to the surface. But Lydie, there's no reason you should have panicked under there. We live in the middle of Lake Superior. If you haven't learned to properly hold your breath, then I suggest we do some training when we return."

Oliver shot him an irritated glance, but Lydie grabbed his hand before he spoke.

"That would be good. Thanks, Julian."

Julian nodded, looking satisfied.

"I will speak with Matilda, and return shortly," he told them leaving the yurt.

****

"So, what's the plan?" Oliver asked Julian that evening when he found him in the open-air kitchen.

"Binda will take me to Meghan tomorrow," Julian said, stirring a spoonful of honey into his tea.

Lydie wandered into the kitchen and sat on a bench that faced the ocean far below.

"How are you feeling?" Julian asked. "Matilda gave me some slippery elm for your throat. I'll brew you a cup of tea."

"Much better," Lydie said, trying not to rub her throat. Physically she did feel better, but the figure from the water had not left her thoughts.

"Are you sure she won't try and hurt you, Julian?" Oliver asked. "Binda did try to wipe Sebastian's memory."

Julian sighed and sipped his tea.

"She won't," he reassured him. "Binda was sufficiently contrite at our last visit. More than anything, she wants to free Meghan from the dream wood and we're her only hope for that."

"Because if Clyde dies, Meghan would be free?" Lydie asked.

"That's our theory, yes."

"His magic has a pretty long reach," Oliver said, dubious. "I mean we're talking a non-witch who's somehow keeping his magical mother trapped, controlling a bunch of Vepars, and stalking all the rest of us?"

Julian nodded, thoughtful.

"I do agree with you, Oliver. He might be a non-witch, but he's spent centuries creating his shell of power. It never pays to underestimate evil."

"If Abby had died in the woods, would Clyde have died?" Lydie asked, her voice low.

"Let's not even talk about that," Oliver started, but Julian interrupted her.

"No," Julian stated abruptly. "Her mother still lived and the magical objects - the dagger, the amulet and whatever else he created all those years ago."

"Then why did Victor stop her?" Lydie's voice shook, but she continued asking.

"Because Kanti has destroyed most of the bloodline and Clyde's hold is less and less stable. He had to save her to keep Kanti's lineage alive. But let me tell you something else."

Lydie turned to face them at the grave tone in Julian's voice.

"I believe there is something special with Abby's baby. We've come to three-hundred years since Clyde originally set upon this path of power and immortality. Faustine believes that three-hundred years marks a turning point. He wants that child."

"Vidya?" Lydie asked, tears filling her eyes.

Oliver gave Julian a look hoping he'd get the hint and stop talking, but he continued.

"Sometimes we don't understand a trajectory until it's too late. We're trying to dive in front of Clyde. I want to know his next move and my gut tells me that Faustine is right. He wants that baby."

"Am I interrupting?" Kit appeared outside the kitchen and Lydie jumped.

"You scared me," Lydie said, putting a hand over her heart.

"I'm sorry, Lydie, for scaring you and even more for what happened today. I shouldn't have taken you to those caves and I feel dreadful about it."

"Come on in," Oliver grumbled. "We were just changing the subject."

"It's okay, Kit. Don't feel bad. I panicked. I got turned around and couldn't find my way out."

"I have to admit, Lydie, I'm surprised that happened. Why didn't you just swim up to the light?" Kit asked.

"There was no light," Lydie said, looking between Kit and Oliver's skeptical faces. "There wasn't. Maybe it got cloudy outside and the light wasn't shining through."

Kit nodded, but Lydie knew she was not convinced.

"I brought some refreshments." Kit held up a tray of chopped fruit and vegetables. "And some sorbet. I thought it might help your throat."

Lydie took it, grateful that Kit and Oliver seemed to have dropped the subject of what happened in the cave.

****

In his dream, Sebastian stood in the center of a familiar forest. He watched the sharp outline of the trees and shrubs, oddly visible in the night. He could see every leaf. Crickets and tree frogs let out their long throaty chirps and bellows. Rivulets of energy flowed from a gossamer pool on the forest floor - like arteries and veins snaking from the earth into his legs. He could see the liquid light traveling into his feet, up his calves and thighs. When it reached his heart, a rush of ecstasy burned through him.

Intoxicated by the power, he stared at the dark mound on the earth the energy flowed out of. He took a step closer, sighing with pleasure. He wanted more. He needed more, but as he drew upon the source, his foot hovered in the air. He set it down, but dared not step closer. A slender white arm protruded from a heap of clothes. Along the pale wrist, Sebastian saw the dark pattern of an elephant tattoo, its body a mosaic of geometric shapes.

Sebastian woke, gasping, and soaked in sweat. His feet tingled as if the milky substance from the forest floor continued to pour into him. Abby slept beside him, her breaths low and deep. Beyond her, tucked in the baby bed, he saw Vidya's tiny form. Swallowing the bile rising in his throat, he pushed off his blanket and climbed from the bed. Careful not to wake Abby, he found a pair of pants and hurried downstairs. In the kitchen, he gulped a glass of water and paced the room. He had recognized the arm on the forest floor. It belonged to Ezra, familiar because of the Ganesh tattoo inked on her forearm. He had been standing over her dead body in the Ebony Woods.

"But it was only a dream," he told the silent kitchen.

Helena slept upstairs. He could wake her, confide the dream to her. Helena understood dreams. Surely, she could put his mind at ease, explain that dreams were merely symbolic, that he had not been absorbing energy from Ezra.

The microwave clock blinked 4am. It was early, too early to be as wired as he felt. Except wired didn't describe it. The lights in the kitchen released sharp beams that drove into the center of his brain. The ceiling fan in the living room sounded like a fan in an industrial warehouse. His skin prickled and suddenly, he couldn't stand the feeling of fabric. He pulled off his pants, switched off the lights, and turned the fan to low. Still, a cacophony of sounds and sensations intruded. He heard the water lapping against the shore. It seemed to drag every grain of sand across the beach. He pressed his hands over his ears and collapsed onto the couch, shoving a pillow over his head.

Ezra was in the Ebony Woods. It might have been a dream, but he knew that much to be true. And he didn't dare wake Helena because he could feel the buzz of Ezra's energy flowing through his veins.

****

"It feels weird to say this," Oliver told Kit that night as they sat on the stairs outside his yurt, "but I'm seeing someone."

Kit looked at him and smiled.

"I know. You didn't have to stress about it. What happened between us was just fulfilling needs, no strings attached. I sensed her then, but figured you knew better than me where things stood. I'm happy that it's moved up a notch for you."

Oliver smiled and felt embarrassed that he'd been dreading mentioning Ezra to Kit. He should have known that Kit would take it in stride.

"It hadn't started when I was here before. I'd met her, but there wasn't any more to it. I just thought there could be…"

"And now there is." Kit pulled a small wooden figure from her pocket and flipped open a switchblade. It was a tree. She carefully shaved along the edge gradually exposing another branch.

"What is it?" Oliver asked, admiring her skill.

"The Mother Tree. I'm making it for Matilda. She has a birthday in two weeks."

"It's beautiful."

"Thanks. Do you want to tell me about her, Oliver? I get the feeling, you're itchin to talk."

He laughed and put his face in his hands.

"Is it strange for me to talk about her?"

"Of course not." Kit looked at him sideways. "I don't mince words, Oliver. When I say I'm happy for you, I mean it. There's no secret emotion I'm not sharing. I consider you a friend. The physical stuff was just bodies meeting their needs. Don't let it mess with your head."

He laughed.

"I'm usually the one that feels that way. It's been a long time since I had a relationship that complicated that aspect of my life. Her name is Ezra."

"And Ezra didn't join you on this adventure into the outback?"

"No. To be honest, I didn't ask her."

"I hope not because of me," Kit said.

"No, well not really. You crossed my mind, but she's rebuilding her coven."

"It was destroyed?"

Oliver sighed and ran a hand through his hair. He'd filled Kit in on the basics of the curse during his last visit. Over the next half hour, he brought her up to date on all that had transpired since their getting abducted at Abby's wedding and ending with Vidya's birth.

"Blimey," Kit mumbled. "And I thought we were in a shit storm with Binda. You've been living in a nightmare."

"It hasn't been a picnic, that's for sure. But that's why I didn't bring her. She's trying to get her head around Victor's betrayal. She's also busy twenty-four-seven. She's like you in that way. Always movin and shakin."

Kit smiled as she whittled her tree.

"Idle hands and all that," she told him with a wink. "And now you're hoping to get Meghan to reveal some bit of goods on this Clyde character? So that you can get rid of him?"

"Yes, unfortunately he has Victor now, which means he's been restored to power. When I first heard about this curse business, I figured it was

Dafne's paranoia. Now it's become this huge beast that's infiltrated all our lives. I want normal again, but so much has changed, I'm not sure that even a curse-free future will feel normal."

"Normal is hardly an appropriate word for your life anyway," Kit told him. "But there's nothing wrong with wanting to feel safe, peaceful. I did a bit of sleuthing after you guys left and uncovered a few old journals that Binda kept. After she'd visit Meghan at the pond, she'd jot down notes, no doubt thinking she'd reveal how to get into the dream wood."

"Did she?"

"No. But she did mention a pocket watch that belonged to her son, Eugene. Apparently, Clyde coveted this watch, but when he killed Eugene, Megan had it. Eugene had given it to her to clean just the day before his death. After he was murdered, Clyde badgered Meghan about the pocket watch. He wanted it badly, but Meghan told him she had no idea what happened to it. She said the murderer must have stolen it, which of course didn't satisfy Clyde because he was the murderer and knew it was not in Eugene's possession when he killed him."

"Okay, go on," Oliver encouraged, not really sure why the watch mattered.

"The pocket watch is here. I found it. Meghan revealed its hiding place to Binda. When Meghan and Clyde came to Australia, Meghan tucked it inside a conch shell and enchanted it. The shell was built into the fireplace of that old cottage out in the woods. The one where Binda took Sebastian. After I read Binda's notes, I assumed she would have taken it, but she never did. I found the shell, chiseled it out, and voila: Eugene's pocket watch."

"I guess I'm still not following."

"It's a bargaining tool, it's bait, Oliver."

"Wow, I'm dense," he chuckled. "That's amazing, Kit. And exactly what we need, a way to draw him out. Something that he wants so badly, he's willing to put himself at risk to get it."

"I'll grab it for you tomorrow. It's in my room."

"Does Binda know you have it?"

Kit shook her head.

"I'm not sure if she even remembers Meghan telling her about it. The journal entry was more than a decade ago. I think Binda was so consumed by love and grief during those talks with Meghan that she ignored a lot of the details. Fortunately, for us, she wrote them down."

Oliver squeezed Kit's knee.

"You're a lifesaver, Kit. I can't thank you enough."

She smiled and inclined her head.

"My pleasure."

They both paused as they heard someone moving up the trail from the Sky Mothers' compound toward the yurts. Matilda appeared at the cliff edge. When she spotted them, she hurried over, her face ashen.

"What is it?" Kit jumped up.

"It's for you, Oliver. A call from home." She held out a cell phone.

"I didn't even know you had service out here," he said, taking the phone.

"Only on this line," Matilda explained. "I'm sorry," she added.

Oliver frowned at the phone almost afraid to put it to his ear. Who would be contacting him in Australia? Why hadn't they tried for Julian instead?

"Oliver." He heard Abby's voice loud and clear. He had expected her to sound far away, half a world away in fact, but she could have been standing in front of him.

"What is it, Abby? Are you okay?"

"Oliver, it's Ezra."

"What? Tell me!"

"She's dead, Oliver."

CHAPTER 12

Oliver stood with the phone held to his ear and tried to let the words sink in. Ezra was dead. That's what she had said. For an instant, he expected to jolt awake. He would be flooded with the relief that comes after a nightmare. He'd sit up in his bed at Ula and realize he'd never gone to Australia, Ezra was fine, and in a few hours he'd wake to Bridget's pancakes and welcome a new day. Instead, seconds ticked by. Matilda hurried off to Julian's yurt. Kit watched him with wide, concerned eyes. He wanted to hand her the phone and just walk away, distancing himself from Abby's words and the news they carried.

"I'm so sorry, Oliver," Abby told him. "She met with Victor, and he took her. He killed her." In the background, Oliver heard a baby cry - Vidya. Sebastian came on the line.

"Oliver? Oh God, man, I don't even know what to say. Abby tried to save her. She ran to the place Victor took her, but didn't find them. We searched for her…" but Sebastian trailed off as if he couldn't stand to share anymore.

And then Julian was there, pulling the phone from Oliver. Matilda took Oliver's elbow and Kit held his hand. They guided him back toward the Sky Mothers. Lydie appeared from the forest, disheveled, woken no doubt by Julian.

"Oliver?" she asked and her voice was small and scared.

He dropped to his knees, and she ran into his arms. They hugged. Oliver smelled mint and eucalyptus in her hair. Lydie said nothing, but holding her made the moment a little more real.

"It's okay, Lydie," he whispered. "It's okay to cry."

Her tears rushed hot onto his shoulder, soaking his t-shirt. After a while, he stood, holding Lydie's hand tight in his own, thinking if he didn't let go, he could hold it all in a little longer.

Matilda and Kit settled them in the breezy hallway. They brought tea and cookies. Oliver shoved three of the cookies in his mouth, struggling to chew. His tongue was sandpaper dry. He forced them down and then drank tea. He still hadn't spoken, not a single word.

Ezra was dead. That's what Abby said. That's what the faces of everyone around him said.

Kit settled next to him.

"Here," she said, handing him a large hunk of obsidian. He needed the earth in that moment, a powerful mineral mined from his element. He took the rock and leaned back on the couch, closing his eyes. A tiny stream of reality flowed into him as he connected to his element. Ezra was dead. Victor murdered Ezra.

Julian walked in, handing the phone to Matilda.

"Tell me," Oliver said, looking him in the eyes.

Julian sighed and shook his head. He looked sad, angry, and defeated.

"Ezra sought Victor out. She asked him to meet her in Trager."

"Damn it," Oliver bellowed slamming his fist onto the glass table. It exploded and shards of glass flew into the room, but Julian stopped them with a flick of his wrist. The cookies and tea smashed on the floor, but he swept those into a pile that Matilda motioned out of the room.

"Maybe you need more time," Julian started.

"No, now. I need to know right now," Oliver snapped.

Lydie snaked her hand into Oliver's and squeezed.

"Ezea wore a camera. It was streaming in their apartment when Kendra returned home. Kendra called Abby."

"She videotaped it?" Oliver asked, horrified.

"Not her death," Julian corrected. "But their conversation. Kendra called Abby and described the location and Abby recognized it. When she arrived, they were already gone. The video disconnected after Victor took her."

"Did they find her? How do they know she's dead?" Oliver asked, hopeful.

"Sebastian found her in the Ebony Woods this morning."

Oliver closed his eyes. Rage blotted out his grief and threatened to erupt.

"I have to take a walk," he said, standing and striding from the compound. He ran into the forest, hard and fast, knowing he couldn't outrun the pain, but he could try.

****

"Sshhh..." Abby rocked from side to side, holding Vidya tight against her. Sad and exhausted, she pressed her lips against Vidya's forehead.

Sebastian had hung up the phone and returned to the living room where Faustine and Helena stood talking.

"Kendra, Dante and Marcus should be here anytime," he said.

Abby walked to the window and watched the waves rolling in from the turbulent lake. The day had been windy and rainy and a match for Sebastian's discovery that morning. Abby had told him to wait for Faustine before checking the Ebony Woods, but he insisted that he'd be careful and doubted he'd find anything. Two hours later he returned, soaked, muddy and streaked with dark brown stains that Abby knew were blood. He'd carried Ezra's body from the woods and laid her in the back of his car. Now her body lay in the shed outside, wrapped in a sheet. As Abby watched rain pelt the roof, her stomach rolled.

Twenty-four hours earlier, Ezra had been alive. Why hadn't she told anyone of her plans to meet Victor? Abby was shopping only blocks away when the meeting started, but it hadn't mattered. Now she was dead.

Vidya snored against her and Abby laid her in the little bassinet they kept in the kitchen. She pulled out a kitchen chair and sat. She thought of the silence after telling Oliver the news. Though he'd said nothing, she'd felt his emotion as if he were in the room. A wall of disbelief and denial had slammed in front of him. With a single phone call, she shattered the joy only just beginning to make its way into his life.

She listened to Sebastian, Faustine and Helena. They felt that Victor or Clyde, whoever he was at this point, was raising the stakes. But was it true? Hadn't he already tried to kill them all once? Abby touched the spot on her throat, no longer tender, where the ski rope had grown taught. Her hands shook as she pulled them away. In the days after Victor had tried to perform his ritual, Abby had often shaken uncontrollably. When she thought of that night, her knees felt weak. Now, with the arrival of her precious child, she could hardly stand to give the thought of death a space in her mind. If she lost her daughter, she'd go insane. She might live another hundred years, two hundred years inside a grief she didn't even know existed. She still didn't know, not truly. But she also hadn't been prepared for the enormous, unfathomable love she felt for her child. It was unlike anything that had ever existed in her life and it terrified her. The vulnerability of that love made her want to pack Vidya and Sebastian in their car and drive to the other side of the world.

Or something much darker. If she didn't run away then she had to eliminate the threat. She couldn't live in fear of Victor. She would not allow him to grow strong and create an army of Vepars to stalk her and her family for the rest of her life. A part of her wanted to race out the door and into the night. She could find him. If she opened herself enough, he would find her. But she had to be smarter this time. She'd made impulsive mistakes before and put herself and others in danger. It was time now to be strategic.

****

"I'm so sorry, Oliver." Kit spoke from behind him the following morning.

He hadn't returned to the Sky Mothers the previous night. He ran for hours, climbed trees and jumped from cliffs into the dark ocean. When he'd grown exhausted enough to sleep, he lay on the beach and prayed he wouldn't dream. He had walked back down the beach that morning and busied himself in the kitchen outside the yurts making coffee and scrambling eggs.

He turned and offered a smile.

"Thanks Kit. Sorry I went MIA last night. I'm not one to sit around when grief strikes. I have to get it out."

"No need to explain," she offered. "And I brought a bottle of Kahlua to spike your coffee if you want to take the edge of."

"Yeah, top me off." He held out his coffee, and she poured in a hefty portion.

Kit made her own coffee and took a seat on a bench. The silence stretched out and Oliver appreciated that she didn't expect him to talk. Although part of him wanted to.

"Oh good, you're back," Julian announced, walking into the kitchen and giving Oliver's shoulder a squeeze. "I think Lydie feared you ran into the Outback never to be seen again."

Oliver sighed.

"I should have stayed to talk with her."

Julian waved a dismissive hand.

"Lydie's a big girl. It's best you follow what's calling out to you in those moments. That kind of news has a process that's different for everyone. Lydie went back to her yurt and drew by candlelight. I had a nice long meditation. Everyone did what they needed to do. This morning, I'll get our plane tickets changed. I plan to talk with Binda in two hours and we'll be on a plane back to Michigan tomorrow."

They had intended to stay for five days, but under the circumstances, Oliver too wanted to return. Although the thought of stepping foot on Michigan soil knowing Ezra was no longer in the world made him feel like flinging his pan of eggs off the cliff.

"Lydie's still sleeping?" he asked, trying to shift his mind away from the anger threatening to overwhelm him.

"Yep, late night for her."

****

Victor stood on the upstairs balcony of the old house. It had once belonged to the coven known as the Serpent House and though there was evidence of them everywhere, it held a residue of filth. Something darker, danker permeated the walls, the floorboards and even the furniture, which had largely gone to rot.

Of the Vepars, only Alva and Tobias had been allowed in the house and now Victor, the third to ascend, or was it descend? He didn't quite know. A strange thing had happened the night he burned the L'Obscurite. As their bodies crumpled and writhed, their hair in flames, their skin melting like candle wax, their pain coursed through Victor. He felt - not only - the burning of their flesh - excruciating - but whole lifetimes of pain, trauma, rejection. Ethel's years of abuse at the hands of her poverty stricken, drunk mother. He experienced a brutal whipping with a hot leather belt that Sabre was dealt at only three years old by his stepfather. As the burning went on and their power surged through him, so too did their anguish, their sorrow, their purity. He had fallen to his knees and wept. He had ripped at his own face and neck and still bore the scars where his fingernails tore away flesh. Somewhere in the night, he thought he had heard the other Vepars mocking him, laughing at him. He had lost consciousness, and did not awake in the singed Ebony Woods, but on a mildewed mattress at Snake Island.

The amulet had pulsed against his chest and the dagger was clutched in his hand. He lay in a dirt room beneath the house, hearing it groan in the whistling lake winds. Next to him, the emaciated body of Clyde breathed slow and deep. Tubes ran between them and Victor understood that he was merely a source of power for Clyde.

He stared at the beach, focusing on a particular rock. Honing his energy on that single stone, he brought his hands toward the sky. The rock did not move. It lay still and heavy growing smooth in the surf. His earth element had abandoned him. He was no longer a witch.

"Then what am I?" he asked. No one answered, nothing answered. The collective consciousness of a million witches who had traveled the earth had grown silent. He no longer had access to their memories, their thoughts, their wisdom.

The only peace he found was in the body of the skin-walker. In that dark, primal space, he left behind the remembered pain of the L'Obscurite and perhaps worst of all, the pain of Ezra as she passed from the land of living into that of the dead. Her prone body, lifeless on the forest floor, haunted his thoughts. When he first saw her in the warehouse he experienced a moment of such profound regret that he slipped away and allowed Clyde to consume him. Now she was gone.

A strange pressure inside his head signaled that Clyde had come to possess him. Victor stared a final time at the gray horizon before his vision grew blurry. Clyde had returned.

In Victor's body. Clyde was a young man again. Lean, fast and starving. He starved for freedom. As the fresh lake air hit his face, he gulped it in, wishing he could become a giant and lean his huge mouth to the water, drink until satisfied. He starved for power. He needed this body forever. In only a few weeks, he would lose his hold over Victor. He could still possess him as he had Alva and Tobias for centuries; however, there was never enough energy to hold their form. When a new century neared, he was lucky to get hours in the bodies of his sires, it was often minutes and drained him for weeks.

He strode through the house, brushing his fingers over the old paintings, the curtains and the long wooden rail that flanked the grand staircase. He did not notice the dust and grime that coated everything. In his mind, Serpent House stood as regal as she had in her prime when witches roamed the halls casting magic, keeping the likes of him out.

He snarled at the memory, their haughty, critical eyes always watching him. He could never visit Serpent House in those days, but he had found ways. Rowing to the island at night and watching them from the trees became a nightly escapade. His mother and Eugene toasted their happiness, their magic, while he was expected to sit at home, eating mush and reading the words of some old bore who knew nothing of dreams.

Stepping onto the porch, he dropped to his knees, inviting the beast within to emerge. Unlike the other Vepars, Clyde relished the sensation of becoming a skin-walker. The delicious stretching as his skin extended and burst, wings erupted from his back. He was in the air before the transformation had finished, flying over the lake, dropping low and feeling the splash of the turbulent water as it rolled beneath him.

CHAPTER 13

"Lydiebug?" Oliver stuck his head in Lydie's yurt.

He caught a glimpse of her splotchy face before she rolled away from him. She hiccuped a sob, trying to muffle her cries in the blankets. Oliver sat on the edge of her bed and touched her shoulder.

"I'm sorry I ran off last night, Lydie. I shouldn't have…"

"That's…" Lydie started and then broke off on another long sob. "That's not why I'm crying," she continued.

"Will you look at me, Lyds? Come one." He gently pulled her toward him and after a moment, she stopped resisting and allowed him to draw her back.

"I'm sorry, Oliver. I…I…" but her words were lost in a whimper. Tears streamed down her red face and she used her sleeve to wipe her running nose.

"What is it, Lydie?" he asked, understanding that her cries surpassed her sorrow for Ezra, a witch she barely knew.

Lydie closed her eyes and shook her head as if she couldn't bear to say what was on her mind.

He waited, holding her hand and wishing he could read her mind.

After several minutes, she spoke.

"In the cave yesterday," she paused.

"When you passed out?" he asked.

Lydie nodded.

"I followed something in. I thought it was a fish."

"It wasn't a fish?"

Lydie nodded again. She pushed the covers off and sat up, reaching for a notebook on her bedside table. Handing him the notebook, she scooted away, pulling her knees into her chest.

"I saw a dead person. After I woke up, I was sure I imagined it, but now I think… No, I know it was…" she didn't speak her name, but Oliver read the truth in her face. Lydie saw Ezra in the cave.

He looked down at the drawing in the notebook. Lydie had perfectly depicted the cave, shading the shadows and crevices. Looking up at him from the center of the drawing were Ezra's eyes. The picture only vaguely resembled the witch, the short hair and tattoos were there, but her face was distorted by death - still he could not deny the eyes.

"I didn't say anything," Lydie continued. "If I had said something…" her voice cracked and a fresh wave of tears poured down her cheeks.

Oliver shook his head, swallowing the lump in his throat, and setting the drawing aside.

"No, Lydie. No. Don't you dare take the blame. By the time we were in that cave, it was too late. That's probably why she appeared. There's nothing you could have done. Okay? Please, Lydie. For my sake, don't blame yourself, not even for a second."

Lydie blew her nose into her blanket.

"You're not mad at me?" she asked.

Oliver stared at her, incredulous.

"Lydie you're my family. I'm so grateful you were with me when I heard what happened to Ezra. I could never be mad at you."

He pulled Lydie into a hug and she released a sigh into his shoulder, pressing her wet face into his shirt.

****

"She won't talk to you. It's best if you ask me your questions and I speak with her myself," Binda told Julian. She held a large opal in her hand and meticulously cleaned the glistening stone.

Julian sighed. He didn't have time to risk upsetting Meghan, but he wanted to speak with her directly. If she outright refused, he'd come up with an alternative plan.

"I need to talk to her. There are questions that might only arise when I'm in her presence and I can't risk missing that guidance."

Binda narrowed her eyes at the stone, but said nothing. After a minute of silence, she nodded.

"Fine. I will meet you in one hour by the waterfall."

An hour later, Julian followed Binda into the forest. Oliver had wanted to join him, but Binda nearly refused to take either of them if that were the case. Julian sensed that Binda's upset lay in her fear of losing Meghan once and for all. Perhaps bringing another witch to the pond to question her would set her off and she'd retreat into the dream wood forever.

They wound through the trees and Julian marveled that Binda ever stumbled upon the pond in the first place. She held out an arm and Julian stopped. Over her shoulder, he saw the dark still pond. Binda moved to the edge and leaned toward the surface.

"Meghan?" she called. Her voice grew softer and more feminine. It was an interesting transformation to observe. The water lay still and silent.

Binda touched her fingers to the surface.

"Meghan, it's Binda," she tried again.

Julian stepped closer to the water, watching the dark pool for any movement.

"We've come to talk about Clyde," he yelled. "Unless you don't care to know what he's up to."

Binda pulled back from the water and gave him a venomous glare. She appeared ready to chastise him, but then stopped. The water undulated. In the center of the pond, Julian watched a woman's face materialize beneath the surface. Her black hair fanned out and created an unnerving Medusa-like spectacle.

The water opened and a horrible shriek of grief and anger exploded.

"You have my Clyde," the witch howled.

Binda fell to her knees sobbing. Julian stepped closer to the water.

"Answer my questions, Meghan. And I'll tell you everything I know."

The water thrashed soaking Julian and Binda. He wiped it away from his face, wrinkling his nose at the foul smell. The water was hot and likely teeming with bacteria.

When the pond calmed, she spoke again. "Why would I help you? You brought me a fake amulet and intentionally deceived me."

Julian fought the urge to remind her that it was she who created the dream wood that lured innocent hybrids into an eternity of doom and eventual death. He had not forgotten about the old man who died at the Sky Mothers after fifty years trapped in a hell of her creation, but he bit his tongue.

"We had no other option. You were holding Sebastian against his will. Another witch stole the original amulet. I didn't realize it was a fake when I returned to America to retrieve it."

"You stole them both. You stole all my sons."

Binda wiped her face and stood away from the pond as if she couldn't bear to witness her beloved in such agony.

"They were not your sons!" Julian exclaimed, growing irritated with the charade. Either Meghan was supremely manipulative, or she truly had gone insane. "They were Sebastian and Liam, two innocent men that you trapped in your sick little world. And I've had about enough of your games, Meghan. You might be the ruler down there, but up here, you're a voice in a pond. So, here's your last chance. Answer my questions and I'll answer yours or stay down there and rot. At this point, I don't care."

Binda watched him, shocked. He doubted that Binda had ever spoken a stern word to the witch beneath the water.

The water lay perfectly calm. Meghan stared at him with menacing red eyes.

"Ask me," she said finally.

Julian kneeled on the forest floor.

"How did Clyde escape?"

"I need assurances," Meghan interrupted, her eyes darting toward Binda. "What does he have, Binda? What can you take to secure his promises?"

Binda started to speak, but Julian silenced her with a look.

"We're not negotiating," he said, sharply. "You've been given your choice. Take it or leave it."

Julian braced himself for another outburst, but the water remained still. Her eyes, on the other hand, were lit with a rage that Julian would not soon forget.

"My son tricked me," she hissed. "He cried and begged me to stay with him in the dream wood. But he had been manipulating my magic. I never created the dark layer. It was meant to mimic the rest of the dream wood, but offer an additional layer of protection to prevent him from running away. In his attempts to change the magic, he poisoned it. The world died. I entered not knowing what he had created. He lured me in and then he vanished."

"He wasn't a witch. Correct? How did he perform magic?"

"He learned magic. He learned to steal it from others, to channel it into objects that he drew power from."

"I see. And you're not sure how he escaped from the dream wood?"

"I have my suspicious," she said.

"Such as?"

"Clyde and I fled to Australia through a portal in space. A stone in the forest. I believe he brought it into the dream wood and concealed it. Then he begged me to come into the deepest layer. I was astonished at what had happened. Why were the trees dead? The earth stank of decay. I did not even see him slip away. He was there and then he was gone."

"Oh Meghan," Binda groaned, reaching toward the water.

"Why didn't you use the portal as well?"

Meghan laughed a mean, derisive sound.

"Don't you think I would have? I did not know the portal was here! I still haven't found it! It is a conclusion I have come to after centuries of contemplation."

"I see." Julian thought about the room that Liam discovered in the area he called the Forest of Purgatory. A space that was undetectable by Meghan and her magic. Could Clyde have hidden it there?

"When Clyde returned to America, he started performing dark magic to become immortal," Julian told her. "We know he had an amulet and a dagger, but according to the book he studied, he had to create three objects that would siphon power from others while also containing a part of his and their souls. Do you know what that other item might be?"

"Immortal," Meghan muttered. "He's trapped me here to steal my energy for eternity? No, no, not my son, my troubled boy. For three days I labored with my youngest son. Oh, how he cried and struggled to grow, that yellow skin and those dark, sad eyes. Eugene was big and strong and strapping, but Clyde was sickly. It wasn't fair! Can't you see that it was not his fault?"

She started to mumble and drift beneath the pond's surface.

"Meghan," Julian said and when she didn't respond, he yelled. "Meghan!"

She stopped shifting and turned her red eyes back on him.

"Did he steal something from you, Meghan? Something that he could use to contain your magic?"

"Clyde?" she murmured. "Hundreds of years, centuries ago this all happened. I don't know," she screamed and Julian clamped his hands over his ears as the sound reverberated through the forest, shaking his eardrums.

"I'm so tired," she muttered, again shifting beneath the water. "I'm ready to pass on. Isn't it time? Why am I still here? Binda, you have to help me! You have to end this for me."

Binda crawled to the water's edge.

"Oh Meghan, if only I could. I would die with you in an instant."

"Help us put an end to this," Julian told her urgently, moving closer to the water. "If you're ready to pass on, you'll be able to. You can end this eternal life on your terms."

"Yes," she screamed, and the sound echoed. Birds fled from the branches of trees raining leaves onto the pond's surface.

"Think back to the day he disappeared. What was your last experience with Clyde? Did he take something from you?" Julian asked, not having a clue what sort of item Clyde used to steal a piece of Meghan's power. He did it though - of that much Julian was sure. He stole her magic, and he locked her in the world that she had built for him. A world she created to protect him. A world she created out of love.

Suddenly Meghan disappeared.

"What happened?" Julian demanded, turning to Binda. "Did she leave?"

Binda peered into the dark water, her face expectant.

Several minutes passed and suddenly ripples broke the placid water.

"I had a ring," she said. "It was a special ring given to me by the witch who first discovered my magic. The ring contained a pearl that could sense my enemies. If an enemy was near, the ring turned black. I never took it off, but when we arrived here in Australia it was gone from my hand. I believed the energy of the portal pulled it off or perhaps it was the price I had to pay for our escape…."

"Describe it?" Julian asked.

Meghan shook her head back and forth as if struggling to recall it.

"It was a large opal set in a silver band. You'd never suspect it was magic unless it revealed itself to you."

"Okay that's good, great even. Meghan tell me about the portal. What did it look like?"

Meghan sighed and paced beneath the water.

"It's not extraordinary, a stone the size of a mango. Its color is the ocean on a stormy day. But there is a light. You can see it, feel it, if you encounter this stone, you stay away from it. But it conceals itself well. Burrowed deep in the mud, waiting to change someone's life forever." Meghan started to mumble under her breath. Julian strained forward to hear her then thought better of it and backed up.

"You found this stone in Michigan? How did you come to know its power?"

"I prayed to the four elements the night that my beloved Eugene left this world. I prayed that Clyde would be granted mercy. Please, I called to the Goddess, let me keep one child. When I opened my eyes, the stone seemed to glow from the forest floor. I brushed away the ferns surrounding it and knew my prayers had been answered. I raced home and packed a bag. I waited until Clyde arrived early the next morning. We ran back to the stone. When we touched it, the world vanished around us. We stepped into a northern Michigan forest and stepped out in the outback of Australia."

Julian frowned, considering her story. He obviously knew that portals existed. The bewitched mirrors of All Hallow's Balls were proof enough. Still - to discover one in nature seemed cause for contemplation.

"Binda, go find Liam and ask him if he saw a strange stone in Clyde's cave room in the dream wood."

Binda scowled at him and started to speak, but then she glanced at Meghan's face in the water and stood abruptly.

****

Dante, Marcus and Kendra sat at Abby's kitchen table. None of them spoke. Kendra picked at a silver bracelet encircling her right wrist. Marcus, red eyed, leaned his chin on his folded hands and stared out the window. Only Dante appeared alert, but also at a loss for words.

Sebastian stood at the counter, meticulously slicing garlic into paper thin squares. Abby carried the coffee pot to the table, but stopped when she realized everyone's cups were full.

They had arrived at Abby and Sebastian's home in angry tears. At their insistence, Abby and Sebastian took them to the abandoned warehouse and afterwords to the Ebony Woods. It was a somber experience standing in those woods where only weeks earlier they nearly died. They all came out alive that night, this time one of them had not.

Kendra cried openly, falling on the forest floor where Ezra's body had been discovered. Dante tried to console her and Marcus ran to the bushes to vomit. Abby sought Sebastian for comfort, but he had been rigid and silent. When she tried to find his eyes, he refused to look at her. He stared into the cloudy sky or deep into the woods. He seemed to be searching for anything to fix on to avoid making eye contact with her. She thought she understood. Discovering Ezra likely brought back memories of Claire's death.

When they returned to the house, Sebastian insisted on cooking though Abby doubted anyone would eat. She heard Helena singing to Vidya in the next room and wished she could grab her baby and crawl into bed. Snuggled beneath the covers, she might be able to pretend that Ezra still lived.

Faustine and Elda walked in from the hallway mirror.

Elda went to the table and leaned down, wrapping her arms around Kendra and whispering into her ear. She repeated the action with Dante and Marcus. Abby noticed a settling of the surrounding air. A peaceful lull descended over the table.

"I know this is difficult to speak of right now," Elda said, sitting down. "But did Ezra leave final wishes? Did she have a desire for burial or..."

"Cremation," Dante said. "She was always very clear about that."

"With her ashes scattered in the..." Kendra's voice broke, but she managed to go on. "In the community garden."

Faustine paused next to Sebastian, but Sebastian pointedly ignored him. Abby wasn't surprised, but wished he'd make a little effort. It only caused more strain when he became so moody.

"If you would like, I can take care of that for you," Faustine told them. "Or if you prefer, we can bewitch a coffin of sorts for you to transport her back to Chicago?"

His cool, slightly accented voice, sounded far too clipped and short for asking such questions. Abby prickled at the insensitivity coming from Faustine and Sebastian. Before she spoke in anger, she left the room, peeking in to see Vidya asleep in Helena's arms. She walked out the door, leaving the porch and following the beach. The lake reflected the gray sky.

The curse was winning. Clyde was winning. As she moved briskly through the humid day that foretold of rain, her body grew cumbersome. As if her skin, weighted with water, had begun to sag and get heavy. She turned and waded into the lake.

The cold bit her ankles, knees and then thighs. It rose up her hips, along her ribs and finally devoured her as she dove beneath the surface. Her shorts and t-shirts fanned in the water, weighted, but barely noticeable as she drove forward. The rain arrived in a rush. When she surfaced, it fell in huge fat drops. Abby rolled onto her back and opened her mouth. The lake and the rain electrified her. It erased her lethargy and made every thought crystal clear.

Abby had to be the one. As she paddled backwards, watching her legs kick sprays of water to meet the rain, she understood that was her destiny.

Before Vidya, she did not have the courage. But now that had all changed. The curse had to end with those who started it. Abby descended from that original pair, but she needed Kanti's help and the time for playing it safe was over.

CHAPTER 14

"Abigail," her mother said pointing out the window. "You just drove right by the tea shop. See." She tapped on the passenger window.

"I know, mom," Abby told her, daring a quick glance at her mom before merging onto the freeway.

"Where on earth are we going?" Becky asked. "Don't tell me you're dragging me to some pub. I don't care what people say about craft beer. Beer is beer. Frankly, it's a barbarian drink. Not to mention we have an infant with us, Abby."

Abby took a deep breath and prepared for her mother's reaction.

"We're not going to the tea shop. We're going to New Orleans."

Becky's mouth fell open, and it took her a moment to gather her words.

"Excuse me?" She narrowed her eyes as if waiting for the joke.

"We're going to New Orleans. I have something I need to take care of."

"And you're telling me this now? Is this like the spa?" She hissed looking around wildly like she might fling open the door and jump.

Abby hit the lock button and then regretted it when she saw the fear in her mother's face.

"I'm sorry, I should have explained, mom. But hear me out. Do you remember the curse that I told you about?"

"Of course," she snapped, fumbling in her purse for a cigarette that Abby immediately pulled from her hand.

"You can't smoke with Vidya in the car," Abby told her.

Becky glared at her daughter and then pulled out a stick of chewing gum, popping it into her mouth and then immediately unwrapping a second and a third piece.

"There's a woman in New Orleans who can help me. But I have to see her alone."

"But," Becky turned and looked out the back window as if she couldn't believe Lansing was fading from view. "But why am I going? And why didn't you tell me? And why do we have Vidya?"

"I couldn't tell Sebastian because he wouldn't have understood. He would have freaked out and, honestly the other witches would have as well."

Becky grimaced at the word witches.

"Is it dangerous? Are you out of your mind? Taking your mother and your newborn baby? Abigail Daniels turn this car around right now!"

"It's Hull, mom. Abigail Hull. And it's not dangerous. I wouldn't put you in danger, but I have to do it alone and I needed someone I trust to stay with Vidya."

Becky looked ready to argue, but seemed to pause on Abby's last words.

"Me? You trusted me to stay with Vidya?"

"You're my mom. I trust you with my life, my child's life," Abby said, again daring a glance at her mother who chewed her gum slowly with a tiny smile on her lips.

Becky nodded as if coming to some conclusion.

"Why didn't you leave Vidya with Sebastian?" she asked after a moment.

"Because he'd never understand my leaving without her and honestly, I'm not comfortable leaving for a weekend without her. There's too much at stake right now."

"But where does he think you are? What did you tell him? And what about your father? Abigail, he's expecting me home for dinner."

"I called dad on my way down. I told him I was whisking you away for a girl's weekend. I told Sebastian the same thing." She left out that she'd also told Sebastian that her mother was despondent over not getting more time with the new baby and Abby wanted to appease her. Moreover, she insisted that she needed to get away after Ezra's death.

"Oh." Becky seemed satisfied with the answer. "Well I never have been to New Orleans."

****

"Hey mate, Kit told us about your girl back in the states. I'm right sorry to hear about it," Liam told Oliver, offering him a frosted glass filled with a fizzy beverage. "That's an Aussie Dark and Stormy right there. Thought it'd suit you and if I check my watch," he glanced up at the sun. "It's after twelve or close enough so a cocktail is surely in order."

"Cheers," Oliver told him taking the drink and tapping it against Liam's own. "Thanks for the condolences and the drink."

Oliver didn't offer more regarding Ezra. He was doing his best not to think about her.

"I would have liked to see Sebastian again, brothers in battle and all that," Liam told Oliver.

"Yeah, well, he's fighting the new parent battle, and I'd describe his personality as Night of the Living Dead meets Oscar the Grouch so I promise you, you're not missing much."

Liam grinned. He had put on some weight since escaping the dream wood. Oliver saw hints of the man he'd been before he went in, though his eyes still held a haunted look.

"I'd take a grumpy Sebastian over this last year of my life any day of the week. I really would love to help him though, pay him back for getting me out of that nightmare. Any curse developments? Kit filled me in on what you're up against. Sounds nasty."

"That's why we're here, breaking curses, meeting with evil witches. All in a day's work," Oliver laughed. He picked up a pink shell and held it out. "Like this one, Lydie?" he called.

"Yeah," Lydie responded. She was squatting further down the beach, combing the sand with her fingers. She had insisted that she wanted a box of shells to take back to Michigan and enlisted Oliver as her helper.

"I don't envy ya mate. That sounds like a stressful job. I'm sincere though. If you guys need help, I'll come back with ya and fight some evil."

Oliver appreciated Liam's desire to help.

"The truth is we're mostly scouring documents, searching for patterns, that kind of thing." Oliver took a long gulp of his drink. It burned a bit going down, but he hoped it might also loosen up his body. He felt taut, like a guitar string pulled too tight. He might snap at any moment.

Lydie made her way back to them, holding a yellow bucket nearly overflowing with shells.

"I don't think those are going to fit on your carry-on," Oliver told her wryly.

"Oh, they will. I've got a shrinking spell, I'm itching to try out. I was planning on using it on your sandals just for fun but this seems more productive."

Oliver reached to pinch her, but she jumped back, swatting at him.

"I'm Liam," Liam told her, extending his hand.

"Lydie," she replied, sticking her tongue out at Oliver.

"Liam!" They heard Binda's strong voice carry across the beach and all three turned as she moved swiftly down the stairs by the pool.

"Crickey, what've I done now?"

"You could take your chances with the sharks instead," Oliver offered, extending an arm toward the ocean.

"Any day of the week," Liam murmured under his breath. Lydie suppressed a giggle as Binda charged across the beach, her face as rigid as a statue.

"At your service," Liam called, sweeping forward in a bow.

Binda frowned, stopping just in front of him.

"Did you ever find an odd stone in Clyde's room in the cave. One that glowed?"

"Blimey." Liam scratched his head. Oliver sensed that Liam knew of the stone, but didn't want to tell her. "I don't remember, Binda. Since getting out, that year of captivity is a blur."

She narrowed her eyes at him, but said nothing more. She turned on her heel and stomped off the way she'd come.

"She reminds me of Miss Trunchbull from Matilda," Lydie whispered as if the retreating figure might hear her.

"Is that an ogre?" Liam asked.

Lydie giggled.

"Basically."

"Why didn't you tell her the truth?" Oliver asked Liam.

Liam shrugged, clearly not disturbed that Oliver had called him on the lie.

"I was trapped in that place for a year. The only solace I had was that little room in the cave. If I tell Binda about anything in there, she'll tell Meghan how to find it. What if another hybrid stumbles into the dream wood and gets trapped? They'll have nowhere to hide. I respect Binda. She's been around a long time, but she's Meghan's number one supporter. She could have told Hannah I was alive, put her fears at ease. She was talking to Meghan after all, she knew I was trapped in there, but she didn't. She let Hannah believe that I had run off or died or whatever. I don't owe her honesty or anything else."

"Good point," Oliver said. "What was it? The stone?"

Liam shrugged.

"I never got that close to it. I saw it once tucked way back in a crevice in the wall. I would have had to prise it out. Maybe I should have since they seem to want it."

"Refills?" Hannah called, holding up a pitcher. She was standing next to the pool wearing an ankle length white dress with slits all the way to her thighs.

"I am blessed," Liam murmured.

Kit walked next to her wearing a pair of white cargo shorts and a black t-shirt.

Oliver smiled and waved at her, amazed how between the two women, he found Kit infinitely more beautiful. Attraction was a mysterious thing.

****

"Are you ready, child?" Leona's soft hands grasped Abby's wrists. Abby noticed their smoothness, like they'd been left in water for too long, pruned and silky.

She nodded and allowed Leona to guide her behind a curtain. The room smelled of incense and rose oil. A veil of smoke hovered in the air and created the illusion that spirits already occupied the space, perhaps they did. A round table, cloaked in a black cloth, sat in the center of the room backed by two chairs. Leona gently guided Abby into one and took the other herself, moving easily despite her blindness.

Leona reached again for Abby's hands across the table.

"It ain't wise to invite such an angry spirit inside," Leona muttered, "but promises have been made, assurances..." She stated the second part as if reminding whatever entity stood in the room to keep their word.

Leona started to breathe long and deep. Abby counted one of her breaths, it lasted nearly forty seconds on the exhalation. Leona's blueish eyelids rested on the folds of skin beneath her long dark lashes. The smoke in the room seemed to drift closer to Leona. It hovered and then started to coil in front of her face. In a flash, Abby saw a great wave of it vanish into the woman's mouth. Leona released her breath, but the smoke did not emerge.

Several minutes passed. Abby's heart thumped in her chest. She noticed a rivulet of sweat slithering from beneath her armpit. The room seemed to grow stifling and smaller as if they were trapped in a madman's funhouse and soon they would be crushed within the dark walls.

"Breathe," she silently reminded herself.

Leona's features began to change. Her posture shifted and she no longer slumped forward, but sat tall and erect, her head held high. Though Leona was still there, Abby saw another face as well. Leona blinked and opened her eyes, watching Abby sharply. Her cloudy eyes were replaced with keen, dark eyes. Her mouth was set in a grim line.

For an instant, Leona's hand tightened in her own. The strength behind the touch did not belong to the old woman and Abby started to shrink away, but the woman held on.

"Kanti?" Abby asked, finding her voice.

The woman nodded.

"I need you to tell me about the curse. How do we break it?" she continued, her hands trembling in her lap.

Though Abby was distracted by the sharpness of the woman's glare, she also knew that they had limited time. Leona had told Abby that she exhausted quickly when acting as a conduit for spirits and the tether snapped easily.

"It is not a curse," the woman said and her voice wrapped Leona's in a husky deep sound, "but an invocation. You think I would curse my own child? Blood of my body?"

The woman let out a short harsh sound and Abby shrank away.

"I died to save her."

"How do we end it? How do I stop him?"

Leona, Kanti, slowly closed her eyes. Her lashes seemed longer, darker. When she opened them, they seemed like long shadowy hallways of melted brown. Kanti had been beautiful, mysterious, wild. Even the tiniest glimpse that Abby could see through the form of the old woman revealed as much.

"The dagger, the amulet, the ring, and last Clyde himself. If you destroy his body first, he will remain. We are his power and we live in those things. You live in them as does your child, your husband, your ancestors…"

Abby frowned.

"Where are they, Kanti? Where are those things?"

"You know," Kanti whispered and Leona's face reemerged and then flickered out.

Kanti let out a low hiss.

"Snake Island?" Abby asked.

Kanti offered a tiny, almost imperceptible nod.

"Invite me in," Kanti whispered. "When it is time, wear the amulet and invite me in."

"And you'll help me destroy him?"

Kanti nodded.

Abby held tight to Leona's hand already feeling it grow weaker in her own.

"Where is Clyde, Kanti? Do you know where's Clyde's body is?"

Again, she hissed and Abby understood.

Snake Island. Everything she sought was on Snake Island.

CHAPTER 15

Abby had not intended to spend much time in New Orleans after her visit with Leona, but her mother insisted they walk downtown for dinner before calling it a night. Abby had rented a hotel room in the French Quarter and as she experienced on her prior trip, the smells and sounds of New Orleans intoxicated her. Her mother, pushing Vidya in a stroller, appeared equally enthralled.

"Look at that," Becky said for what must have been the fiftieth time. She pointed out old buildings, street musicians, sculptures, food vendors and even complete strangers wearing beads or bright clothes.

Abby nodded and offered the occasional comment, but mostly she thought of Kanti. Her magnetic eyes were burned into Abby's thoughts. They had been powerful, angry and filled with despair. After Leona broke the connection, the woman had barely been able to hold her head up. Her assistant had helped her to a couch to lie down. Abby had tried to pay, but Leona waved her away, saying 'Darlin, by the time this is over, you'll have paid more than your fair share.'

Abby tried not to dwell on what she meant.

"We'll have dinner here," Becky announced, turning abruptly into a dimly lit restaurant. The tables and booths glowed in the light of small red candles. The host seated them in the back, and Abby slid into the booth that faced the doorway. She had not forgotten where they were. Victor had destroyed the leader of the L'Obscurite, but in those kinds of clans there was always a new one ready to take over.

As if in response to her thoughts, Audra, the young woman that had helped them months before walked through the door flanked by two witches. Abby recognized them as witches immediately. Their aura was different, larger and more solid than the humans around them. Helena had taught her how to see their unique shape and she found herself mildly impressed with her ability to do so. Her pride was dashed when she realized they could also sense her and they were dangerous.

Abby cringed into the corner of the booth, cupping a hand over her face.

"Sit up straight," Becky chastised, grabbing for Abby's shirt. "You're fidgeting."

Abby fought the urge to kick her mother beneath the table or better yet to use a silencing charm on her.

"Mom," she whispered under her breath, then thought better of it, pulling a pen from her purse and writing her mother a note on a napkin. "We need to leave RIGHT NOW!"

"That way," Abby mouthed at her mother, pointing behind her toward the kitchen.

Becky glared at her daughter as if she'd lost her mind. The witches stepped to the bar and one glanced their way. She was tall and broad with sharp features and dark green eyes that absorbed them in an instant. With the tiniest gesture, she touched the elbow of the other witch, a man with a pointed black beard and a pair of devil's horns sticking from a headband on his long black hair.

Abby had already lifted Vidya from the stroller and tucked her into a baby wrap across her chest. Becky stood fumbling with her purse and nearly dropping it on the floor. As the contents started to spill Abby flicked her wrist and they shot back inside startling her mother.

Audra had noticed them as well. She made eye contact with Abby, recognizing her immediately. Abby saw her eyes flick down to Vidya's head poking from the wrap across Abby's chest.

Audra lifted her glass, which appeared to be filled with bourbon and knocked it hard into the glass of the witch wearing devil's horns. He had ordered a whiskey drink as well, but the bartender had lit his on fire. When the drinks collided, the glass smashed and the long alcohol sodden bar lit on fire.

"Go," Abby told her mom, shoving her toward the kitchen. Becky ran through the double doors, nearly slipping on the greasy tile floor. Abby steadied her and pushed her towards the back. The kitchen staff, clad in white linen, stared at them surprised and the chef pointed an angry finger shouting at them that they could not be there, but already Becky had pushed through the back door and into the alleyway. Abby did not think, she shoved her mom down a dark alleyway and whispered an incantation of invisibility putting a finger to her mother's lips. She didn't have an elixir to aid in their vanishing, but an intention combined with her magic would hopefully block them enough to escape.

The dark alley stank of urine and rotted food. Abby pressed her mother against the wall. When she started to protest, Abby cut her off with a hand over her mouth.

In the light of the street they'd departed, Abby saw the witch with the black beard emerge. He walked slowly, pausing and cocking his head to the side before moving on. The broad witch followed him, her hand clamped on the bicep of Audra whose face remained impassive. Abby fought the urge to help. It would only put them in danger and Audra had already told

Abby that her family's store was controlled by the L'Obscurite.

Abby waited several minutes after the two witches had disappeared. Silently, she nudged her mother toward a well-lit street and climbed quickly into a cab.

Later that night, Abby and her mother ate at a little diner off of highway fifty-nine. To Abby's surprise, Becky devoured her burger and French fries and then insisted on a brownie sundae for dessert.

"I'm happy to see you've gotten your appetite back, mom," Abby told her honestly. Abby's own appetite felt rather suppressed after their encounter with the L'Obscurite.

"Me too," Becky agreed, pushing her sundae toward Abby. "Try it, Abigail. The homemade vanilla ice cream is divine."

Abby took a half-hearted bite and nodded.

"I'm really sorry, mom," she said, adjusting Vidya who had fallen asleep after Abby breastfed her. "I promised no danger…."

Becky dismissed her with a wave of her spoon.

She looked at her conspiratorially across the table.

"To tell you the truth, Abby, it was rather exciting, wasn't it? I mean if they'd found us in that alley, I would have peed my pants. But all in all, I think it went well."

Abby stared at her mom, mouth agape. Becky had returned to her sundae and was scooping spoonfuls of melted ice cream into her mouth.

"Did you see the person about the umm…," Becky dropped her voice to a whisper, "the curse?"

Abby smiled and nodded her head.

"Yes. And I couldn't have done it without you. Thank you, mom."

Becky beamed at her across the table.

"I'd say we make a pretty good team. Or I guess it's a threesome now," Becky said inclining her head toward Vidya who led out a long gurgling burp.

****

"Here's the watch," Kit told Oliver, handing him a small velvet bag. He stood next to the Range Rover as they prepared to leave Sky Mothers for the airport.

He dumped the contents into his palm. The gold was tarnished, and he had to prise the lid open. The glass was spider-webbed, and the numbers faded.

"Nothing to write home about, is it?" he asked, turning it over.

"Not today, but three hundred years ago was another story."

"Thank you, Kit. I appreciate this more than I can say."

Kit stepped into him and before he said more, she pulled him against her and kissed him long and deep. When she stepped away, the warmth left his body. He took a deep breath and grinned.

"I'll be seeing you, Oliver," she winked and turned, walking back toward the Sky Mothers.

Inside the Rover, Lydie rolled down the window.

"What was that?" She asked making a gagging face.

"A goodbye kiss," Oliver laughed, watching Kit wistfully.

"Get in the car, Romeo," Julian barked.

Oliver jumped in and closed the door, holding the pocket watch.

"It's not much of a bargaining chip, but better than nothing," Julian observed.

"There's more," Oliver told him. "When Binda asked Liam about the stone in Clyde's room, he lied. He saw it crammed in the wall and couldn't reach it. What was it?"

"The portal he used to travel between Australia and America," Julian told them. "Meghan was right - that's how Clyde escaped back to America. The question is, does it still work?"

****

"Hey! Where are you sneaking off to?" Sebastian grabbed Abby around the waist before she walked out the door. "I've only had you for fifteen minutes and you're already leaving?"

She leaned into his kiss and then pressed her face against his chest.

"I left Vidya's blankie in my car," she said.

Since returning from New Orleans, she'd been carefully phrasing her answers to evade Sebastian's inquiries. She hated lying to him.

She had concealed her trip to avoid upsetting him, which didn't make the lie okay. Trust was such a fragile thing and if he believed she had lied about her trip, he might start questioning other things. After she had dropped her mom in Lansing, she'd driven straight home often checking her rearview mirror with the vaguely irrational fear that the L'Obscurite had followed her. She did not believe they had recognized her, only that they recognized she was a witch in their territory. Still, when she had first walked into Vidya's nursery, the memory of the doll tucked in the bassinet sent a shiver down her spine.

"I missed you," Sebastian said, kissing her nose. "It was weird spending a whole night in this house without you, especially after…"

He didn't say the words, but she understood - Ezra's murder. Though she had left for a day and night, it didn't change all that had transpired before. The truth was that she'd gone to New Orleans because of what happened to Ezra. She couldn't stand idly by as Clyde destroyed them.

****

"How are you?" Abby asked Oliver, finding him alone on the widow's walk, gazing at the rising sun.

Lydie, Julian and Oliver had returned from Australia late the night before.

He tilted his head and looked up at her, offering a small smile.

"Is it terrible if I say fine?" he asked. "I sort of shift in and out of sadness. One minute, I'm angry and sad and the next, I'm completely numb. This morning I'm numb."

Abby handed him a cup of coffee and then carefully perched her own on the rail before sitting next to him.

"Wow," she breathed, catching her first conscious glimpse of the sun as it rose. The base of the horizon glowed bright red with a mushroom cap of flaming orange at its center.

"It's a great reset for your element and your energy. Sunrises and sunsets are powerful. When I trained with Julian, I used to meditate during the sunrise and sunset every day. Dafne did it too, though for her it was by choice. I grumbled about it. I liked to sleep late. Who wants to wake up to Michigan in February for a sunrise when it's negative twelve degrees?" He chuckled and shook his head. "But now looking back, I realize it made me a better witch and a better man. My body, my brain, my element, my spirit - everything was in balance."

"I can imagine," Abby agreed, noticing how the sun seemed to cleanse her as it rose. "And I'm so very sorry, Oliver. Maybe saying it doesn't matter, or help, but I can't not say it. I'm so sorry."

Oliver reached for Abby's hand and held it in his own. He traced his finger over her moonstone wedding ring and then gave her a squeeze before releasing it.

"I appreciate it. A part of me feels like I don't deserve all this sympathy. It should be for Kendra, Dante and Marcus. I only knew Ezra for a few months. Why am I allowed to grieve?"

Abby shook her head.

"Love doesn't work that way. It's not measured in time. When Sebastian disappeared, I felt..." the memory of it created an immediate fist in the center of her chest. She rested her hand over her heart space and continued. "Like I wanted to die. I didn't want to go on. I'd only known him for months. At least that's what my head told me, but my heart didn't reduce love to something as insignificant as time."

Oliver shifted and looked Abby in the eyes.

"Thank you for saying that. Maybe I'm trying to live in my head on this. Goddess knows I want to. I've never been a good griever. I'm the funny guy. The funny guy is not supposed to mope around. He's supposed to cheer everyone else up when they're crying."

Abby smiled.

"You do, Oliver. You're always making me smile, and everyone else, but you're more than all that. You've got all kinds of layers. It's okay to hurt and to mourn someone you cared for."

Oliver sipped his coffee and returned his gaze to the sun.

Abby perked her ears for any sound of Vidya, awake in the house, but everyone, her baby included, still slept. When she did wake, Sebastian would get up with her. She slept in a small bed attached to their own so they heard her the moment she stirred. It hurt to feel so full of gratitude as Oliver sat empty beside her. Abby had Sebastian and now Vidya. Oliver had lost his new love and believed he did not even deserve his sadness.

"What does your heart need?" Abby asked.

"My heart?" he glanced back at her.

"Yeah, what can we do to comfort your heart this morning? Pancakes? Sebastian's famous cinnamon rolls? A walk on the beach? You name it and it's yours. Before you answer, it's perfectly acceptable to tell me you'd rather be left alone."

He grinned.

"My mom used to make me chocolate chip pancakes on my birthday," he admitted.

"Yes, those sound awesome. You finish your coffee and then come down to the kitchen. Chocolate chip pancakes it is," she told him.

"Wait. I don't want to change the subject, but I'd rather not put this off," Oliver said, grabbing Abby's hand before she walked away. "We need a way to make Clyde aware of this watch." He pulled something from his pocket and held it out.

Abby looked at the tarnished gold pocket-watch.

"What is it? I mean, I can see what it is, but what does it have to do with Clyde?"

"It belonged to his brother, Eugene. Apparently, he wanted it and his mother pretended it disappeared after Eugene's death, but really she hid it in Australia. Kit found it for us."

Abby touched the watch.

"Hmmm, wow. That's good, right? I mean he'll want it so we can..."

"Set a trap," Oliver sighed. "Since that worked out so well last time."

Abby knew that he referred to Ethel and the L'Obscurite.

"We'll be in Chicago tomorrow. Let's ask Dante," Abby said.

CHAPTER 16

"I should have been here," Oliver sighed.

He stood with Kendra, Abby and Sebastian on the edge of a Chicago park. The flowering trees spilled white and purple flowers onto the grass. People walked the pathways holding hands, licking ice cream cones and laughing. It was surreal. Abby's eyes kept drifting back to Kendra's hands where she clutched a plain wooden box that held Ezra's ashes.

Through her tears, Kendra shook her head.

"You couldn't have stopped her, Oliver. Ezra did what she thought was right. She trusted Victor, after all that happened, she still assumed he wouldn't hurt her." Kendra's voice broke, and she sank to the grass. Oliver sat with her and wrapped her in a hug.

Tears flowed down Abby's cheeks as well. She nuzzled her face into Vidya's hair. She slept in a wrap pressed close to Abby's chest. Sebastian rubbed Abby's back. He too looked ready to cry.

"Here comes Marcus and Dante," he said, his voice low and rough.

The two men gathered Kendra into their arms and they stood hugging and crying. After several minutes, Kendra led them toward a flower garden that Ezra planted the previous year. They each took a handful of her ashes, Oliver too, and released them into the flowers.

"Ezra always told me when she got stressed about life, she remembered that we're stardust, destined for better things. Shine bright, little star." Kendra said, fighting the sobs trying to steal her voice.

After they spread her ashes, the witches returned to the new loft that Ezra and the others had moved into several weeks before. Abby was grateful they no longer lived in the loft they previously shared with Victor. Their new home seemed eerily quiet as if it were as lost as the witches who occupied the space.

Kendra ordered coffee and pastries from a shop that delivered. Abby took the delivery and assembled the food on a large wooden coffee table surrounded by colorful pillows. She unwrapped Vidya, fed her, and laid her on a blanket on the floor. Sebastian lay next to her, watching the tiny bubbles of spit that popped from her mouth as she slept. The three remaining Guerilla witches sat close together, none of them speaking.

Oliver leaned on a pillow close to Abby and picked at the seam.

Abby tried to imagine their experience. In a very short span of time one of their closest friends, the creator of their group, had betrayed them and now only weeks later he had killed one of their own. She struggled to reconcile the Victor she had cared for with the monster who so carelessly destroyed the people he once loved.

"What can we do?" Abby asked. "How can we help you guys through this?"

Dante looked up and offered her a half smile. His eyes were red rimmed.

"We'll be okay. It's hard to conceive right now, but we're survivors. Ezra taught us that." He smiled as if remembering. "But we can help you by giving you a copy of the video of Ezra's last day. Maybe there's something important…"

He trailed off and an icy shudder slid down Abby's spine.

She had not watched the video, but heard Ezra's voice and Victor's during their final meeting. She feared witnessing the last moments of Ezra's life. Obviously, it upset Kendra as well. She pushed her hands over her face and cried in great heaping gasps for several minutes.

"We're not vengeful," Dante went on, hugging Kendra close to him. "I loved Ezra and though it's hard to admit, I loved Victor too. We don't intend to hunt him down and make him pay. We're just not those kinds of witches. We do want to know what happens though. We'll help when you need us, but we've all agreed that we need to rebuild our lives here. We can't return to Trager and become obsessed with this. It's already taken two of us."

"Yeah, of course," Oliver replied. He shifted on his pillow and offered an awkward knee-pat to Kendra.

She stopped crying, but her face was red and splotchy.

"Why did she go there? Alone? I just don't get it…" Kendra started, pausing when another tear slid down her cheek.

"Because she still had faith in Victor. It's like you said, she wanted to believe he was still good, that he wouldn't hurt her."

"But why didn't she take one of us. Why go alone?" Kendra wrung her hands and then shook her head as if accepting defeat.

Vidya made a gurgling sound and opened her eyes. She blinked up at Sebastian.

"Hi beautiful girl," he told her, leaning down and kissing her forehead.

Abby scooted close and lay down on the blanket, taking one of Vidya's tiny hands in her own.

"She's beautiful, Abby," Dante told her, standing and walking over to the baby. "Thank you for bringing her today."

He sat down and offered one of his fingers to the baby. She clutched it in her own.

Kendra's already drawn face seemed to pinch with grief at the sight.

"I have to go lay down," she mumbled, standing and stumbling toward her room.

"I'll tuck her in," Marcus told Dante, offering the others a sad smile before following Kendra out.

Abby took advantage of their time with Dante alone to bring up the watch.

"Dante, I hate to ask about this now, but we have a pocket watch that we believe Clyde would want," she started.

Oliver fished it out of his pocket.

"We need to make Victor aware of this. Any idea how?" Oliver asked.

"You figure since Ezra was able to contact him, I should know how as well?" Dante asked.

"We hope," Abby said.

Dante nodded. "Let me think about it. My head's not clear, but I'll call you in a day or two and see what I can come up with."

****

"That was rough," Oliver murmured as they drove back to Trager City. They had driven down that morning in Oliver's VW van.

Abby sat in the backseat, rubbing Vidya's satiny little toes and watching her peaceful face in sleep.

"Yeah, I feel terrible for them. And for you, Oliver," Abby added.

"How are you holding up?" Sebastian asked, giving him a side-long appraisal. "I can drive if you want to catch a nap, check out for a couple hours?"

Oliver shook his head.

"I'm better driving. Gives me something to focus on."

"I'd like to get my hand on Victor," Sebastian muttered.

Abby reached forward and squeezed his shoulder.

"Let's not go there right now, okay? Vidya gets agitated when we do. We could all use a few hours of peace."

****

Abby waited until Sebastian and Oliver left to do a perimeter walk around the property. She put Vidya in her bassinet and retreated to her bedroom. In her diaper bag, she fished out a small velvet pouch and set it on the bed. What had gotten into her? She had snatched the bag when she saw it on the shelf at Kendra's loft in Chicago. Something in her just reached out and grabbed it while no one was looking. She remembered the first time she laid eyes on the bag at the All Hallow's Ball nearly a year before. That was the night she first met the Guerilla witches. In a way, that night marked the beginning of the curse's appearance in all their lives.

She untied the tiny silk ribbon and stared at the weird bones nestled against the soft fabric.

She didn't have a bone to use with the magic. After all, Victor was still alive. She did however have a ring that he used to wear. She saw it sitting on Kendra's bureau in Chicago and snatched it, feeling terrible for doing so. Would it work? The last time, Dante performed the magic she had not been included. She had, however, listened closely and remembered the words he whispered into his glass. Now she intended to perform the magic herself.

****

Hours after everyone retired to bed, Abby listened to the creaks of the house, waiting until she was confident that Sebastian and Oliver slept. She crept down the stairs, stopping in the kitchen for a glass and a bottle of juice before retreating to the study and closing the doors firmly behind her. She sat on a rug, and poured a glass of pomegranate juice which sparkled in the lamplight.

She placed a large bowl of water before her and set a hunk of volcanic rock in its center. Tying a piece of string around the ring, she attached the opposite end to her ring finger on her right hand. It would help to keep part of her grounded in case the magic drew her away from her body and she struggled to return. Dropping the bones into the glass followed by Victor's ring, she whispered Dante's words and took a long, fast gulp.

For several seconds nothing happened. Disappointment and relief rushed through her. As she started to lift the glass, her fingers vanished and the room tilted away from her.

Blinking into an unfamiliar landscape, she tried to get her bearings. She stood at the edge of a forest looking out at the choppy waters of a lake. The night sky sparkled with stars and a half moon. In the trees, she heard creaks and groans, but there was little wind. When she glanced up, she saw huge creatures perched on the branches, their weight slowly buckling the wood beneath them - skin-walkers. Around her feet thousands of snakes slithered and writhed.

For an instant, the snakes vanished as the moonlight was blotted out. Abby looked up to see a hulking form flying in front of the moon - another skin-walker.

She stood numbly watching the creature and realized she could hear more of them, dozens. A thud to her left nearly sent her sprawling, but she was not in her normal cumbersome body. Lighter through this magic, really not there at all in the physical sense, she was able to move swiftly away. She stared at a hunk of bloody flesh. Her eyes bulged, and she fought a scream bubbling in her throat. A tiny splotch of fur revealed it was likely deer flesh, but that recognition brought her little peace.

She wondered if any of the beasts were Alva or Victor, but doubted it. She remembered the Vepars she had first encountered when Devin had sent her on a death-mission to save her parents who weren't in danger. They had snarled and fought like animals. The one she had killed in particular seemed more beast than human. The memory of their blood-lust made her want to call out to her body and end the magic.

"Snake Island," she whispered. Dante's secret magic had taken her to Snake Island.

She moved from the forest along the beach to the water's edge. In the distance, she saw a house. Three stories tall with faded weather-beaten wood, it looked ready to collapse into the steady thrum of Lake Michigan's surf. She followed the line of the woods, occasionally glimpsing a skin-walker, but gaining confidence as they ignored her.

They can't see me, they don't have a clue that I'm here, she silently reassured herself.

At the rickety porch that surrounded the base of the house, she paused. A broad black door led into the home. Could she walk through it? She took the steps slowly, cringing if they made a sound. When she tried to step through the door, she realized she was not as ghostly as she believed. Her form stopped, unable to push through the wood. She touched the handle and felt the cool metal against her fingertips, pulling them quickly away.

Dante's strange magic unnerved her. She was not astral traveling, but she was also not physically present. Her unease only increased when she recalled Victor's dark energy consuming her when she had attempted to pull the witches back from the magic the last time it was performed. She pictured her physical body slumped over in the study. What if she somehow got trapped in this dimension of almost formlessness? Would Sebastian wake up to find her unresponsive? Would the witches of Ula have some way to draw her back?

Refusing the tumult of thoughts churning in her mind, she twisted the handle, stepped into the house and quickly closed the door. A musty odor greeted her. A grand staircase faced the door, its merlot colored carpets faded and mostly rubbed away. The dark rail revealed a thick layer of dust marred by fingerprints. A chandelier creaked overhead swaying like a pendulum, or perhaps the hand of a clock ticking the time there was left before it would pull free of the sagging ceiling and crash to the floor.

Kanti told her that Clyde's body, along with all the objects he bewitched, were on the island. Abby wanted the amulet in particular. With Kanti's help, she believed she could end Clyde once and for all.

A vast parlor opened to the right of the front door. She peeked in, scanning tabletops, fireplace mantel, searching for items lying about. It was a strange scene. The old house was clearly occupied and yet seemed abandoned, haunted even.

Julian and Elda had relayed what they learned from Nora about Serpent House. Abby could imagine it in its prime. A lavish dwelling place filled with witches embarking on the promise of the New World. Nora had described walking into the study and seeing Eugene for the first time. Abby moved through the parlor where two glass doors stood open to what she recognized as the study. A huge old desk piled with curling yellow papers sat near an enormous window with thick, dark curtains drawn to cover the view of Lake Michigan beyond. Abby searched through the office quickly. She did not touch anything, but scanned the items on the desk, ran to the bookshelves and studied the spines of books, looking above them for anything tucked into dark spaces.

The sound of footsteps thumped overhead, and Abby let out a little gasp. She listened as the footsteps pounded down the stairs, and she quickly tucked herself behind the heavy curtains. She peeked out, not sure if she could be seen and not daring to find out.

Victor strode into the room looking disheveled and grubby. His black hair hung in greasy pieces over his head. His eyes were rimmed in purple sleeplessness. Against his dark robe, Abby saw the pulsing red jewel nestled within the golden snake. Amazingly he took the necklace off the moment he closed the study doors. He looked around as if afraid someone would catch him. When the snake pulled away from his body, he let out a long, strangled sigh and sank to his knees. He pushed the necklace away with his foot and sat, trembling, tears rolling down his face.

Abby understood the regret in his eyes. She heard it on his breath, sensed it in the hunch of his shoulders.

He opened his cloak. His chest, where the amulet had lain, looked red and raw. He touched his fingertips against it and winced. For several minutes, he sat that way, unmoving. Finally, he stood, snatched the amulet by its chain and plucked a velvet box from a desk drawer. He dropped the necklace inside with shaky hands. All the while his eyes darted everywhere as if he knew that someone watched him.

For a moment, Victor's eyes settled on her. His dark pupils locked on her own. Seized by panic, she reached through space for her physical body. Serpent House and Victor's sad, angry eyes disappeared.

Abby came to, still sitting on the floor. Her glass of juice had fallen over. A dark red stain seeped into the cream carpet. She held her hand above the stain and drew upward. The stain vanished, and the juice hovered in the air for a moment before she directed it back into her glass. She nodded, smiling, continually amazed at her developing abilities. A silly one, perhaps, but useful nevertheless.

Snake Island

The clock blinked 2am. For that moment, she knew where the amulet was hidden. If she hoped to steal it, she had little time to waste.

CHAPTER 17

Elda took another bite of her pudding and then set her spoon down with a clatter against her porcelain plate.

"Is everything all right, love?" Bridget asked, looking at Elda with concern.

Lydie sat up straighter across the table and her eyes darted toward the window as if she expected to see a raven or some other dark omen hovering nearby.

"Yes, oh yes. I'm sorry I startled everyone." She stood, smoothing her hands down her dark cloak. "I've been summoned to the cave. It hasn't happened in so long I didn't recognize the sensation."

"Water down your spine," Bridget murmured, nodding. "I haven't felt it in ages myself."

"Why?" Lydie demanded. "Is something wrong?"

"I'll know soon enough, but I think not. Only lightness surrounded the call."

"But why?" Lydie asked again. "I mean who would call you there?"

"That's the beauty of the cave, my dear. You can contact any witch in the world. Of course, they might not hear you right away, but the cave is how we've communicated safely for hundreds of years."

Lydie wrinkled her brow.

"Why does it always seem so hard to reach out to anyone then? The witches in Chicago? Even Abby sometimes," she asked.

Elda smiled, sitting on the edge of her seat.

"New witches often don't understand the sensation for many years, so many elder witches choose not to bother with the caves until the witch is old enough to recognize the call."

Lydie frowned. "How will they ever recognize it then?"

"Bless your pea-pickin little heart," Bridget told Lydie, giving her a motherly smile. She waved Elda toward the door. "You go on now, I'll tell Lydie all about the cave of elders and by the time I'm finished, you'll be back with your news."

Elda stood and offered Bridget a little curtsy.

"I promise I'll answer any other questions you have later, Lydie."

Elda moved swiftly toward the dungeons of Ula. Settling into the velvet-backed chair, perched on a stone slab, she slipped from her body into the astral plane. Elda opened her eyes to the cave of elders. She moved into the tunnel to the right and drifted toward the glowing flames that filled the mouth of the cave. The witch Ellen, that Elda had met previously, stood at the split in the cave watching the night sky. Her white hair flowed long over her blue cloak.

"Elda." The witch moved toward her and clasped her hands. The soft coolness that accompanied physical contact in the astral world moved against Elda's hands. "Thank you for coming."

"Of course," Elda said. "Has something happened to Nora?"

Ellen shook her head.

"Not exactly, though she is the reason I'm here. Since you left, she'd been having vivid dreams of her time at the Serpent House with Eugene. Powerful memories have returned, and she feels compelled to share them with you. We hoped you might return and speak with her."

"Yes. I can come tomorrow. Will that work for Nora?"

"It will."

****

Abby swam hard and fast. Her body streamed through the frigid water, but the cold did not reach her. She had eaten one of Helena's pepper plants and swam nearly two hours before returning to the house. Sebastian, holding Vidya, sat on the porch with Helena and Oliver. They drank coffee and watched the early morning fog drifting off the lake.

Abby walked from the water, her muscles warm and hard beneath her skin. Surrounded by her element, the weariness of the world fell away. Sometimes she imagined swimming until she reached Wisconsin, not to run away, just to go hard enough that she left their present moment behind. Perhaps they wouldn't have to break the curse, she could just burst through some time/space continuum and on the other side, they'd all be free.

"I've got a fresh cup with your name on it," Sebastian called, holding out a mug of coffee.

Abby toweled off and waved.

"Let me grab my robe."

Abby had not told Sebastian, but she had an ulterior motive for her swim. She wanted to get comfortable in the water for long periods of time. She practiced holding her breath and had surpassed four minutes. That afternoon she planned to return to Snake Island.

****

"We'll be back before you know it," Elda promised Lydie who stood on the dock at the lagoon's edge. The castle towered behind her and low drifting clouds crowded the turret's peaks. Aepa, Helena's Siberian husky, rubbed along Lydie's back legs and nearly pushed her into the water.

"Back off, Aepa," Lydie told the dog, rubbing her ears. She would be alone at Ula with Faustine and Bridget until Oliver returned that afternoon. She half considered jumping through the mirror to see what he and the others were up to.

"I'll be fine," she promised.

Elda and Julian climbed into the Boston whaler, Faustine at the helm. They were going to visit Nora, the witch in Montana, who had known Clyde centuries before. Oliver had told Lydie most of the details though the history of the curse had become so cumbersome it gave her a headache to think about.

She returned to her Dream Room in Ula and climbed into the tree house settling onto a butterfly chair with her notebook. She wrote a long letter to her Aunt Camilla. She wanted to tell her everything about the curse, the deaths of Max, Dafne and now Ezra, and the fear that chased her everywhere. Sleep had become a stream of nightmares punctuated by thought-riddled periods of exhaustion. Instead, she wrote about the weather, Abby and Sebastian's new baby and the hope of seeing her aunt again soon.

****

Sebastian ran his hand beneath the faucet.

"Perfect temperature," he told Vidya, gently lowering her into the mesh baby bathtub propped in the sink.

She cooed and blinked at him with her shining blue eyes. His eyes.

As the water rolled over her, her eyes opened wide, and she caught her breath.

"Did that surprise you?" he asked, cupping the water in his hands and opening it over her belly.

She smiled and closed her eyes, falling asleep.

He took the duckie washcloth that Abby's mother gave them and squirted it with soap. It smelled of lavender. He washed beneath Vidya's chin, her feet and under her arms, unable to tear his eyes from his daughter. He and Abby had created this tiny, perfect being. When he thought of the depth of his love for his daughter, his heart felt like it might explode within him.

Other feelings arose too, darker feelings. He imagined Claire, his beloved sister, stolen before she ever experienced that kind of love. She would never have a daughter. She would never fall in love. Clyde was behind it all. An ancient monster who'd been sucking, stealing, raping the lives of others for his own sick, greed-filled desire. He started to squeeze the cloth, the soap oozing out and he immediately dropped it. Julian had warned him about mastering his thoughts. With Vidya, he couldn't afford to lose control. Whatever powers he had, they were explosive and uncontrollable. He remembered the crow in the woods the day that Julian had been trying to train him in meditation. He had killed it and not even known he held it in his hands. He turned off the water and took several long breaths, envisioning the thoughts floating away on Vidya's soap bubbles.

"I will focus only on love when I am with you," he told Vidya, though she slept soundly now.

"Oh my, is it bath time?" Helena asked, sweeping into the kitchen in a long red and purple dress. Her auburn hair was braided and her wrists jangled with gold bracelets. A sweet smelling mist seemed to hover around her. Sebastian blinked as if he might be hallucinating.

"Oh, don't worry, honey," she laughed, waving her hand to dispel the mist. "I was conjuring a bit of honey love."

"Honey love?" he asked, sniffing at the air. It did smell a bit like honey.

"An old charm I discovered in a book of shadows when I was just a girl. It infuses a house with sweetness, takes the edge off, so to speak. With all the sadness lately, I wanted to lighten your house up."

He smiled.

"Thank you."

"What a lamb," Helena whispered, touching Vidya's slippery soft cheek. "Have you ever seen such an angelic child? Sound asleep in water. She might take after her mama."

"I hope so," Sebastian said. "Do you want to finish up here? I thought I'd check the gas in the lawn mower."

Helena cocked an eyebrow at him. He wondered if she could sense his anxiety.

"I would love nothing more than to wrap up this little bundle and rock her. You go get stuff done."

He left the house and walked to the shed, mostly for the sake of appearances. After pretending to check the gas, he left and walked into the woods.

Discovering that he descended from Clyde had been a blow. Abby did too, of course, but the lineage of the men told a much darker tale. Alva, Tobias and Victor were all men from that blood line. They were seduced by power and control. Sebastian's own thoughts often veered toward that darkness. He'd been obsessed with killing Tobias. Since Claire's death, it had been the single motivating force in his life. That rage had not dissipated with Tobias's death, but instead shifted. Now Clyde consumed his mind. He wondered if Clyde experienced that rage over his brother's power. Was it Clyde's rage that lived inside of Sebastian now?

He flexed his hands staring at the lines of blue vein snaking to his fingers. He remembered the power from his dream of Ezra. Her life force had flowed into him. It terrified him to admit it, but he craved the sensation.

****

"They called it Snake Island," the old man told Abby, pulling off his worn ball cap and slapping it hard against his thigh. A spray of sweat flew from the hat before he returned it to his head.

"Snake Island?" Abby asked, looking at the choppy Lake Michigan waters. She wasn't surprised to hear him speak the name, but it unnerved her just the same.

Anyone who grew up near the great lakes knew they held as many stories, and ghosts, as the ocean. Massive bodies of water that were major passageways for trade and travel were bound to be filled with secrets. She had never heard of Snake Island until Lorna mentioned it months before, but she knew the lake held dozens of islands, large and small, that rarely saw more life than an errant squirrel or bird.

"Probably five miles off the shore here, give or take," he continued, pointing into the fog that blanketed the lake.

"Do people live there?"

He laughed and shook his head.

"Not anyone in their right mind. Used to be an old man who called it home, a snake charmer people said, but I was a boy then, so he's long since turned to dust."

Unless he's immortal, Abby thought.

"Does anyone go out there? Tourists?" Abby knew the answer, but asked it anyway.

He hooked his thumbs into the belt loops on his grease smeared jeans.

"Not likely. Some's say you can't never find it twice. What do you want with it, anyhoo?"

"I'm writing my thesis on insect life that has been largely untouched by modern man," she lied. After she saw Victor remove the amulet at Serpent House, Abby knew she needed to figure out how to return to the island in her body. She had tracked the man down online. He was known locally in Trager as an old-timer with stories about local folklore. He was also cited in the book that she and Sebastian had found in Rod's loft that referenced Snake Island.

"Bugs?" he nodded as if it was a completely logical answer. "Probably won't find too many out there. Snakes and all."

"Good point," she agreed. "Well I guess, I'll keep looking. Thanks for your time."

She shook the man's hand and returned to her car. When she watched him climb into his pickup and drive down the rutted four-season's road that they'd followed in, she stepped back out of the car.

Five miles out was a long swim, but Abby was not concerned. She could do it. Or she could return to Trager and tell Sebastian her plan. They could rent a boat and drive to the island together. She would lose time and the element of surprise. Worse, she would put Sebastian in danger. One way or another, she would get that amulet and she would do it alone.

She stripped out of her clothes, revealing the black one-piece swimsuit she put on that morning. Over that she layered a short-sleeved wetsuit. Her body created ample heat, even in frigid water, but the wetsuit would add a layer of water surrounding her body, which would enhance her element when she left the lake. Using the same invisibility potion she had discovered at the Sky Mothers, she quickly swallowed the contents of a glass bottle tucked beneath her seat. It burned a trail into her belly and she didn't hesitate, running for the water. Twenty minutes to the island, ten minutes inside and twenty minutes back was her plan. She needed invisibility for just under an hour and in truth, she had no idea how long the potion lasted, but an hour seemed about right.

For the first several miles, she swam an easy breast stroke. As she drew closer, she felt a subtle shift as the dark energy trembled through her body. With each thrust forward, the feeling intensified. She no longer doubted that the entire island had become a part of the evil being who occupied it.

In the dense fog, Abby swam close to get a good view of the island. The trees on the edge of the island were large and huddled close together. They blocked the interior from view, but already Abby felt her stomach plummet at the sight before her. She counted five skin-walkers. They sat on the trees' huge limbs. Some of them tore at fleshy things grasped in their taloned hands. A wasteland of carnage spread over the beach. She saw mounds of bloody flesh, rib cages and other bones. To her immense relief, much of it had fur, and she hoped that the skin-walkers preyed on animals rather than humans.

She swam slowly around the perimeter of the island. Loud shrieks that echoed across the water revealed many more skin-walkers hiding in the darkness of the trees. The Serpent House gradually came into view. Three stories high, the house seemed to sag forward as if the tide slowly pulled it into the lake. Lights blazed through the windows, but still the house seemed dark.

Abby kicked her legs and watched. Every few minutes, a shadow paced in front of a lit window, but she couldn't make it out.

The cloudy sky made time hard to determine, but she couldn't waste a moment. Sebastian believed she had gone into town to the library. They didn't have the luxury of flexibility in the midst of all that had transpired. If she were more than ten minutes late, he would start searching. Not to mention Vidya would need to eat soon. Abby already felt the tingling sensation as her breasts started to get heavy with milk.

The shadow paused in front of the window. Abby's skin crawled. Whoever stood inside now looked out. Could they see her? Was it Victor?

She dove beneath the water and swam to another location. When she emerged, the shadow no longer stood silhouetted in the square of light.

Lifting her hand above the water, she saw only the tall dark trees of the island beyond it. For now, she was invisible.

Running across the beach, she glanced behind her at her footprints, swearing under her breath and using her element to wipe them away. They smeared, but no longer resembled an actual footprint. She wiped her feet in the beach grass and crept across the porch, pausing at the door.

Slowly she turned the handle and slipped inside, closing the door and searching the entryway. No one stood watching, waiting. Staying close to the walls, she hurried through the parlor. The study doors were closed, and she pressed her ear close to the glass, listening. No sound from within. Grimacing at the creak as she pushed the door open, she slipped inside and closed it. The study was empty.

What if the amulet was gone? If Victor had already returned it to his chest? But when she opened the drawer holding the velvet box, she knew instantly that the ouroboros lay inside. The box itself seemed to pulse and when she touched it a warm throbbing met her fingers. She opened the case and lifted the necklace out, hesitating for only a second before slipping it over her head and tucking it beneath the wet suit.

Upstairs she heard footsteps. They moved from one end of the house and back again. Was Victor pacing through the rooms? The amulet pulsed against her skin. She wanted to rip it off. But no, she had to keep going. She was so close now. The footsteps pounded down the stairs and Abby knew she had to get out, fast. If Victor found the amulet gone, he would know she was inside. She flung open the study window and climbed out, dropping ten feet to the sandy beach. She lifted her hands and, drawing on the energy of the water, she pulled the window back down. Halfway it got stuck and made a terrible screeching. Though it was too high to see inside, she knew that Victor or someone else had entered the study. She turned and ran for the water, focusing on the shoreline where she'd parked her car, knowing her body would intuitively guide her there. As she swam away from the island, she stayed beneath the surface for long periods of time. The invisibility charm had not worn off, but she felt safer beneath the water.

CHAPTER 18

As Julian turned onto the rutted dirt road that led to the Winds of Change Farm, Elda noticed how different this visit felt from the previous. Low dark clouds hung in the sky capping the Montana mountains in a slithering white mist. She felt the rain building and wondered if thunder and lightning would accompany it. A house full of witches during a thunderstorm was one of her favorite experiences; the energy raced through the air like darting hummingbirds.

When Ellen greeted them at the door, she wore overalls splattered with mud and Elda noticed bits of straw sticking from her braid.

"Our mare Flame birthed a slick little black foal last night. She's been named Lit by Jeremy, her unofficial owner and my grandson." She gestured at her clothes in explanation. "I'm going on twenty-eight hours awake and fixin to collapse into my bed before y'all leave. My daughter Penny is in the kitchen baking bread so just give her a holler if you need anything."

Ellen left them at the room they'd visited before. Nora sat in her wheelchair next to the window. She slumped over as if in sleep. As the door creaked open, she startled awake and blinked at them several times before recognition passed over her features.

The coffee table had been set with a pitcher of tea and a plate of scones. Elda and Julian settled on the couch.

"You caught me dozing," Nora told them, smoothing flyaway hairs behind her ears. "Don't worry though, I do it more often than not these days so you weren't seeing anything unusual."

Julian laughed and Elda smiled.

"Rainstorms are perfect napping weather," she offered.

"That they are," Nora agreed. "And this one's waitin to take me home, but I wanted to speak with you first."

Elda frowned, but Julian seemed unperturbed by the comment.

"You'll die soon?" he asked as if it were the most ordinary question in the world.

"Tonight," she told them nodding and offering a small, but genuine smile. "And boy am I ready."

Elda understood that death for witches often arrived as a welcome departure from a long, harried life. Still she'd rarely encountered anyone who met it with the ease of the witch sitting before them.

"I wanted a look at Flame's little girl before I left. She'll be a firecracker that one. And of course, I wanted to pass along my memories to both of you. I'm sure the dreams have come for that very purpose."

"How does your family feel? Do they know you're leaving soon?"

Nora nodded, looking at the window toward the barn where Elda sensed most of the grandchildren hovered around the new baby horse.

"I've been here for three hundred years, my dear, they've gotten their fill of me." She laughed and her eyes lit for a moment as if remembering lifetimes of family come and gone. "We talk openly about death here on the farm, always have and always will. Some of us have been around for centuries and others have barely seen a year before our spirit called us home. That's the mysterious beauty of this life. But we're all together, here, on the other side, the space between. They'll wish me well and celebrate with a big potluck tomorrow afternoon."

Julian nodded, smiling. "I hope for a similar farewell when it's my time."

"Then make it known now while you've still got lips to speak it," Nora reminded him.

Elda took his hand and squeezed.

"It is known," she told him.

Nora smiled and nodded. "Now that we've gotten the death conversation out of the way, let's talk about good and evil."

"Perfectly light conversation for tea and scones," Julian said picking up a scone and taking a bite.

Elda let out a short dry laugh and then hiccuped, surprised at herself. All three of them started to laugh until Nora's laugh became a harsh deep cough.

Elda rushed to her side and placed her hands over the old witch's chest helping encourage breath back into her lungs.

After several moments, Nora held up a hand.

"Thank you, oh my. I'd better be careful or I won't get this story out after all," she whispered, reaching for a glass of water on the window's ledge. She took a shaky sip and closed her eyes before touching the pink rosary that lay coiled in her lap.

"Can we get you anything else, Nora?" Julian asked.

"No. I'm right as rain now," she murmured, taking a big breath. "My nights have been rather exciting since I last saw you both. I've been walking the halls of my past and," she smiled fondly, "I forgot how wonderful those years were at Serpent House. It has been a gift to revisit those days and I want to thank you both for that."

"We didn't do anything," Elda started, but Nora silenced her with a wave.

"I know you didn't intentionally do anything, but some energy wants me to remember in order to help you. I'm grateful and felt it prudent that you are aware that there are entities in the universe rooting for you. You are not battling this darkness alone."

Elda smiled and put her hand over Julian's, feeling as if a ray of sun had suddenly come streaming into the room.

"My grandfather was very involved in the native American tribes of the Great Lakes region. In those days, much of our country was composed of tribes and many, if not most, of the American witches were native American. My grandfather worked closely with several Algonquin tribes. They shared magic, language, tools and most of all knowledge. After Eugene came to Serpent House, my grandfather took him on as an apprentice of sorts. In addition to studying the ouroboros and other items they discovered with the Egyptian artifacts, my grandfather taught him about the tribes. He even took him to meet some local shamans and the magical children who would eventually become the healers and the seers."

"Kanti," Elda breathed.

Nora looked up sharply.

"Yes, Kanti. I had forgotten her name all these years, hundreds of years." She shook her head as if she hardly believed it herself. "Until four nights passed when I woke with her name on my lips. I believe I forgot her because my grandfather tried to shield me from the horrors committed by Clyde. After Eugene's death, my grandfather no longer spoke much of the tribes and I never asked why, too caught up in my own pain to notice."

"Your grandfather knew that Clyde kidnapped Kanti?" Julian asked, frowning.

"Not right away," Nora continued. "We didn't know Clyde had returned at all. My grandfather assumed Meghan took him far away and we would never hear of him again. It was only later when Rowtag, the shaman of Kanti's tribe, contacted my grandfather and told of her abduction. After that we started to hear the stories. Stories of torture and murder. My mother told me those stories after I insisted I wanted the truth. I'd overheard my grandfather speaking the name Kanti. The tribe wanted revenge, justice perhaps, but that is not the witch's way," Nora spoke bitterly as if she disagreed with that stance. "We moved here to Montana. We had stayed in Serpent House several years after Eugene's death, but we could not rebuild our coven. We fixed the house after the fire, but it was haunted, plagued. It never felt the same and the snakes on the island started to reproduce in large numbers. Before Eugene's death, the snakes had been friends to the coven, but they grew hostile. They attacked on-sight, unprovoked. We abandoned the island and Trager City. My uncle, who was not a witch, had moved to Montana when I was just a child. In letters to my father he described the wild beauty, untouched by man. We followed him and built The Winds of Change Farm."

"That's how Clyde learned of Kanti," Julian said. "From the work your grandfather was doing with the tribes."

Nora nodded.

"The guilt followed my grandfather for the rest of his life. He was the link between Clyde and the murdered child of their tribe."

"They knew she was murdered?" Elda asked. "We've been researching and haven't found anyone to substantiate that."

"Rowtag, their shaman, was as powerful a witch as you or me. He knew when she died, that it was violent and…" she paused and pursed her lips. "Not final. She did not pass peacefully from our world. Rowtag told my grandfather that Kanti visited him, but it was not the friendly encounters of a ghost who has moved to another realm. She was angry, tortured and trapped. She nearly drove him to madness and I believe the other members of his tribe eventually pressured him to leave. They could not stand the stories he told of her captivity in the world between worlds. My grandfather learned that Rowtag raved for days after a visit by Kanti."

"Did Rowtag try to find Clyde?" Julian asked.

"I believe that he did, and he sought my grandfather's help, but my grandfather refused. He knew what the shaman would do to the man Clyde and wanted no part in it. The shaman insisted that he needed Kanti's bones. He told my grandfather the bones had to be buried on sacred ground for Kanti to pass into the afterlife. He said if the bones were not at rest, the spirit would be confused. He was sure that Clyde was moving Kanti's bones and that he'd done something to the bones and perhaps to the burial ground to keep her tethered to the earth realm."

"Wait," Elda held up a hand, thinking. "In Dafne's journal she wrote that Tobias wore an amulet on his chest, the ouroboros, but fifty years later, Alva dug up Kanti's bones and the amulet hung around her neck. And the bones had been moved from the place on the map."

Julian nodded. "To the base of the tree."

"You found the girl's bones?" Nora asked.

"Yes, on Abby and Sebastian's property, which continues to disturb me," Elda murmured.

"And me as well," Julian agreed. "Clyde has been having those bones dug up and reburied for hundreds of years."

"To ensure that Kanti's spirit cannot transition to the afterlife," Elda said.

Nora yawned and covered her mouth.

"I'm sorry," she sighed. "It's not the story. I'm quite fascinated in fact. It's this old body, she does what she wants these days."

"Of course," Elda told her. "Do you have more to tell us, Nora? If not, perhaps we should leave you to your rest."

"One more thing," Julian interrupted. He pulled a folded map from his back pocket. He opened it and moved closer to Nora.

"Does this area have any significance to you?" Julian pointed to a place on the map and Nora frowned, nodding.

"Eugene grew up on that peninsula. His house was right about here." She tapped her finger in a space on the map.

"Abby and Sebastian own those woods now. They live there," Julian muttered.

"And that's where Clyde buried Kanti," Elda finished.

****

Abby ruffled the blonde curls on Vidya's head watching her sleeping face over Sebastian's shoulder. He looked hilarious wearing Vidya strapped in a pink baby carrier across his chest. Perched on his head was a hat with a little umbrella to block Vidya from the sun. Additionally he wore a back pack stuffed with bathing suits, bottled water and trail mix.

"We could have used a magic bag from Ula," Abby told him. "It would have made this trek a bit easier.

He turned to her and grinned.

"Do you doubt my carrying abilities? I'm a beast of burden, honey."

"I see that." She laughed.

They followed a trail that wound through the woods and ended at a steep climb through a pine forest.

"Doin okay?" he asked as they climbed higher.

"Yeah," she said. "Feels good to make this body work. I spend so much time nursing Vidya, my butt's starting to feel like a pancake."

"Well it's a sexy pancake," Sebastian told her.

She grinned and reached forward, pinching his butt.

"Whoa there," he called over his shoulder. "Don't get me excited or we'll have to stick Vidya in a tree so we can have some private time."

"In a tree?" she asked.

"Yeah. The birds will watch out for her."

Abby nodded. They probably would. They had been following them through the woods, many flying from tree to tree overhead, and a few hopping along the dirt path.

The trees ended and the pine needle floor gave way to sand. As they reached the top of the hill, Abby gasped. They stood at the top of a blowout sand dune that edged Lake Michigan. The dune sloped at least one-thousand feet to the sparkling turquoise water below.

"Surreal, isn't it?" he asked.

"It looks like something from a travel magazine," she whispered.

"It is. Sleeping Bear Lakeshore is considered one of the most beautiful places in America," he told her, dropping the backpack and adjusting Vidya.

"How did you find this place?" she asked.

"I asked a couple guys in town the other day. They drew me a map and everything. Said it's a totally unknown dune, and I had to swear not to tell anyone about it and prove that I was a local before they'd tell me how to find it."

She laughed.

"I can see why they want to keep it a secret."

"Care for a swim?" he asked.

"That's an awfully steep hill," she mentioned, touching Vidya's cheek.

"You'll see, babe. Piece of cake."

Sebastian started to trot down the dune and Abby followed. Soon her strides had become long jumps that sent her scissor-kicking into the air. He watched her, wide-eyed, as she flew more than twenty-feet into the air during one jump.

"I'm jealous," he called.

"Want me to hold Vidya and you can try," she asked, panting a bit when she stopped.

He shook his head and kissed Vidya's temple.

"Some other time when it's just the two of us," he told her, but his eyes looked sad as he spoke and Abby felt the little pinpricks of unease that had been cropping up more and more lately.

Sebastian had been insisting on little day trips claiming that he and Abby needed normal family time. However, during the brightest moments, he tended to look more grief-stricken than joyful. Though she had asked him about it, he always shrugged her off. She circled back to the belief that his new daughter brought up painful memories of his family, but that didn't quite ring true.

As Abby moved closer to the edge of Lake Michigan, she thought of Snake Island. Just miles from where they stood, the island sat teeming with skin-walkers, Victor patrolling the halls of the old house. Did he know she had stolen the amulet? Would he soon be coming to get it back?

CHAPTER 19

"And then we'll dangle the watch like a hunk of red meat for a lion and just wait for him to pounce," Oliver told Lydie grinning.

"A lion?" she asked, skeptical.

"A juicy red flower for a honey bee, a fresh virgin for a vampire, a delicious brain for a zombie. I'm sure you get the point," he continued.

He lay stretched out on a long wooden log that was actually a pillow in Lydie's dream wood. She swung lazily from the tree swing, an ice cream cone in one hand.

"This feels surreal," Abby said, looking back and forth between them. "Like we're actually in a Halloween Special where we sit around planning to defeat the monsters while eating ice cream in our tree house."

"The ice cream is killer though, right?" Oliver asked, holding his own cone up in the air in a kind of salute. "No pun intended."

Abby shook her head and smiled. One thing could always be said for Oliver - he knew how to bring the level of stress down several notches.

"It is good ice cream," Abby admitted. "Bridget is a culinary genius. Of course, now Sebastian's going to spend all day in the kitchen trying to learn how to make it."

"Yeah, but then you'll have homemade ice cream all summer," Lydie piped in.

"I should check on Vidya," Abby told them, standing from the sand dune she'd plopped down on.

"No," Oliver waved her back down. "Helena told you she'd come get you. Don't deprive her and Bridget of their hour of staring at a sleeping baby. Though," he dropped his voice, "they may be siphoning her youthful innocence into some giant cauldron they'll later boil down and turn into an elixir that they'll sell to the common folk for millions of dollars." He let out a high cackle and Lydie kicked a fuzzy slipper at him.

"Not funny," Lydie said.

Abby rolled her eyes and took another bite of her ice cream.

"You two are a tough crowd today," he laughed, popping the last of his cone in his mouth. "Lydie have you trained that cat to retrieve ice cream yet?" he gestured at Garfield who slept on the porch of the tree house over Lydie's head.

"I'm still training him not to bite me when I pet his belly. And not to hide for two days when he sees Aepa."

"Speaking of Aepa, where is that fur bag? I haven't seen her all day," Oliver asked.

"With Faustine. I think she's imprinted on him. It drives Helena nuts," Lydie explained.

"Imprinted?" Oliver asked. "Have you read Twilight too many times?"

Lydie stuck her tongue out at him.

"When are Elda and Julian coming back from Montana?" Lydie asked Oliver. "Elda promised to show me a Book of Shadows written by a teenage witch."

"A teenage witch?" Oliver screwed up his face. "Sounds hormonal."

Lydie flicked her fingers and a mushroom pillow next to Oliver burst into flames. It extinguished immediately with no sign of having been burned, but gave him a good scare, nonetheless.

"Tonight," he told her holding up his hands in surrender. "Now please refrain from burning me alive."

"I was hoping to look at Dafne's journal," Abby announced, changing the subject. She'd been wanting to ask about the journal since they'd arrived at Ula that morning, but had refrained. The topic of Dafne always shifted the mood for the Ula witches, but she couldn't wait forever and now that she had the amulet, she wanted to know how to use it.

Lydie's face darkened, but Oliver offered an understanding smile, sitting up.

"It's in the library. I can get it for you," he said.

"Have you read it?" Abby asked.

"Bits," he admitted. "There's a lot there. She wrote about her entire life. Sometimes I can handle it and other times, I just can't."

Lydie said nothing, but Abby had the distinct impression that she had not read the journal. Lydie grew tight-lipped when Dafne came up, or Max. In the immediate aftermath of Max and then later Dafne's death, Lydie had seemed enraged that no one spoke of them, but then she too grew silent about the witches.

"Thanks, Oliver."

Abby stood and followed Oliver into the hall. She waved goodbye to Lydie who offered her a tight smile and a half wave.

"How is Lydie doing?" Abby asked when they were alone in the library.

"She's..." He paused as if searching for the right word, "adjusting. Like the storm is over and she's a tree just settling back into place, letting her roots dig deeper. Though I get the feeling, she's waiting for the next tempest to arrive."

"Well, she's not wrong to do that," Abby said.

"Unfortunately, I agree. I wish she could enjoy life in the meantime though. I know it's not easy and I wouldn't want her to pretend everything is okay, but she just carries that haunted look everywhere she goes, like she never takes a breath that's not followed by a sad thought."

"Oh," Oliver said, holding up an envelope that he dug out of the desk drawer. "I completely forgot Dafne wrote you a letter too."

"She did?" Abby asked surprised.

The cream envelope displayed her name in sharp black cursive. She took it, and Oliver handed her a letter opener. She slid the blade along the seal and took the folded letter to a chair.

Dear Abby,

If I'm gone, you're the only one now. Not that I would have been much help. Like the Lourdes, the death of my friends and the horrific betrayal by the man I loved destroyed me. The Lourdes was not much help to me, but at least she was proof that we could survive the curse, that everything in us could die and yet still we lived. You will likely face this alone, hopefully with more knowledge. I have done my part to leave that behind. If I have succeeded, you will never read this letter. It will all be over. But alas, I am a witch and intuition tells me that I will never return to Ula to burn these letters. Still, I race towards my death with willing and open arms. I hope that you never understand why that is.

I have many things I would like to say to you, an apology for the way I've treated you, for the havoc I've caused in your and Sebastian's lives. I am sorry. However, the purpose of this correspondence is much larger than all that. It is a call to your highest good, Abby. How much are you willing to sacrifice to end this evil once and for all? I ask you to see beyond the heartache it has caused you. See beyond how it destroyed me and the Lourdes. This evil has lived for centuries, it has fed on the lives of countless witches and humans. It will continue to feed long after you're gone if you let it. By then it will have consumed you and all that you love.

I was a fool to assume that removing Sebastian would end the curse. I knew so little then. Shocking that it was only a few short months ago and now here I sit writing these letters with this mystery desperate to pour out of me. In my selfishness, I keep it from you. I will try to defeat it on my own. I owe you all that much and I must admit it is also an act of self-preservation. Perhaps I will tell you later when I am triumphant.

Abby paused, biting her lip. She imagined Dafne sitting at a desk in her room scribbling those words by firelight knowing in some deep part of her that by the time they were read, she would be gone.

I have often wondered was Tobias evil? And now I believe the answer is no, but let me tell you this, evil runs in his blood. You might say it runs in ours as well, but it appears differently for the men, perhaps there is a darkness in them that is called forth. Do not trust Sebastian, Abby. What a terrible statement. Yes, I know, but I'm telling you, anyway. He might resist the darkness, but it will come. It will consume you and all you hold dear.

****

Long after the witches of Ula slept, Abby crept back to the library, settling into a chair close to the fire. She opened the thick leather-bound journal that Dafne had left behind. Lines of cramped cursive filled the pages. Seeing the words caused Abby to think of her own journal and recommit to writing her life down on paper. Without Dafne's diary huge parts of her life would be missing from her story. Abby wanted to leave that legacy for her child as well. Someday Vidya would be able to look at Abby's life through Abby's eyes.

Not wanting to waste time, she flipped to the end where Dafne would have spoken of the amulet since she had only just discovered it before her death. Next to a crudely drawn image of the ouroboros Dafne had written an incantation along with a series of herbs and stones for protection. Of course, Dafne had been unable to do the possession her way. After being intercepted by the Vepars, she was imprisoned and the possession was forced upon her. In the end, she killed herself to escape it.

"But there is a way," Abby whispered tracing her finger over the snake. Galla had already put a barrier over Abby to block psychic invasion. Kanti could not possess her when she wore the amulet. However, Abby could invite her in and she intended to do just that, but not yet. The time would come when Abby would be ready to enlist Kanti in the destruction of Clyde.

CHAPTER 20

Abby walked to the porch where Julian and Elda sat at the patio table. She and Sebastian had returned that morning and a short while later Julian and Elda had come through the mirror as well.

"I have green tea or lemonade?" she asked, holding up two pitchers.

"Lemonade would be great," Julian answered. "But have a seat, Abby. We have something to discuss."

Abby filled their glasses and sat down, feeling her heart skip a beat. Had they somehow discovered that she had the amulet and what she intended to do with it?

"Where's Sebastian?" Elda asked before they began.

"At the store. Diapers, baby wipes, and he saw some sling online that's apparently perfect for daddies. He was checking the baby store in town to see if they had one." Abby smiled imagining him with Vidya tucked close to his chest.

"He's a good man," Elda said.

"Yes, he is," Abby agreed wondering if it was Sebastian they wanted to talk about.

"Abby, Elda told me that you found this house in a dream," Julian interjected.

Abby nodded.

"And we found out yesterday that this property belonged to Clyde's family. He grew up here. In fact, I'm almost positive I've seen the remnants of his childhood home," Julian continued.

Abby grimaced. The news surprised her and yet...hadn't she known they were led to the house?

"The stone wall in the woods," she said looking at Julian. "That was his house?"

"Yes. That's why he buried Kanti here. This was his home. It was familiar to him."

"And we think Kanti led you here to find those bones," Elda said.

Abby turned and looked at the house. Her eyes always settled on the bay window jutting from Vidya's nursery and her stomach twisted at the idea of letting it go.

"Why do I love this place?" she asked them. "Is it all part of this curse? Somehow Kanti has manipulated me into connecting with this house in order to set her free. What in this life is me?" She stood abruptly and kicked a pot of geraniums. The ceramic cracked and dirt and flowers scattered across the deck. Inside, Vidya started to cry.

Abby stuck her fist in her mouth and bit down, welcoming the sharp sting of her teeth. She started to hurry inside, but Elda stopped her.

"Let me," she told her, putting a hand on Abby's arm. "Take a little walk, Abby. Find your center. I understand why you're upset."

Julian avoided eye contact as Abby left the porch walking into the woods. She strode through the trees until she found the stone wall. She snatched a branch from the ground and whacked it against the stone. Bits of dirt and wood flew into the air as the branch snapped in half. She kicked the wall, letting her breath out in a rush as a hunk of it crumbled. She stared at the small pile of rubble and noticed one of the stones seemed to have words etched into the surface. She saw the initials E + N roughly carved into the rock. Eugene and Nora. He must have carved their initials after he met her at the Serpent House. Though Abby had not met Nora, she had heard her story, and the appearance of those ancient initials made her heart leap into her throat. She muffled a sob as she sat heavily on the wall, turning the stone again and again in her hand.

"What do I do?" she asked. The forest sounds answered her in the shrill call of crows and the scampering of squirrels and chipmunks. Unfortunately, she didn't know their language and instead sought Sydney's face in her mind.

"Sydney, if you're out there somewhere, I need your help. I'm drowning here."

Abby tilted her head and watched the sunlight slanting through the trees imagining that Sydney might suddenly appear. Instead, the sound of a car engine and the slamming of a door found her. Several moments later, Sebastian called her name. She stood, tucking the stone in her pocket and walked back to the house.

****

"Do you think we should sell the house?" Abby asked Sebastian that evening. They sat in the side yard next to a roaring fire that Sebastian built in the fire pit. It was a warm night and seemed ideal for their first bonfire of the summer.

Sebastian poked at the fire with a metal stick, his face impassive. After several minutes, he turned to her.

"No. It may sound crazy, but I love this house. It's our new beginning. Vidya was born in that tub." He pointed to the rock bath that he and Oliver had built. "We already have memories here."

Abby sighed and watched the flames devour the logs that Sebastian had cut from their forest. It had felt like a new beginning, but how many horrifying experiences could they have before it would become a nightmare?

"I'm scared, Sebastian."

He dropped the poker and moved his folding chair close to hers. He sat down and wrapped his arms around Abby, pulling her into him.

"I'm supposed to say brave, manly things right now, but I'm going to opt for truth. I'm scared too. But running away isn't going to save us. Fighting back, conquering Clyde once and for all-that's our only hope. Kanti wants that too, Abby. She wants to rest peacefully. She brought us here because she knew that would be the fastest way to end this thing."

Abby looked at the house. Inside Helena rocked Vidya to sleep. Lydie and Oliver played Monopoly at the kitchen table. And upstairs, the ouroboros sat breathing in a little boxy, calling out to its master who at that moment might be coming to reclaim it.

"But are we safe here?" she asked finally.

Sebastian grimaced.

"Are we safe anywhere?" he asked, returning his gaze to the flames.

****

"Let me show you how it's done," Oliver told Abby and Vidya.

Abby sat on the porch transplanting several chamomile plants that Helena had brought from Ula. Abby tipped one of the plants and held it in her palm. Each time she glanced up at the house, the lake, or the forest, she remembered that Clyde had called it home.

Oliver rubbed his hands together and held it over the bundle of roots. The tiny white shoot started to break apart and grew longer. He fanned his hands out, and the roots stretched toward him.

Vidya watched him intently, releasing a sound like a giggle.

"Did she just laugh?" Abby asked, surprised. Though Vidya watched them carefully and often smiled, her only laughter had seemingly come from gas.

"Of course, she did. I'm hilarious." He grinned and wiggled his fingers so the roots danced.

Abby held out her palm and blew at Oliver. A spray of water shot toward him and hit him square in the face.

"Oh no, you didn't," he growled, throwing a handful of nothing at Abby that turned into mud splattering against her right shoulder.

"Oliver!" she spat, jumping up and ducking behind a lawn chair. She created a bubble, sneaking a peek to see that he hovered near the porch steps, and sent it floating across the deck toward him.

"Clever, but too slow," he called, dodging aside. She shot a burst of water at the spot that he jumped into, catching him in the chest.

Vidya laughed again, and Oliver clutched his chest in mock horror.

"Vidya, your mother hath struck me dead." He slowly collapsed to the porch, letting his eyes close as he made obnoxious gurgling sounds.

Abby stood and Oliver flicked his fingers at her. Another ball of mud caught her right between the eyes.

"Ah," she shrieked, clapping her hands together so that a sheet of rain poured over him.

He laughed and held a hand up to shield his face.

"You need the bath more than me," he called as she wiped the mud off her forehead, mostly smearing it into her hair.

****

Sebastian and Helena stood in the kitchen watching them. Helena had also brought fresh asparagus for Sebastian. He stood washing and chopping it, but mostly sneaking glances at Abby and Oliver.

"Vidya loves it," he said.

"It's magic. What kid doesn't love it?" Helena responded, though she sensed Sebastian's unrest. He was jealous of Oliver. What man wouldn't be, but there was something more in his demeanor and Helena couldn't quite place it - perhaps defeat. She thought of Bridget's dream. Was the wheel of fate truly spinning for Sebastian? Could they somehow skew the outcome in their favor?

"It's more than magic," he said, not taking his eyes from Abby who had just been splattered with mud. "It's harmony. Abby and Oliver are like instruments that are in tune and I'm the kid beating on a frying pan with a wooden spoon."

Helena laughed, but she forced it. It hurt her heart when Sebastian spoke as if he were an outsider.

"Love is not meant to be easy, Sebastian. Clichés like 'opposites attract' exist because they do. There is growth in loving the person who does not always resonate with us. Abby loves you, fiercely, blindly, without question. Don't ever doubt that."

He smiled and looked at Helena from the corner of his eye.

"I don't doubt it, Helena. But blind love is dangerous."

****

Sebastian walked purposefully through the woods. Recent rain had resulted in a burst of dense growth that he waded through gradually, inhaling the earthy smells of pine and mud and a hundred plants that he could not name. In summer, the rock wall was nearly buried in green. Ferns, vines and bushes crawled over the crumbling stone.

He stared down at it, remembering the previous winter when he'd followed his own footprints through the snow to the wall. That night he'd found a single black hair that belonged to Dafne. It was the first night that he realized the darkness was calling to him. He had little to no memory of that night, but now he understood the significance of that stone wall. It was the foundation of Clyde's childhood home. He had buried Kanti at the place where his life began.

He dropped to his knees and ran his hands along the rock. Sebastian didn't know what he searched for, but groped with his fingers growing desperate. Pulling plants from the earth, he flung them behind him, dirt raining over his head as he uprooted every weed and flower along the wall. A butterfly bumped his face and he shook his head. It returned, flying into his eye and he batted it away. The butterfly struck the wall and he stared at the copper wings dotted in black spots. They fluttered and the butterfly took flight again, this time perching on Sebastian's hand.

Claire had told him that she appeared as butterflies. He closed his eyes and rocked back. Gently, he blew the butterfly and she flew away.

"I'm sorry, Claire," he whispered as he dug into the dirt.

"Damn," he yelped as his finger jammed against something hard. He pulled his hand out, but the world rolled away from him. He fell into a black void, screaming, flailing, and then a burst of light and heat surrounded him. He felt his body rocketed backwards and then it stopped as if he had struck a brick wall. He lay sprawled on the ground, gasping and shaking. Lying perfectly still, Sebastian kept his eyes closed, willing the world to stop swimming.

Finally, his heart slowed to a steady thud, and he opened his eyes. A rock wall met his vision and when he recognized the room, he scrambled to his feet. He was in Clyde's cave tucked in the dream wood mountain. He was back in the Forest of Purgatory.

****

"Good grief! Did you fall in the mud?" Abby asked when Sebastian walked through the door, streaked with dirt and twigs.

He smiled and shrugged, picking a slug from his shirt. "I decided to do some weeding."

"Weeding?" she asked, surprised. She sat in a gliding chair breastfeeding Vidya who had mostly fallen asleep, but occasionally latched back on and proceeded to dribble most of the milk down Abby's side.

"Yeah. I thought a garden would be cool, right? Didn't you say you wanted a garden?" Sebastian kicked off his shoes and walked to the refrigerator. He pulled out a pitcher of ice tea and poured himself a glass. "Want one?" he asked.

She shook her head no, noticing how little eye contact he'd made with her since walking in the door.

"I need a shower," he said, leaning down to kiss her forehead before heading for the stairs.

She watched him, biting her lower lip and then glanced toward the doorway through which he'd come. She wondered what she would find if she went to investigate the garden he spoke of. Upstairs, she heard the shower turn on.

CHAPTER 21

Dante set up the web cam. Several days after they had left Chicago, Dante called Oliver with a plan. Of course, Abby knew where to find Victor. He was living on Snake Island, but they wanted to draw him away from his place of power. She couldn't exactly deliver him a letter. It had been Dante's idea to upload a video, convinced that Victor still monitored some of their online network.

"Do you really think this will work? Abby asked Dante.

He nodded, adjusting the camera.

"I can see that someone has been hacking into our network. Fortunately, we started a separate one that we've moved a lot of our information onto, but we want to keep the old one live because we can potentially feed him information. This is the perfect opportunity."

"Not to make light of the situation, but does anyone else feel like we're about to film something raunchy?" Oliver asked, holding up a fur lined throw pillow on one end of the couch.

"That's a Kendra decor item," Dante sighed. "Marcus tried to refuse it a place in our perfectly outfitted home, but she persisted."

Abby grinned and shook her head. "I'm happy someone can joke. I feel like I might throw-up."

"That's because you're breastfeeding and haven't eaten a crumb today," Helena told her, tucking a curl behind her ear.

"I can't. I'm too nervous. I don't even know why. It's a web cam for Pete's sakes," she murmured, looking again at the damaged watch. Would this work?

"How come Sebastian got to stay home with the baby?" Oliver asked. "Shouldn't you be the one with the baby excuse?"

Abby rolled her eyes at him.

"Yes, but Sebastian would be crawling up the walls right now if he were here. I figured I was the safer bet."

"Good point," he replied.

"Okay, we're almost there," Dante said. "I just need to login to Victor's network and we'll be live."

"Live?" Abby asked, feeling her stomach clench.

"Yes, but Victor doesn't know where we live. Okay? And we did a lot of shielding on this place."

"Let him show up," Oliver snapped. "I'd love a little face-to-face time with that backstabbing piece of…"

Helena held up a hand to shush him. "Intentions are powerful things my dear Oliver. Don't invite him here with your mind. This place leaves us far too vulnerable."

Dante left the room and returned a moment later.

"Ready, set, action," Dante announced as he pressed the black button on the camera.

Abby stood frozen for a moment, before she remembered that it was she who had to speak to Victor, lure him into their trap. She took a seat on the couch and squared off against the lens, watching the little red light.

"Victor, this message is for you or should I say for your master, Clyde."

Abby leaned forward on the couch and opened her palm, revealing the watch cupped in the center of her hand.

"Does this look familiar to you? I believe it belonged to your brother. The brother you murdered. The brother who was truly magical. How sad to spend centuries coveting someone else's power."

On the other side of the room, Dante, Oliver and Helena watched her. Oliver gave her a thumbs up.

Abby took a deep breath. She imagined Victor watching the video, feeling that misplaced rage given to him by Clyde. Why would he sacrifice his life to join Clyde?

She swallowed the lump forming in her throat and continued.

"This watch means nothing to me, but I'm willing to make a deal with you. Meet me, answer my questions and I'll hand it over. I'll be waiting for you in the Ebony Woods on Friday at 2pm."

Dante pressed the button on the camera and the tiny red light disappeared. It was done unless of course you considered that they'd just told Clyde that she possessed something he desperately wanted. Sebastian was at home, hopefully safely rocking their little girl to sleep. Would Victor wait for their meeting or attack them in the night? Did he know she'd stolen the amulet?

"Let's get home," she announced, handing the watch back to Oliver. She feared Sebastian and Vidya alone in their house.

****

"Why are you wearing that?" Abby asked, startling Sebastian from his reverie.

He'd been stirring a pot of white bean chicken chili and watching Lake Michigan through the window. He blinked to clear his mind.

"What?" he asked, glancing down at his t-shirt and expecting to find he'd put it on backwards.

Abby strode across the room and poked his chest.

"That watch! Why are you wearing it?"

She looked upset, maybe even angry, and he stared at the small gold disc hanging from a chain around his neck. He had no clue how it had gotten there.

He frowned.

"Huh, I don't know." He looked again at the furrow of her brow and the grim line of her mouth. "Why? What is it?" He felt confident he had never seen the watch, let alone put it on and yet there it was.

"It was Clyde's brother's watch, Sebastian. The one that Oliver brought back from Australia. We took it to Chicago today. Remember?"

Sebastian frowned and lifted the bit of gold. He slipped the chain over his neck and set it on the counter.

"That's really strange," he murmured. "I swear Abby, I don't remember putting it on." Her expression had shifted, and he saw fear in her eyes.

He knew that he needed to offer a better explanation, but frankly he didn't have one. He turned his attention back to the chili trying to ignore the weight of her stare boring into his back.

****

"He digs up the bones every what? Fifty years? Takes the amulet out and then buries them again. Why does he take the amulet out?" Oliver asked.

He sat in a boat with Elda, Faustine and Julian. They drifted in the calm Lake Superior water. Oliver was perched on the bow of the Boston whaler, his leg draped over the side. He had returned from Chicago and filled them in on the webcam video.

"Because it's charged," Julian said. "He puts it with Kanti's bones to restore the connection to her power. Then he moves her bones to ensure she continues to drift, ungrounded, in the realm of spirit. He digs it back up when he feels it has regained its power."

"And before she becomes too powerful herself," Elda added. "Perhaps he waited too long the last time he placed the amulet with her bones and that is how she started to make contact with the physical world."

Faustine stood at the helm, his hands gripping the large silver wheel, his eyes focused on the horizon.

"We have to ground her bones. Bury her in the consecrated earth of her tribe," he said.

"Do we know where that is?" Oliver asked.

"I'm sure Nora could tell us. I'll go to the cave when we return, hopefully she is still with us," Elda responded.

"What does that mean? She's dying?" Oliver asked, swinging his leg into the boat and facing them.

"Yes, and soon. Let's return right now," Julian agreed.

Faustine started the engine, and they sped back to the cliffs of Ula.

Oliver watched the castle rising in the distance and felt a pang of love for the towering home of Ula. For years he had felt the castle beginning to stifle him, but recently something had shifted, the death of Ezra perhaps, and suddenly he could think of nowhere he'd rather be than paging through a book in the library, drinking a cup of coffee while Lydie threw a ball of yarn to one of her cats.

He sighed and leaned over the boat watching the water race by - ripples of his reflection there and then gone.

****

Abby closed the bedroom door and leaned her head against it. She held the watch cupped in her hand. It seemed to burn though she knew she only imagined it. Why had Sebastian been wearing it? After creating the video in Chicago, she had returned the watch to a small box tucked in the far back corner of her suitcase. She had meant to retrieve it and pass it off to Julian. Not only had Sebastian dug it out, but he put it on and seemingly had no memory of doing so.

After leaving the kitchen, Abby had bypassed the living room where she heard Helena and Lydie in a boisterous conversation. Why hadn't she stopped? Told Helena immediately about Sebastian wearing the watch? Why did there always seem to be a reason for keeping secrets where Sebastian was concerned?

She returned the watch to the box and stuffed it inside a huge ceramic vase in the corner of the room. She whispered an incantation and directed her fingers toward the box, watching it disappear. It had not actually vanished, only changed shade to blend with the vase surrounding it.

The door slid open and Sebastian stuck his head in.

"Hey, I'm sorry about that just now. I should have said more…"

Abby sighed and moved to the bed, hoping Sebastian had not seen her looking into the vase. She sat down and folded her arms across her chest.

"I'm worried about you, Sebastian. You're supposed to be protected and yet somehow you have no recollection of finding that watch and putting it on."

"You're right. And believe me, I'm worried too. I'm going to find Julian tomorrow and tell him what happened. We'll try new spells, whatever it takes." He sat next to her and pulled one of her hands into his own.

She smiled at him, but the words from Dafne's letter sat heavy in her mind. "Don't trust him."

****

"I have coordinates," Elda announced striding into the library with a map. "Sadly, Nora has passed; however, Ellen was able to get an exact location from a map in Nora's scrapbook and she gave me the coordinates. I doubt it's still an Indian reservation, but judging from the map I'm guessing it's wooded and isolated."

"So she accurately foresaw her death," Julian commented.

Elda nodded, putting a hand over her heart. "Ellen said her passage was peaceful."

"The one person who could tell us about Clyde is dead?" Oliver asked.

"I believe she told us all that she knew," Elda reassured him.

Faustine walked through the library doors behind Elda, his face grave. "We have to find her bones first."

"What?" Julian spun from the window and Oliver saw a glimmer of fear in his eyes.

"They're gone," Faustine said, holding out his palms to reveal their emptiness. "The box is gone."

"Victor must have taken it after Abby's wedding. When…" But Elda didn't finish the statement and she didn't need to. When he drugged them all and using his magic moved them from Ula to the Ebony Woods where he had intended to sacrifice them in order to help Clyde rise to power.

"Why didn't we think to look then," Oliver muttered.

"Because we had other things to worry about," Julian reminded him. "And we didn't recognize the significance of the bones."

Faustine took a deep breath.

"I need some time in the tower. Let's meet back here in two hours." He strode from the room.

"Lydie and Helena are at Abby's," Elda murmured. "Bridget is making breakfast for dinner. Is there anyone I'm missing? Are we all accounted for?"

"Yes, Elda. Come take a seat." Julian led Elda toward a chair by the window. "It's been a long day, relax and we'll create a plan when Faustine returns."

Elda nodded again stroking the pendant around her neck. She leaned her head back in the chair and her eyes drifted closed.

Julian gestured for Oliver to follow him from the library.

****

Sebastian waited until Abby slept soundly. He had a few hours at least before Vidya's first wake-up and only Helena remained in the house with them, hopefully sound asleep. He crept from the house and closed the door quietly before sprinting into the woods. He found the stone wall and lifted the large birch branch he'd placed over the hole. The portal was a mud caked rock, about the size of a softball. Without gloves he had not wanted to touch the stone a second time. Unable to remove any of the mud, he hadn't seen exactly what kind of stone it was.

Sliding thick, sheep-skin gloves over his hands, he reached into the hole and brushed the rock with his finger bracing for impact. Nothing happened. He sighed, relieved. He intended to travel again, but wanted to investigate the rock first. He flipped on a flashlight and balanced it on the stonewall as he lifted the rock. Using a dishtowel, he wiped most of the of mud away and examined the rough surface. A purplish-blue sheen seemed to cover the stone and despite its density, a light emanated from somewhere within it. He turned it over, looking for any other distinguishing traits, but found none. Had he passed it sitting on the beach, he would barely have noticed it.

He checked his watch. Only fifteen minutes had lapsed. He still had time. Of course, if he got trapped in the dream wood, time would be irrelevant. No one would have a clue. He would simply disappear without a trace.

Slipping off a glove, Sebastian closed his eyes and pressed his palm against the rock.

****

It took less time to come down from the dizziness that accompanied his travel through the portal. Sebastian rubbed his eyes and surveyed Clyde's cave room, considering looking around, but deciding against it. Time was limited.

As he moved through the Forest of Purgatory, Sebastian's feet sank into the soggy earth, and he wrinkled his nose at the putrid smell that seemed to rise up from everywhere. He had expected Meghan's dark phantoms to descend upon him the moment he stepped from Clyde's secret room, but he found only silence. He walked to the gnarled trees beneath the pool of water that he knew to be the pond in the dream wood. In the Forest of Purgatory, it was a strange floating mass of dark water.

He paused and glanced back toward the cave he'd left behind. He was balanced on the precipice, facing a choice that once made could not be undone. He could turn, walk back to the cave, climb into Clyde's room, and touch the purple stone that would send him back to Trager.

He cupped his hands around his mouth and called out.

"Meghan!"

The phantoms appeared from the misty darkness. He closed his eyes as they surrounded him.

CHAPTER 22

Abby woke, startled, and blinked into the pink light of the room. The salt rock lamp had been a gift from Helena to help balance the energies in their bedroom, and also to offer a sleep-friendly night-light for the baby. Rolling to her side, she watched Vidya. Her daughter slept soundly, her tiny pale eyelids fluttering beneath dark lashes. The other side of the bed lay empty and cool as if Sebastian had not been there for some time.

Pushing the covers off, Abby slipped from the bed and took the gold silk robe from the chair by her bed. The robe was long and hooded and Abby felt like royalty whenever she wore it. Oliver had given it to her after his last trip to Australia. Matilda made robes for other covens and when Oliver spotted the golden silk, he thought Abby would love it. Matilda insisted that the Sky Mothers wanted to give the robe as a gift and would not accept payment, which Abby appreciated. Had it merely been a gift from Oliver, Sebastian might have taken offense and then she would have felt awkward every time she wore it.

Moving down the stairs slowly, Abby listened for sounds of Sebastian. More importantly, she allowed her energy field to open so that she might sense him. Had he slipped out into the night on some mysterious business that he wouldn't tell her about? She tried to strike the thought from her mind, but it sat there heavy and unmovable.

The front door was locked, and she saw Sebastian's sandals sitting neatly beside the rug. Still she pulled open the door and stepped into the warm night. Stars and a sliver of moon crowded the sky. A cacophony of crickets and tree frogs filled the night air, and Abby watched tiny lightning bugs blinking in the darkness.

"Hey. Did I wake you?" Sebastian spoke from behind her and Abby whirled around, startled.

He stood silhouetted in the doorway, shirtless, his hair tousled.

Abby sighed and stepped into him, chastising herself for doubting him. She wrapped her arms around his naked waist and inhaled his scent, nuzzling the soft hair on his chest.

"Mmm," he breathed, kissing the top of her head and then tilting her face up to meet his. He found her lips and then kissed her neck, sliding her robe off one shoulder and then the other. It pooled in a silk heap at their feet. He picked her up and carried her to the porch laying her on a chaise. In the darkness, she could not look into his eyes, but she felt them moving over her. As he traveled down her body, she pushed her hands in his hair, massaging hard into his scalp. She arched back and moaned when he moved into her. As they made love, she tried to lose herself in the sensations of their bodies. She wanted to, needed to, but when she'd slipped one of his fingers into her mouth, she'd tasted dirt and felt the grittiness of it against her tongue. It hadn't been there when they went to bed. He had taken a long shower and clipped his fingernails afterward. Sometime in the night he'd been digging.

****

"Victor has to bury the bones on Abby and Sebastian's property," Julian told Oliver as they walked further from the castle toward the sand dunes on the north end of the island.

"What makes you say that?"

"It's part of the magic. Those woods are significant in some way. He can't move them far or he would have by now. He digs them up every fifty years or so. Why not take them to a lair? To a safe place? He has to leave them there."

"Then you believe that Victor buried them in the same place?"

"The same relative space, yes."

Oliver rubbed a hand through his blonde hair. His eyes felt dry and grainy. He needed to go to bed, but adrenaline kept him awake.

"Okay," he announced, shoving the exhaustion down. "What do we do? I'm not keen on popping into Abby and Sebastian's house in the middle of the night.

Julian nodded.

"Morning is only a few hours away. Catch some sleep. I'll talk to Faustine and we'll meet in the breakfast room tomorrow," Julian told him, turning to walk back towards the castle.

****

Julian and Oliver moved stealthily through the woods. They had not told Abby and Sebastian that they intended to search the property for a new burial site.

"Look here," Oliver said, jogging to the stone wall. The dirt surrounding the wall was disturbed and some of the wall had been demolished.

Julian squatted down and touched the earth.

"Abby came out here the other day and had a go at the wall," he said. I could hear her beating on it from the porch after we told her this had been Clyde's home."

"Can't say I'm surprised," Oliver commented. "But that looks like digging."

Julian looked at the hole Oliver pointed to.

"Yeah it does, but it's pretty shallow for bones. Six inches down the earth is packed hard. It's only the top soil that's loose," Julian said, pushing his fingers into the hole.

"Would Abby have been digging though?"

Julian shrugged.

"Sure. We're hunting for more items, right? We know Clyde bewitched the amulet, the dagger, possibly a ring, but no one has seen the ring. It could be buried here somewhere."

"Maybe we should have told them," Oliver said, looking frustrated. "If they've been out here digging, it'd be helpful to know that."

"We will," Julian said, standing and brushing off his pants. "But let's take a look around first."

A rustling sound caused both of them to pause. Julian held a finger to his lips and then waved a hand over through the air. When they moved, their footfalls did not make a sound.

"Abby?" Oliver asked, surprised.

Abby was on her hands and knees in the forest, a small shovel clutched in her hand, a streak of dirt on her face.

She reeled away from the sound, clutching her chest.

"Oh," she breathed. "You scared me half to death." She looked behind them. "I didn't hear you."

"What are you doing?" Julian asked.

She opened her eyes wide and glanced at the shovel. She took a moment to answer and Oliver wondered if she were weighing the possibility of a lie.

"I'm looking for Kanti's bones," she admitted finally. "Victor buried them here. He had to, right? It's part of Clyde's magic. He can't afford to lose the connection to Kanti."

Oliver grinned, but Julian gave her an irritated glare.

"You didn't think it might be dangerous for you to come out here and dig alone?"

"I did revealing spells first," she retorted, looking equally miffed. "And I'm not helpless, you know? Should I sit in my house knitting booties while you take the risks, Julian?"

Julian sighed.

"Did you find anything, Abby?"

She looked sheepish.

"No, but I'm getting close. I can feel it."

"Then we better get to work," Oliver announced. "Yeah?" he looked at Julian expectantly who only shook his head in defeat.

They created an ever-widening circle from where Abby had been digging.

"This is it," Julian announced after several minutes. Abby and Oliver both ran to where Julian stood. The disturbed earth revealed recent digging, but it was the air above the ground that told them magic had been performed there. A heavy greenish vapor hovered over the altered ground. Abby shivered and rubbed her arms despite the warm day. She did not mention that Sebastian had been digging just the night before.

"Don't get too close," Julian told them. "This magic is meant to keep us out and keep her in. I would like Faustine to have a look."

"I'm on it," Oliver said, trotting back to the house.

"Where's Sebastian?" Julian asked.

"Helena took him and Vidya to an herbalist. He wants to learn to make medicine for Vidya and since most of Helena's medicine is magic, she figured he should learn from a human."

Julian raised his eyebrows.

"And they wanted to give me a few hours to myself."

"And this is how you chose to spend the time?" Julian frowned.

Abby shrugged and wiped dirt from her face.

"When the urge strikes…"

Oliver returned with Faustine a short time later.

Faustine carried a heavy black cloak and a brown leather case. He slipped the cloak on. It concealed his entire body, leaving only two mesh slits for his eyes. From his case, he took a glass bottle and a gold ladle.

"You didn't know Faustine was a mad scientist, did you?" Oliver whispered, nudging Abby.

She shook her head, watching Faustine intently as he stepped into the green haze. He vanished completely and Abby stumbled back, shocked.

"Oh my god! What happened?" she asked, looking wildly at Julian whose face was unsurprisingly calm.

"It's the suit, not the magic," he explained. "When the suit comes into contact with a toxic entity, it shields the witch inside it, completely as you can see."

"A human couldn't perform this kind of magic, right? Or a hybrid?" Abby asked forcing her voice to sound neutral.

Julian studied her.

"I find it hard to believe anyone except an experienced witch could perform this magic. But that is a strange question Abby. Why do you ask?"

Abby started to respond, but was interrupted when Faustine re-emerged. The glass bottle appeared empty, but Abby could see tiny, nearly transparent, green particles adrift beneath the glass.

Julian opened the case and held a black canvas pouch to Faustine. He placed the bottle inside and the four witches waited.

"Dramatically, the magician pulled a green rabbit from the pouch!" Oliver exclaimed.

Julian shot Oliver an annoyed look, but a tiny smile cracked Faustine's lips.

He reached into the bag and retrieved a roll of parchment. He carefully loosened the twine and opened it.

"Exponentia Acidum," Faustine read. "Antidotum," Faustine trailed off, reading silently. "Abby do you have fennel in the house? And gold jewelry of some kind?"

"Yes," Abby said. "I'll go get it."

She sprinted back to the house and flung open the cupboards, wishing that Sebastian were home while grateful that he was gone. He knew the spices better than she and it took her nearly five minutes to dig out the container of dried fennel seeds tucked in the back of the cabinet. She grabbed a gold bracelet that Nick had given her on their first anniversary wondering why she'd ever bothered to keep it.

Back in the forest, a small black folding table had appeared with a mortar and pestle. As Faustine crushed and stirred, he whispered words that Abby did not understand. Julian stood over his shoulder, occasionally making suggestions.

Oliver slipped closer to Abby.

"Kind of makes you feel like an amateur, huh?"

"That's an understatement," she admitted. "How did they ever learn all of this?"

"Living, I guess. And I get the feeling the old ways were a bit stricter with education."

"Right you are," Julian interrupted as Faustine poured a sprinkle of the mixture into the bottle. A tiny explosion of light occurred within the glass and the green particles vanished.

"I was educated in a coven that did not allow speaking during the first year of training. It ensured that all magic had its roots in the energetic realm," Julian explained, a gleam in his eye.

"The world has changed much since that time," Faustine agreed. He scooped a handful of his concoction from the pestle and threw it into the green haze. Light shot in every direction and the green faded and disappeared.

"Wow," Abby breathed.

"There came a time when some witches believed it might be best if new generations discover magic for themselves. If you seek a teacher, then you might learn spells of old. If you do not, then it is hard to say what magic you will amass in your lifetime," Faustine continued.

"It was a tactic," Julian added. "To reduce the power of young witches who were at times volatile and impulsive. It can be dangerous to give all your secrets to such witches."

"Humph," Oliver grunted. "I'm offended."

Julian winked.

"I would teach you all the ways of the witch, Oliver. You know that."

Oliver grinned.

"I'm afraid I've lost my discipline to be a student, Julian. I prefer this kind of learning now." He waved his hand at the woods.

Abby realized, though she hadn't heard Faustine's words, she knew the magic he had performed. Some part of her had recorded his movements, his sounds, his mixture. Just as she'd repeated Dante's magic to follow the bones, a part of her was always absorbing the magic being performed around her. Likely Oliver was as well.

"Now it is time to dig," Faustine announced.

CHAPTER 23

"So, this is the place," Abby murmured, pressing her hand against a gnarled oak tree. She had expected to recognize it from her visions of Kanti, but it looked like a thousand other forests she'd walked through.

"This is it," Julian agreed. "There's a boulder formation over there. Some of the Algonquin elders added it sometime later to mark their dead."

"We're standing on an Indian burial ground?" Oliver groaned. "Great! Now we'll all be haunted for life."

"Very funny," Abby grumbled.

Sebastian squeezed her hand.

"You okay?" he asked.

Abby nodded. She was, but still the memory of Kanti's last morning, on the ground they now stood, made her feel as if she might cry. One of the first memories that Kanti revealed to her occurred that fateful day when she was stolen by the hulking giant as she sang to the fire. Her tribe slept, unaware that their gifted child was embarking on a horrifying journey that would end in her death and a curse that would span centuries.

Abby's turbulent emotions didn't end there. Sebastian's strange behavior, his wearing Eugene's pocket watch, and the holes she found along the old foundation on their property all pointed to a very disturbing conclusion. Sebastian had begun keeping secrets again. She could have told Julian, Faustine and Oliver the day before when they discovered Kanti's bones, but instead she remained silent.

A man with dark ruddy skin stepped from the shelter of trees and Abby's heart leaped. Julian had tracked down an Algonquin elder who had agreed to perform a proper burial for Kanti. He tilted his head in her direction, his long black hair braided over each shoulder. He had black streaks painted across his cheeks, forehead and chin. When Julian presented him with the bones, he knelt on the ground and wrapped them delicately in birch bark. He dug the grave slowly, singing a song in the language of his tribe.

Abby fell back toward the trees as did the other witches and Sebastian. They watched the man place the bones gently into the ground. He buried them and chanted for nearly a half hour before quietly disappearing into the forest.

****

That night, Bridget made a feast at Ula. Prime rib, heaping dishes of candied yams, buttered rolls, salads and desserts lined the long table in the dining room. The candelabras blazed and the witches' voices carried through the patio doors and high into the night.

Abby savored the food, using one hand to gently rock Vidya asleep in an antique bassinet that Elda had brought from the cellars of Ula. It had been Lydie's bed during her brief infancy at Ula, but before that it had belonged to Miranda, Julian's deceased wife. Though she and Julian had never born children, the bassinet had been her own baby bed and a family heirloom that Miranda treasured. Occasionally, Abby saw Julian sneaking glances at the rocking bassinet, though if caught, he quickly looked away and resumed his conversation.

"She's as bad as a cat," Oliver said across the table, inclining his head toward Vidya.

"Except at night," Sebastian noted, running a hand through his tousled hair.

He looked tired and had been quite hairy that afternoon despite the success at the burial ground. He seemed to drift in his own thoughts. Abby often had to say his name several times before he realized that she had been addressing him.

"Coffee?" Bridget asked, overhearing their conversation.

He shook his head.

"I feel wired as it is. Caffeine will only make it worse," he replied.

Helena started to stand and Sebastian grabbed her arm.

"It's okay, Helena. No tinctures for me tonight. I'm hoping the storm gathering out there will lull me to sleep."

He nodded toward the window where the sky had grown considerably darker.

"Well it definitely won't help me sleep," Abby commented, knowing she would be in for a night of wakefulness due to the rain. As a water element, she noticed that even more than large bodies of water, rain storms seemed to magnify her energy.

"I'm sure she'll keep you company," Helena said, leaning over Sebastian to grab one of Vidya's outstretched hands as she woke and lengthened her pudgy little arms.

"Well, hello," Abby told her, pulling her blanket a bit lower to reveal the onesie that Oliver and Lydie had bought for her in Australia. It was white and covered in little kangaroos of various colors.

"How are things down unda?" Oliver called over the table.

Vidya's eyes opened wide, and she produced a second yawn.

"Sleep all day, party all night, don't ya?" Sebastian asked her, leaning his face close, so she grabbed at his long black curls. He kissed her forehead and watched her a moment more before diving into the huge slice of banana cake that Bridget had placed in front of him.

Abby lifted her from the bassinet and settled her in the crook of her arm. She waved a little concealment spell over her chest before opening her cloak to latch Vidya on. She didn't mind breastfeeding in front of the other witches, they more than encouraged it, but she always felt a little awkward at the moment before her child latched as she sat with her breast fully exposed. In the back of her mind, she could hear her mother hissing with disapproval. Becky was all for breastfeeding; however, she believed strongly that it was best performed in a dark empty room.

Sebastian leaned close and kissed her temple.

"Fancy a boat ride, tonight?" he asked. His eyes sparkled and the tiredness seemed to have vanished.

Wanting to hold tight to this happier version of Sebastian, she nodded.

"I'd love it," she told him.

****

Sebastian stopped rowing. His teeth glowed a startling white in the light of the moon. Lake Superior stretched out around them, ice-cold and still as glass.

The anticipated storm had been fast and fierce, pouring down rain for twenty minutes and then disappearing into the horizon. In the calm aftermath, they had set off in a little rowboat.

"Fancy a swim?" Abby asked.

"Not just yet," he told her, leaning forward and reaching beneath his bench.

Abby looked back toward Ula. Lights blazed in the castle windows. Set high on the cliffs the castle gave Abby chills, much the same way it had the first night she'd seen it. Somewhere within those high stone walls, their baby lay on a blanket as Oliver and Lydie entertained her with magic tricks.

"It's all so surreal," she whispered.

Sebastian sat up holding a box wrapped in shining red paper.

"What do you have there?" Abby asked.

"A surprise." Sebastian grinned, holding up the small box so that Abby could see the dark tendrils of ribbon curling from its surface.

Abby felt a little shiver tickle her spine. An odd sense of foreboding stole over her as she stared at the gift. Swallowing the lump that had formed in her throat, she took the box, forcing a smile.

"What's the occasion?" she asked, twisting her finger through the ribbon and pulling it loose.

Sebastian's smile grew wider. "No occasion. I saw it and knew it belonged to you."

Abby pulled off the shiny red wrapping and tucked it beneath her seat. She held a small black velvet box. When she opened it, her breath stopped as if someone had sucked the air from her body. Black spots danced behind her eyes, but even through that haze of darkness, she still saw the ring. A huge pearl balanced on a tiny silver band. When she grazed the pearl with her finger it flashed black. Abby closed her eyes unable to forget the memory of that ring on someone else's finger - Vesta - the Vepar who had died in the lair the previous autumn.

Sebastian's eyes twinkled.

"It's amazing, right?"

Abby forced a nod while her thoughts ricocheted like bullets through her head. Where had Sebastian gotten the ring? What had led him to it? And what motivated him to give it to Abby?

Thinking fast, Abby pretended to cough, leaning forward in the boat to brace her hands on her knees. Oliver had taught her a basic enlarging spell. She had only used it once during her pregnancy to make her shoes bigger. Silently repeating the incantation, while rubbing her right hand, she drew from the water element surrounding them. A prickling sensation ran along her fingers.

"Abby?" Sebastian stood, the boat wavering. He reached her and started gently patting her back. "Do you need water? I brought some."

She nodded, still feigning her cough. Examining her fingers quickly and convinced they looked a bit larger, she cleared her throat and took a long drink from the water bottle.

"Better," she said. "I think I swallowed a bug."

He laughed, but Abby did not miss the skepticism in his eyes.

"A chocolate one, I hope," he told her.

"Hardly. More like those weird little gnats that you can't see until they're wedged in your throat."

"Try it on," Sebastian said, taking the box from Abby's hand.

"Where did you get this ring?" Abby asked, treading carefully. She wanted to blurt out Vesta's ring - where in the hell did you get Vesta's ring, but bit her tongue.

Sebastian's eyes clouded, and she knew he had created a lie before he spoke it.

"A little shop in Chicago. I saw it in the window when we were there for Ezra's..." he trailed off, but Abby understood, Ezra's memorial, except it was a lie. Abby tried to remember if he had ever been separated from the group and yes, he had gone to the store to get extra baby wipes for Vidya. Still, she felt confident he had not purchased Vesta's ring in a store in Chicago.

Sebastian pulled the ring from the velvet case and lifted Abby's right hand. He started to slide it onto her ring finger, but it stuck at the first knuckle. He frowned and tried again.

"Ouch," she snapped, a bit too dramatically, but he immediately pulled the ring away.

"I'm sorry," he said, looking at her hand in puzzlement. "I was so sure it would fit. And honey, I think your hand might be swollen."

He held it up in the moonlight and Abby realized she had overdone it a bit. Her hand looked like it belonged on the State Puff Marshmallow Man.

"Oh wow," she exclaimed. "I used one of Helena's tinctures earlier on my fingernails. I must have used the wrong one." She laughed and shrugged. "I'm sure it will go down in a few days and then I can try it on."

Sebastian looked disappointed, but didn't push the subject.

****

Abby knocked on Oliver's door, glancing behind her a second time. The hallway at Ula stood empty, the candle-lit orbs glowing dimly.

The door opened a crack and a sleepy Oliver peeked out. When he saw that Abby stood on the threshold, he opened it wide. Abby took in his rumpled boxer shorts and otherwise nakedness feeling even more guilty that she'd slipped out while Sebastian slept.

"What's up?" he asked, instantly alert. He stepped from his room and looked down the hall.

"No emergency," she said. "But I need to talk to you. In private."

She pushed past him into his room. He closed the door and sat back on his bed.

Abby took a seat on a chair, a safe distance away.

"Sebastian gave me this tonight." She pulled the velvet box from her pocket.

Oliver took it and opened the lid.

"Okay…" he looked at her, confused. "It's pretty?"

"You don't recognize it?" she asked.

"Should I?"

Abby bit her lip, hating herself for betraying Sebastian by taking her concerns to Oliver.

"It belonged to Vesta."

"The Vepar?" he asked, touching the ring and jumping back when it flashed black. "That was weird."

"It flashes black when a witch touches it. Or is near it, I think."

"Okay, wait. You're telling me this is a magic pearl ring? Like the one that Meghan lost three hundred years ago?"

"What are you talking about? I just told you this was Vesta's ring. I saw her wearing it. Did Meghan have a pearl ring that…"

"Flashed black when enemies were present," Oliver finished for her. "Yes, that was the third item. Julian wanted to keep the third artifact a secret."

"But why?"

"Probably for this reason right here," he sighed. "How on earth did Sebastian get this ring? And why would he give it to you?"

She grimaced as she heard the words spoken out loud.

"I have no idea."

Oliver frowned, running a hand through his hair.

"You haven't been wearing it?" he asked.

Abby held up her puffy hand in explanation.

Oliver smiled.

"Looks like a clown hand. I kind of like it."

"I used your enlargement spell. I was hoping for something more subtle," she admitted.

"Forget subtle. That was effective. Best to keep it that way for a couple of days. Julian and Faustine need to see this ring."

Abby nodded.

"I know. I just feel terrible. Like I'm betraying him."

"You're not betraying him, Abby. This whole thing is bigger than him. We're walking on the edge of life and death and as you well know, there are no coincidences. We need to figure out how he got ahold of this and why."

"He said he bought it in Chicago," she added.

"And you believed him?"

She shook her head no.

Oliver stood and walked to his desk, rifling through the top drawer. He pulled out a plastic gold ring. A large, also plastic, heart bauble sat in its center.

"A gift from Lydie eons ago," he said, carefully pulling out the pearl ring and laying it on his desk.

"I think that's a poor replacement," she said.

"Not for long." He took out a small circular mirror and laid it on the table. Setting the rings side by side, he whispered an incantation and held his hands over the rings.

Abby watched the plastic ring take on the exact image of the pearl.

Oliver put the plastic ring, now identical to the other, back in the velvet box. He handed it to her.

"So long as he doesn't take it out, we're good."

Abby touched the ring. Though it looked like the pearl ring, it felt like the gaudy plastic piece with the heart.

"Now go back to bed. It will only make him suspicious if he catches you in here."

Abby glanced at the pearl ring on his desk.

"I'm going to take it to Julian tonight," Oliver told her.

"That's going to make it seem like a really big deal. Maybe you should just wait until morning."

Oliver narrowed his eyes at her and she stood, sighing.

"Okay, you're right. Just don't let Julian bust down our door and pull Sebastian out of bed for an inquisition," she told him, pausing in the doorway. "Thank you, Oliver."

He gave her a two-finger salute, and she left, hurrying down the hallway with the fake ring clutched in her hand.

****

Julian and Faustine stood in the oratory. The symbol X glowed from the circle as if awaiting the witches who would not be gathering upon it that night. Julian held a loupe, or jeweler's eyepiece, over the ring and peered into the glass.

"What do you see?" Oliver asked, leaning over his shoulder.

"That the pearl is real for one," Julian told him. "See how rough the surface is?"

Oliver looked through the eyepiece.

"But is it magic?"

"Unfortunately, yes, and not light magic. Just holding it, I get the feeling it's trying to invade me in some way." Julian set the ring down.

Faustine thumbed through a huge antique text, the gold lettering on the spine unreadable.

"Abby is sure that this was Vesta's ring?" Julian asked.

Oliver nodded. "She wouldn't have brought it to me otherwise. It scared her enough to put an enlarging spell on her hand to avoid wearing it."

"It belonged to Meghan. This has to be the ring she described. It turns black in the presence of your enemies. In Vesta's case that would have been witches," Julian muttered.

"It turned black when I touched it," Oliver mentioned.

"I would imagine that is because its previous owner was a Vepar," Julian explained.

"And Sebastian gave it to Abby," Faustine added, staring at the ring grimly.

"Why was Vesta wearing the ring?" Oliver asked. "I didn't get the impression from Abby's visions of her that she was important to Tobias or Alva. Why would they entrust her with such a valuable item?"

"To empower Clyde," Julian said. "We already have the sense that Alva and Tobias started to betray Clyde on some level by assisting Kanti. I believe they wanted freedom from his control. Putting the ring on Vesta meant he pulled power and had more direct access to her than to them."

"How did Sebastian find it? And why did he give it to Abby? Why didn't it give him the creeps?" Oliver continued.

"My concern is that Clyde allowed this ring to leave his possession. We are in the midst of attempting to secure these items for their destruction and one falls right into our lap," Faustine said, setting the book aside.

"Clyde doesn't know that we are aware of the ring," Julian said. "Clyde doesn't know that we have met Meghan, that we know of Eugene, any of it…"

"I wouldn't be so sure about that," Oliver admitted. "We made that video in Chicago. Abby held Eugene's pocket watch out and spoke of Clyde coveting Eugene's power."

"So, he does know and still allowed Sebastian to get this ring," Faustine murmured.

"Wanted Sebastian to get the ring is more like it," Julian said. "These objects give Clyde access to the power of whoever is wearing it."

"Which would have been Abby," Oliver grumbled. "What do we do about this?"

"We confront Sebastian for starters. The Crystal of Sight will help get to the truth," Julian huffed.

Oliver suspected that Julian was angry that despite all his work with Sebastian, the man continued to slip under Clyde's control.

"I tend to agree," Faustine added. "It is clear that Sebastian cannot be trusted."

CHAPTER 24

"That thing looks lethal," Abby told Oliver. He stood over a long wooden table assembling arrows.

"That is the point," he remarked, holding up an arrowhead. "No pun intended."

She shook her head, laughing, and walked to his work station.

Abby picked one of the sharpened blades up and turned it in the light.

"Don't touch the tip," Oliver advised. "They're coated in a salve made from Julian's powder."

"Doesn't that only work on Vepars?"

"Probably, but let's not find out."

Oliver pointed at several of the blades that looked quite crude and misshapen.

"I found those in the land that belonged to Kanti's people."

"Wow," Abby touched one. "If only her family could know that she'll soon be at rest."

"They do know," Oliver reminded her.

"Good point."

"They're done," Lydie announced striding into the room with a tray of feathers. Some were black, others brown and white, but all shone as if sprinkled with gold powder.

"Those are beautiful," Abby breathed.

"Don't touch, please," Lydie chastised her as Abby reached for a feather. "Let me demonstrate."

She lifted a feather and holding it high, spun in a fast circle. The feather burst into flames.

"Oh," Abby jumped back as Lydie released the feather and it burned so hot the flame turned blue. Nothing remained of the feather.

"Damn, Lydie! You have truly outdone yourself," Oliver declared, slapping her on the back.

She did a little curtsy.

"I made those from Vidya's birds." Lydie smiled at Abby who returned her expression with horror.

"Vidya's birds?" she asked, shocked.

"I didn't kill them, silly," Lydia explained. "I've been collecting the feathers for weeks around your house and here at Ula."

"Oh, ha, okay," Abby laughed. "And now we'll be using them to kill Vepars?"

"I will be," Oliver corrected. "Lydie saved a few to make Vidya a dreamcatcher. So, don't worry there will be non-violent use of the feathers as well."

He grinned and Lydie laughed.

"It's going to be sweet, Abby. Helena has a charm that helps draw nightmares into the catcher. She gave me one as a little girl too," Lydie beamed.

"Thank you, Lydie. Maybe you could make one for me as well. My sleep has been terrible lately."

"I'm on it," Lydie announced, heading toward the door.

"Oh, no." Abby held up her hand. "I was only kidding."

"Why?" Lydie cocked her head to the side. "I still have one. So do Helena and Bridget for that matter. They're not just for kids, you know. And they're pretty."

"Take the dreamcatcher," Oliver told her from the corner of his mouth. "Or you might end up with one of these fiery feathers in your arse."

Lydie rolled her eyes at him.

"Thank you, Lydie. I'd love one," Abby told her. She meant it too. Nightmares had plagued her for weeks. She no longer had visions of Vidya. A new darkness had begun to stalk her dreamscape. He was faceless, but she always woke with the sense that it had been Sebastian following her through the dark.

****

"Sebastian?" Faustine stopped him in the library as they were preparing to step through the mirror.

Abby looked at Oliver, her eyes widening.

"You go first," Oliver told her, giving her a little push toward the mirror. "We're right behind you."

Abby stepped through and Oliver followed. Julian waited a moment.

"What's up?" Sebastian asked, stepping toward the mirror. They had only a few hours before Abby needed to be in the woods with Eugene's watch. He had no intention of letting her go without him and didn't want Faustine to catch them up.

"I need you to accompany me to the tower." Faustine told him.

Sebastian glanced at Julian who stood in front of the mirror as if he were blocking it.

"I have to go with Abby," Sebastian reminded them. "If Victor shows up…" He trailed off seeing Julian's grave expression. "Am I missing something?"

"The ring that you gave to Abby is one of Clyde's bewitched artifacts, Sebastian," Julian told him. "You need to go with Faustine."

Sebastian's mouth fell open.

"What? No! I bought it…" but he couldn't exactly remember where he'd bought it. He had told Abby Chicago and that seemed right, but for some reason he had no actual memory of purchasing the ring, no receipt, no proof what-so-ever.

Faustine opened the library door.

"Let's get to the bottom of this, Sebastian. For your and Abby's sake," he said gesturing toward the open door.

Sebastian turned back as if he wanted to shove Julian aside and jump through the mirror, but thought better of it. He stuffed his hands into his pockets and followed Faustine from the room.

****

Abby took a deep breath, trying to focus on the horizon. Julian and Oliver were somewhere in the woods surrounding her and she fought the desire to turn and search for their faces. Sebastian had stayed at Ula. Had Faustine discovered where he got the pearl ring? The jumble of thoughts in her head was amplified by the weight of the gold watch resting in her hand.

She opened the clasp and stared into the cracked face as if it might hold the answers to the questions churning in her mind.

An hour passed and then two. Her butt turned numb so she stood and paced back and forth among the trees.

"He's not going to show," Oliver called, jumping from the branch of a high tree and landing with a thud that startled her. She dropped the watch, bending and quickly picking it up.

"Here," she shoved it at Julian when he too emerged from the forest.

"Best if we head back to Ula and make another plan," Julian told them.

****

Sebastian's eyes darted in every direction as Faustine led him into the circular stone tower. The ceiling soared high above him and staring up at it made him dizzy. He shifted his gaze to the floor, racking his brain for where he had purchased the ring.

Faustine walked up the stone staircase in the center of the room and settled on the stone slab at the top.

"Join me," Faustine called to him.

The heavy wooden door had slammed closed behind them and Sebastian thought if he tried to flee, he would find it locked.

He took the steps slowly, the weight of his feet, or more likely his fears, dragging him down.

Faustine sat on the slab and lifted the familiar Crystal of Sight, positioning it over his third eye.

"Have a seat, Sebastian."

Sebastian sat heavily, balancing his elbows on his knees and putting his head in his hands. He waited.

Faustine closed his eyes, taking a long slow breath.

"Argh!" Faustine's howl echoed through the chamber and Sebastian fell back nearly plummeting off the slab twenty feet to the stone floor.

Faustine ripped the crystal from his head, his eyes watered, and a trickle of blood ran from his nose. He pressed his hands over his eyes.

"What can I do?" Sebastian asked, starting down the stairs. He yanked on the wood door and as he suspected found it locked.

"Faustine, unlock the door," he shouted.

Faustine blinked down at him, lifting a trembling hand. The door clicked open and Sebastian hurried out.

****

"How is Faustine?" Julian asked Elda.

He had waited until Sebastian stepped through the mirror, back to his home in Trager, before asking the question.

Elda wrinkled her brow.

"He's okay, but quite concerned," Elda said, continuing to stare at the mirror where Sebastian had disappeared moments before. "When he attempted to view Sebastian through the Crystal of Sight he said a horrible blackness descended over him. He described the pain as a sledgehammer against his skull."

"Ugh," Oliver groaned. "That's nuts. Why did it happen?"

Elda shook her head.

"He's not sure. Was it insight into Sebastian or a fluke with the crystal? He honestly doesn't know."

"Is Abby safe with Sebastian?" Oliver asked.

"Helena is aware of what occurred. She's going to keep a close eye on things. Tell me what happened with the watch," Elda said, leaving the mirror and sitting on the edge of a chair.

"We were too obvious," Julian confessed.

"The important thing is that he knows it exists," Elda said.

"We need a ruse," Oliver agreed. "Lydie," he said, an idea suddenly striking him. "Lydie takes the watch and acts like she wants to meet Victor on her own. When he doesn't show, she pretends she's going to throw the watch in the lake. He met with Ezra because he didn't see her as a threat. None of us are less threatening than Lydie."

"No," Elda announced. "No, Oliver." She shook her head. "That plan is absolutely ridiculous."

"I want to do it," Lydie announced, barging into the library where she'd clearly been listening at the door.

Julian frowned.

"It could work, Elda. She's a teenager after all. Impulsive, she snatches the watch, plans to give it to him to get him off our backs…"

Elda gave Julian a venomous glare.

"Do you really have no more sense than that, Julian? You would put Lydie in danger to…"

"To end this curse?" he snapped. "To save us all?"

Elda stood, her fists balled at her sides.

"Lydie, you need to leave this conversation. You will not be used as a ploy to draw Clyde in. The fact that Oliver and Julian would even suggest it calls me to question the state of their minds."

"Elda," Oliver said, "we'd be right there with her. We're not going to send her into the woods unprotected."

Elda spun around and glared at him.

"Because all of your schemes go according to plan, don't they?"

She grabbed Lydie's hand and dragged her from the room, allowing the library door to slam behind her.

Julian shrugged.

"We'll talk to Lydie tonight," he said.

Oliver stared at the slammed door. He had rarely seen Elda angry. The thought of defying her made him uneasy.

****

"This is just stupid," Lydie said after an hour. She stood from the log and gave it a good kick. The bark flaked off and revealed a layer of scurrying bugs. She bent down and inspected the ants racing along the ashy surface.

Tucking the pocket watch in her cloak, she pulled up her hood and started picking her way toward the beach. She needed to maintain the facade even with her thoughts and concentrated on doing just that.

Had she really thought Victor would sense her in the Ebony Woods and come after the watch? It had been a foolish plan, one that Max would have boxed her ears for if he was still alive. At the thought of Max her shoulders slumped, and she considered pulling the watch back out and chucking it into Lake Michigan. A little bit of screw you to that bastard Clyde who she now understood was behind it all. And not only the death of her beloved Max and Dafne, but also centuries of horror, babies abandoned, soulmates ripped apart, covens destroyed. Her own parents had fallen to a similar evil. Not Clyde as far as she knew, but then again what were the chances another group of Vepars lived in northern Michigan? They all likely belonged to him, did his bidding.

She took the watch out and flipped it open.

"I hope you rot in Hell, Clyde," she whispered against the cracked glass. She reached back as far as she could. She wanted that watch to disappear and never be found. Cocking her arm, she started to fling it forward, but a hand caught her wrist.

Shock almost paralyzed her, but her instincts took over and she crouched, swinging low and chopping hard with her hand. Unfortunately, the hand that Victor had grabbed stung and throbbed above her head. He easily stepped back before she could swipe his legs from beneath him. She waved her good hand and a wall of fire rose up between them. The watch had fallen into the sand and Lydie grabbed for it with her bleeding hand. She glanced and saw the half puncture of his teeth etched into the flesh of her palm.

Her mind wanted to attack him. Here he was, and she was meant to get her revenge, but already the venom raced through her blood. Her right hand had gone hot, tingling and finally numb. That numbness was flowing into her wrist, now her elbow. It traveled fast, and she had no time. She looked beyond him for Oliver or Julian, but her vision suffered and she could only concentrate on the man, the Vepar, before her.

She fumbled in her cloak, felt for the canvas pouch of Julian's powder, and whipped it out, releasing the bag and sending it whooshing on a breath of fire towards Victor. He twirled away, grinning, his black eyes glowing orange from the fire that raced past him.

An arrow soared from the trees and struck Victor in the back of his calf. His eyes widened, and he howled in pain as he reached and yanked it from his leg. He blinked rapidly, dropping the gold dagger and whirling toward the forest where Oliver pounced onto the beach, another arrow cocked and ready to fire. Julian came from the water and with him a rush of wind that knocked Victor to his knees. A dark foam had begun to ooze from his mouth. Oliver released another arrow, but somehow Victor rolled just enough and it planted in the beach beside him.

Lydie held a steel dagger in her hand and walked slowly toward Victor writhing on the beach. He had begun to transform. His human body contorted, and he screeched and howled. Wings broke through his back, and he opened his wolfish mouth to reveal rows of fangs.

Lydie stalked toward him, not allowing him to escape, but the venom slowed her.

"Lydie, no," Julian shrieked as she reached the Vepar turning Skin-walker.

She plunged the dagger into his chest, intending to hit that hard bulge of darkness that would end his life. She missed. He roared in pain, but the transition had completed. He took flight, his talons sinking into Lydie's shoulders surpassing flesh and grasping the bones beneath. She screamed and kicked and tried to throw fire into the beast's face, but she missed. The skin-walker flew higher moving, over the lake. Dizzy and nauseous, Lydie saw Oliver and Julian standing on the beach behind her. Oliver had sent another arrow but if fell short of the mark.

CHAPTER 25

Oliver cocked another arrow and let it fly. Julian sent a rush of wind and together they honed on their target - the center of the skin-walker's back, right between the wings. It hit home. The screech barely reached them, but they watched him plummeting towards the water. He had released Lydie who hit first. Oliver was already swimming. He'd never swam so hard in his life. He heard Julian beside him, his own legs and arms slicing through the water.

Oliver knew the place she'd gone in and dove below, searching. Julian found her first, wrapped an arm across her chest and swam back to the surface. Oliver looked for the skin-walker, didn't see him and didn't care. If Victor lived, which was unlikely, they'd deal with him later.

They pulled Lydie onto the beach and Julian sent bursts of air into her lungs. She coughed and choked out water, but did not awaken. The Vepar's venom flowed through her blood. Julian pulled out an antidote and poured it into her mouth. Blood streamed from the wounds in her shoulders. Oliver could see bone peeking through Lydie's ripped flesh.

He pulled off his t-shirt and tore it in two. Wrapping the cloth around her bleeding shoulders, he pressed and tried to staunch the flow. She looked ghostly pale beneath him, her eyelids fluttering. Julian held his hands against her chest, his eyes closed, his lips moving with an incantation that Oliver prayed would help. He thought of Elda. She would be furious that they had put Lydie in harm's way. How could they have been so stupid?

"We need to get her to Abby's house," Oliver choked, feeling the sob he'd been keeping at bay rise into his throat. He didn't have time to cry.

They carried her through the woods and loaded her in Oliver's van. Julian drove and Oliver held her, smoothing the hair from her feverish forehead.

"She's burning up," he told him.

"That's good," Julian replied, hands white knuckled against the wheel. "She's pushing the venom out."

"Shit, shit, shit. This was insane. I'm so sorry, Lydie. I'm so sorry." Oliver leaned down and kissed her cheek, but she remained unconscious. Only the rise and fall of her chest gave Oliver a moment of ease.

Julian drove fast down Abby and Sebastian's driveway, slamming to a stop and flinging open his door.

Oliver hoisted Lydie from the back and Julian already had the front door open. Running through it, he called out Abby's name.

"Abby, Abby!"

She hurried from the kitchen, eyes widening when she saw Lydie's bleeding body.

"Oh my God! What's happened? Helena!" she cried out.

Helena ran to the door, Sebastian followed holding Vidya.

"In here," she barked, pushing Julian out of the way and striding into the living room. She whipped a blanket from the couch and spread it on the floor.

Oliver knelt, laying Lydie on the blanket. For a moment Helena, looked up at him and their eyes met. He saw the accusation there and looked away, staring at his feet.

"Abby, the transfusion equipment is in your linen closet, top shelf."

Abby ran from the room. She returned with a plastic tote filled with tubes, needles and glass bottles.

Helena worked quickly, tying off Abby's arm and slipping a needle into the large blue vein. She set up Lydie next, her mouth set in a grim line. Sebastian rocked Vidya back and forth seemingly mesmerized by the scene unfolding. Oliver held Lydie's hand. Julian too stayed silent, standing in the corner.

"Go get Elda," Helena snapped.

Julian's face fell, but he slipped from the room.

****

"We have two out of three now," Julian argued. "The dagger and the ring. Yes, it was a sacrifice, but a worthwhile one."

Elda stomped her foot and a geyser of water exploded from the lagoon behind her.

Lydie slept in the healing room. Abby's blood had begun to heal her, and Helena stayed by her side. Elda, Oliver, Julian and Faustine had moved to the lagoon where Elda looked ready to strangle them both with her bare hands. Faustine too had an expression of disappointment that made Oliver writhe beneath his gaze.

"I specifically forbade you from involving Lydie in this scheme and look at what happened! Lydie nearly died. Would you ever have forgiven yourself? Oliver? Do you both have no sense at all? No moral compass?"

Oliver blushed, but Julian set his jaw defiantly.

"You forbade me, Elda? Is that your place? Are you the leader of this coven and I one of your lowly followers?" Julian spat.

"Julian," Faustine warned, his eyes holding the same threat as his voice. Julian glared at him.

"What would you have us do? Wait until one morning we walk through the mirror to find Sebastian, Abby and their baby slaughtered in the woods, staked to the ground, the newest Vepar sacrifice."

"You're a danger to us all, Julian. Ever since Miranda, you have been unhinged, operating on your own vendetta. I'm tired of making excuses for you. She's gone, Julian. Destroying us all won't bring her back," Elda seethed.

"I won't listen to this," Julian hissed, turning on his heel.

"No," Elda shrieked, throwing up her hands. Julian stopped as icy water seemed to flow through his veins. He stood paralyzed by her magic. "I will be leaving to check on Lydie, the child you nearly killed today."

Elda stomped away, her dark cloak billowing behind her.

After she had disappeared from view, Faustine released Julian. His face turned crimson, and he too stormed off in the opposite direction.

"I'm sorry, Faustine. I can't tell you how sorry I am," Oliver told him.

Faustine considered Oliver, his mouth in a grim line.

"Oliver, I understand that it is hard to question Julian's guidance. He was your teacher and I blame myself for that. I believed that having a disciple would draw Julian back from the edge. Unfortunately, he merely passed his own extreme tactics on to you."

"It was my idea, Faustine. I never thought he'd get near her. I..."

Faustine held up a hand to quiet him.

"It may have been your idea, but the foundation of your learning was formed by Julian. He lost sight of weighing risks a long time ago. He has put you in danger many times. I too have been complicit in his choices. I have been so happy that he has returned to us that I've turned a blind eye to the very behaviors that forced a wedge between us originally. I do not blame you, Oliver. But I do expect you to do better. From this moment on, you follow your heart's advice and nothing else. Your love for Lydie should have eliminated that idea the moment it arose, but Julian has taught you to bypass those insights and go with your head. It is time to live from your heart."

Faustine did not say more. He looked toward the sand dune where Julian had disappeared, but turned and walked back toward the castle.

****

Abby knocked on the door to Faustine's tower and pushed it open a crack. He sat on the floor with his legs crossed and his eyes closed. When he heard her, he glanced up, and she saw the Crystal of Sight suspended between his eyebrows. For a moment he watched her, his eyes twitching as if following a series of images she could not see. He blinked and pulled the crystal from his head.

"I'm sorry to interrupt," Abby said. "Helena asked me to check on you. The Crystal is working then?"

"Come in," Faustine said. He stood and set the crystal on a dark cloth.

Abby hovered just inside the doorway, gazing at the ceiling that narrowed to a point five stories above them.

"It's high," she murmured.

"I work better with the space," he told her. "Abby, is there anything you'd like to tell me?"

She paused, preferring to slip back out the door and pretend she hadn't heard him. But he watched her intently. Knowing that he had seen things she had been keeping a secret, she walked into the room.

"You've been to Snake Island?" he asked.

Abby nodded.

"And you have the amulet?"

She put her hands on her hips and considered what explanation might suffice.

"I needed to do it alone, Faustine."

He nodded, steepling his fingers in his lap.

"I understand those needs, Abby. I have often followed them myself, but there's a reason that witches created covens. We are smarter, safer and stronger when we share the burden. It is hard. We want to protect those we love, not involve them in the danger, but we hurt them much more with our lies."

"I didn't lie," she started and then sighed. "Okay, I lied. I'm sorry. Sometimes it feels like the talking and the planning distract us from actually doing anything. I needed to do something."

"It's valuable information you've found. More so, we have the amulet which we can now destroy and be one step closer to ending Clyde's reign."

"I need the amulet," Abby told him.

Faustine frowned.

"What does that mean?"

"I need to confront Clyde wearing the amulet. Kanti will help me destroy him."

Faustine cocked his eyebrows and Abby could tell he was weighing his words.

"Allowing Kanti to possess you is very dangerous."

"I know that, but Dafne discovered how to allow the possession and still keep Kanti from having control."

"And yet she still killed herself to escape that possession."

"Because she never got to perform the charm that would have protected her," Abby argued. "This is my life, my child's life."

"The amulet gives Clyde direct access to you, Abby," Faustine stated.

Abby frowned and shook her head.

"I'm not wearing it. It's safe."

"I know," Faustine agreed. "You've returned it to our dungeon here at Ula, a wise decision. However, I cannot in good conscience allow you to put that necklace on and invite Kanti into your body."

Abby felt like a child being scolded by her stern father and a part of her wanted to act the part by stomping from the room and slamming the door behind her.

"Teach me, prepare me, whatever it takes. But I am doing it, Faustine. I know this is the way."

****

Sebastian felt trapped. The walls of his and Abby's bedroom seemed to close in. He threw his book at the opposite wall in agitation. He trotted down the steps, listened, and when silence greeted him, made for the front door. Outside the cold night air filled his lungs. He gasped it in and ran for the woods, losing a sandal and then another. He pulled his t-shirt over his head. His jeans felt too tight. He stopped and stripped them down, already running before he kicked them off. Still the pressure continued. His skin seemed to stretch over his muscles and bones like taut rubber-bands. He wanted to rip his skin off. He raced through the woods and burst onto the shoreline. His body seemed to burst with him. He shrieked as he felt his skin tearing away. His lips curled back and his teeth poked sharp into his gums. Something poked and then thrust through the skin of his back. He screamed and fell to his hands and knees. It was agony and ecstasy, burning, tearing, searing pain coupled with that blissful release as the confines of his tiny, powerless body exploded.

He left the beach. Huge black wings opened behind him and he soared out over the moonlit lake. As the wind rushed beneath him, he felt the sensations as it moved over this foreign body, the way it tickled the tiny hairs that had sprouted from his skin. A primal hunger started a rumbling in his belly. He needed to feed.

****

Abby stepped through the mirror, Vidya snug in a wrap across her chest. She felt the rapid beat of her daughter's heart and the warmth of her body and sighed. She had sat with Helena at Lydie's bedside for hours and her lower back ached. She greeted the silent foyer, looking forward to a night alone with Sebastian. It had been awhile. Usually at least one of the Ula witches stayed over, often Helena to help care for Vidya, but equally likely

Oliver, Lydie and even Julian.

"Poor Lydie," she whispered, remembering Lydie's drawn face. She had woken several times, but for no more than minutes before drifting back to sleep. The venom had worn off, but Helena continued to give her an elixir that made her drowsy. She worried that the pain would be uncomfortable when Lydie woke and wanted her to sleep as long as possible.

"Sebastian?" she called. He didn't respond, and she walked upstairs, wondering if he might have taken a nap. He had not gone to Ula with Abby and the other witches. In the urgency of the moment, Abby had not pressed the issue.

Their bedroom stood empty. The comforter was still snug beneath the pillows and the bed looked unruffled. She spotted the book he'd been reading earlier that day. It lay on the floor, splayed open with its spine up. She picked up the book and a little tremor passed through her. Had something happened to Sebastian?

She felt her own heartbeat increasing as she walked back down the stairs calling Sebastian's name. She unwound her wrap and placed Vidya in her bassinet. She turned on the faucet and ran the cool water over her hands and wrists. Closing her eyes, she allowed her awareness to move through the house. She felt…something, but had no word to describe it. She knew the sensations when something violent had occurred and that thickness did not find her. Instead, a gnawing sense of disquiet seemed to blanket the house. Turning off the water, she did a more thorough search, walking through rooms and searching for a note. Sebastian rarely stepped out, even for a walk, without leaving her some kind of message.

****

Sebastian woke shivering. Cold water lapped over his naked legs and thighs. He struggled to sit up, pushing his hands into the wet sand and looking around, disoriented. The moon cast an opal of light across the lake and gradually he recognized his surroundings. He lay on the beach that edged the Ebony Woods, completely naked. His body ached as if someone had pummeled him with a baseball bat. Rubbing his eyes, oddly sticky, he studied his palms and fingers in the moonlight. They were splotched with dark streaks and he didn't need a closer inspection to know that he was covered in blood. He could smell it.

A wave of horror passed through him as he thought of Abby and Vidya.

"No," he whispered, shaking his head. This wasn't a blackout. He remembered. He didn't want to, but he remembered. He felt the cool wind streaking beneath his wings and he saw the man standing on the shore. The man had been alone, drunk, a vagrant most likely. Something prehistoric had overcome Sebastian. He remembered diving for the man, the look of confusion on his face and then...

He clenched his eyes and felt a burst of nausea turn his stomach. He threw up, pressing his bloody hands into his thighs, doubled over. He had to hide the evidence, but when he looked up, he remembered. He had carried the man out over the water; he had already disposed of him.

He broke into a run, his feet like anvils in the sand. Sydney's house rose in the distance and he fought back the sob bubbling in his chest. He had murdered an innocent man. He had turned into a skin-walker and consumed another human being.

CHAPTER 26

Sebastian leapt onto Sydney's porch and tried the door handle, locked. He smashed the glass and unlocked the door, pushing inside and running straight to the shower. His tears merged with the scalding water and he scrubbed until his skin felt raw. The smell of Sydney's coconut soap brought streams of memories - Claire and his parents and summers on the beach. Sydney laughing as she blended margaritas. The summer after his parents' deaths when he sat on the dock with Sydney on a cool autumn day and cried openly. More memories wanted to come. Images of Vidya sleeping on Abby's naked chest as his magic wife smoothed her hand over their child's milky back. Their wedding at Ula as Abby moved into the floating garden, her hair blowing in the cliff-top breeze, the scent of the flowers overwhelming his senses.

He stepped from the shower, grabbing a thick white towel and wrapping it around his waist. The house had been stripped of Sydney in many ways, but he felt her presence. Was she watching him? Judging him for what he had done?

He needed clothes. He could not return to the house naked, but all of Sydney's and Rod's stuff had been removed. In the attic he found several cardboard boxes that had been abandoned. He slipped into a pair of Harold's sweatpants and a law school t-shirt. He looked strange, the clothes too short and wide, his feet stuffed into small loafers, but he didn't have another option. He ran down the driveway and prayed for a trucker or understanding motorist who might give him a ride home.

****

"Sebastian!" Oliver yelled waving his flashlight through the trees. He could see Julian's light closer to the beach.

Abby too was in the woods with a flashlight. Helena and Lydie had stayed at the house with Vidya. When Abby had burst through the mirror insisting that Sebastian was missing, Oliver had feared the worst. Had Clyde somehow taken him?

But like Abby, he had not sensed distress in the house. As he moved through the woods, he sniffed at the air. He smelled something...something that reminded him of the lair he'd been trapped in by the Vepars. It wasn't the smell of a Vepar, but near to it, more animal, more deadly.

Julian appeared through the trees, holding his flashlight down.

"Do you smell that?" he asked.

Oliver nodded.

"And I found this." Julian held up one of Sebastian's sandals.

"Shit," Oliver breathed. "Maybe we'd better get Abby back inside."

Julian cocked an eyebrow at him.

"You think she'll go?"

"Good point," Oliver agreed.

Beyond the trees, they heard the sound of splashing water and then Abby's voice pierced the trees.

"Sebastian! He's here. I found him. Help me."

Oliver and Julian raced to the beach where Abby pulled a naked Sebastian from the water. He leaned heavily on her, sputtering water and breathing hard.

"Are you okay? What happened?" she babbled, tears pouring down her face. "I was so scared. I thought..." but she couldn't finish the sentence.

Oliver watched Sebastian who had rolled on his side and heaved as Abby slapped his back.

"I'm okay," he whispered hoarsely. He took several deep breaths, his eyes closed, and then finally looked at them.

"I went for a swim. I wasn't paying attention and went out too far. The current got ahold of me."

Oliver studied Sebastian's face as he spoke and felt the prickle of a lie. He sensed a similar impression from Julian. Only Abby seemed ready to accept the explanation.

"Holy crap," she breathed. "Thank the goddess you're okay! Here, come on." She stood and helped him stand.

They walked back to the house, Oliver and Julian trailing behind.

Oliver stared hard at the two long bruises that ran down Sebastian's back on either side of his spine. They were ghastly and dark. He felt Julian watching them as well.

****

"You went swimming naked?" Julian asked.

Sebastian sat across the kitchen table, a towel draped over his shoulders and his hands stuffed into his lap. Abby had given him a mug of tea and when he took a sip, they all saw the dark bruises on his fingers. In the light of the kitchen, more bruises surfaced. Much of his skin looked purplish and raw.

"Sebastian, you are covered in bruises," Abby exclaimed, tenderly touching a space on his neck.

His face darkened, and he looked down at his torso.

"I don't know why," he admitted. "I was practicing with my power earlier, throwing some logs and rocks. It must have happened then."

He blinked into his cup and shuddered.

Abby took a deep breath and steadied her hands on the back of Sebastian's chair. Her husband was sitting at the table bruised, near-drowned and clearly lying to all of them. She wanted to believe every word from his mouth, help him upstairs, and tuck him into bed, but how could she ignore the expressions on Julian's and Oliver's faces?

"I'm going to check on Helena and Vidya," she murmured finally. "Maybe you should talk to Julian and Oliver."

Abby didn't say more, but quietly left the room. She knew that he may not be able to come clean with her nearby. Though she had no intention of missing the truth. She hovered outside the kitchen door, listening.

"Sebastian, tell us what really happened," Julian said.

Abby waited, holding her breath, but only silence followed. The seconds ticked by.

Finally, he coughed and spoke. "I was, ummm, practicing in the woods, like I said and then I heard a screech."

"A skin-walker?" Oliver asked.

"Yeah. I ran toward the lake. I didn't see it, but suddenly I was flying. It didn't kill me, but dropped me on the beach by the Ebony woods. There was blood all over the beach. I think it must have killed someone. I took a shower at Sydney's and hitchhiked home. I ran in the lake and made the rest of it up," his voice grew quieter as he spoke until Abby had to strain to hear him.

"Why would you do that?" Oliver asked. "Why not tell the truth?"

"I don't know. I panicked when I saw the blood on the beach. I started operating on auto-pilot."

"Who was the skin-walker? Alva? Did it transform into a Vepar at all?" Julian asked. Abby heard the skepticism in his words.

"No."

"Did you fight it?" Oliver asked.

"I umm…yeah. I mean, you see the bruises, right?" Sebastian's tone had grown defensive. "Of course, I fought it, but it was holding me in talons that felt like steel hooks in my back. I wasn't exactly trying to fall to my death or provoke it to eat me."

"I see," Julian continued. Abby could not see their faces, but she could imagine them. Sebastian's would have grown hard, defiant. Oliver would look amused as if he couldn't believe the story Sebastian was feeding them.

And Julian would hold that careful appearance of neutrality while beneath the surface his mind cranked out a thousand thoughts a minute.

"I'm exhausted," Sebastian said. Abby heard the scrape of his chair on the floor.

She hurried down the hallway and burst into the living room where Helena sat on a blanket with Vidya. Helena looked up and seeing Abby's face, frowned.

"What is it, honey? Is Sebastian okay?" she started to stand, but Abby waved her back down.

Abby walked toward Vidya and then sank down on the blanket next to her, feeling the tears pour over her face. She cried into the little yellow blanket, muffling her sobs against the floor. Her shoulders heaved, and Helena smoothed her hands down Abby's back, saying nothing.

Sebastian was lying, had lied. What had happened? What could it mean that his first instinct had been to hide the real story from all of them, including her?

When she sat up, Helena brushed a finger along her face, catching a tear. She cupped it in her hand and held it close to her ear. Helena grimaced as she leaned into the tear as if told her the story of Abby's pain. Perhaps it did.

"Abby?" Oliver stood in the doorway. "Come to the kitchen for a few minutes."

Abby nodded and stood. Helena reached into a pocket tucked in her flowery yellow dress and produced a smooth black stone.

"Hematite," Helena told her. "For courage."

Abby took the stone and squeezed it in her palm, following Oliver to the kitchen. Julian sat at the table, his chin resting on his steepled fingers, his face deeply troubled.

"You heard all of that?" Julian asked.

Abby nodded.

"And you also clearly detected the lie?"

"Yes," Abby admitted, though she wanted to choke on the word rather than say it. Abby thought of the watch around Sebastian's neck, Vesta's ring, the late night digging.

"What would you like to do about it?" Julian asked.

Abby widened her eyes, surprised. She had expected some fully formed plan already in Julian's mind.

"I..." She paused and glanced at Oliver for help.

"Well, she's clearly not safe here," Oliver said. "I think she and Vidya need to come back to Ula with us tonight and..."

Julian held up a hand.

"I asked Abby."

She sat heavily into a chair, pushing her face into her hands.

"I'm not afraid of Sebastian," she told them. "I'm afraid for him. I can't run away and leave him to face this alone."

"So, you're willing to fight for him?" Julian asked.

"Of course," Abby snapped.

"I'm only checking, Abby. I sense that we're going to have a painful battle ahead, and it may hurt Sebastian most of all, but if you truly want him to stay on the side of light then…"

"Then what?" she asked.

"Then we need to lock him in the dungeons at Ula until we've eliminated Clyde."

Abby stared at him, incredulous. He couldn't be serious. Lock up Sebastian?

She started to shake her head, but Oliver beat her to it.

"Julian, you can't be serious."

"I'm deadly serious. And let me tell you what I think. I think there was blood beneath Sebastian's fingernails. I think there were bruises on his back in the exact place where two wings might have emerged. I think that Sebastian took a life tonight, and he didn't intend to do it, but he was powerless to stop it."

Abby stood, her chair clattering to the floor.

"You think what? That Sebastian turned into a skin-walker?" her voice trembled with rage as she spoke, and worse, with fear.

Oliver too appeared shocked, but Abby saw something else in his face, belief.

"He's gone upstairs to sleep. Or perhaps to climb out the window. But I can tell you what this moment is, Abby. It's a turning point. Until now Sebastian has successfully fought off the advances of Clyde. Tonight, he succumbed and we have all witnessed what waits at the end of that dark tunnel. If we don't take serious action on this night, you will lose him, Abby. You will lose him in the worst possible way."

Abby swallowed the lump forming in her throat.

From the living room, she heard Vidya cry out.

"I need to feed Vidya," she said, turning, but then it was Helena's cry that rang through the house.

Abby raced into the living room nearly tripping over a footstool in the center of the floor.

Helena clutched Vidya to her chest, staring wide-eyed at the glass doors that led to the patio. They had been flung open to the night.

"I'm sorry, I screamed," she said, shaking her head. "I didn't realize…" Helena gestured at the door. "He came through here so fast, it startled me."

"Who?" Abby asked, taking Vidya from Helena's arms.

"Sebastian," Helena said, her eyes troubled. "He didn't speak a word, just plowed through the room. He knocked over the stool. I thought he'd run right through the glass, but the doors opened. I didn't see him touch the handles, but they flung open and he ran out."

Julian walked to the door with Oliver close behind. He stepped onto the porch and stared at the woods where Sebastian had disappeared.

Vidya started to cry, her wails echoing through the house. An owl landed on the porch, its large dark eyes trained on Vidya.

"Ssshhh, there, there. It's okay sweetie," Abby whispered, rocking her from side to side.

Abby struggled to take a full breath. It caught in her throat and lodged there.

"We have to go after him," she said finally, handing Vidya back to Helena after her cries had subsided.

Helena snuggled the baby close, tucking her beneath her chin.

"Of course, you have to," Helena agreed.

Julian shook his head.

"It's too late, Abby."

"Excuse me?" she snarled, feeling an explosion of anger at his words.

A pitcher of water on the coffee table exploded.

Julian whirled towards it, blowing hard. The glass stopped midair. Oliver held his hands up and the pieces gathered in a pile in his palms.

"You need to learn to control your temper," Julian seethed. "If not for our sakes, then for hers." He pointed at Vidya and walked from the room.

Abby's face grew hot, and she clenched her eyes shut. She started to walk out the door, but Oliver caught her hand.

"I don't believe it's too late," he told her. "But Sebastian needs space right now. Don't chase after him. It will only make things worse."

Abby clenched her teeth and forced the blue ball of energy building to dissipate and flow back into her body.

****

Sebastian ran through the trees not bothering to sweep branches aside as they pricked his face and caught in his hair. Tears streamed from his eyes. An itching sensation tore at his skin. Like before, he felt trapped in his tiny, weak body. Except this time, he knew how to escape it. He raced toward the end of the peninsula and then crouched, still running, his skin ripped apart and the skin-walker emerged. His taloned feet tasted the water's edge and he soared. As his eyes scanned the trees, he saw a hunched figure below him. A pentacle glowed from the man's chest and Sebastian almost circled and returned to the shore, but the sensations of the primal body he inhabited blotted out the image. Out over the crashing waves, he flew. Somewhere in the night a voice called out for him. He could not escape his destiny.

CHAPTER 27

They talked loudly and over one-another. Abby tried to concentrate on their words, but they streamed into a single sound that passed through her head without comprehension. Julian's hands shook as he spoke. Oliver interrupted, his eyes darting back to Abby.

He mouthed something at her. "Are you okay," she thought his silent words said, but she did not respond. Instead she gazed numbly at the witches' faces in the library of Ula. Elda stood close to Faustine anxiously clutching the pendant at her throat. Faustine nodded, asking lightning fast questions that Julian blurted answers too. Helena spoke to the witches, to Vidya, to Abby, but still Abby stood perfectly still. Even Adora had joined the fray. Each time she spoke her voice shook. She wanted to know things, urgently, she feared they were under attack, but somehow her questions hung unanswered in the sea of words.

Oliver moved close to her, grasped her elbow.

"Abby, I think you should sit down. You're white as a ghost." He tried to nudge her toward a chair, but she resisted.

It took all of her strength, but finally she broke her silence.

"I need a minute, Oliver. Alone. I'm going to take a walk," she pulled away from him and opened the library door.

"I'll go with you," he said.

"No." She stared at him, hard. "I said alone."

Pretending to walk toward the castle doors, Abby stole a glanced behind her as she moved through the golden hallway. Oliver had watched her for a moment before closing the door to the library. Abby changed direction and ran to the stairway at the end of the hall. Rushing down, she sought the dungeon room that contained dangerous items of magic. She had hidden the amulet there and knew Faustine would have placed the ring and the dagger there as well. In the room, she plunged her hands into boxes, disregarding all of her training. If she touched an item bewitched with dark magic, it could injure her, but she didn't care.

Already knowing the amulet sat in a black velvet box on a high-shelf, she saved that for last. Someone had placed the dagger in a glass box, suspended inside with tiny golden clamps. Prising the box open, she grabbed a black cloth from the work table and wrapped the dagger within it. Despite the cloth, meant to hinder the magic inside, she felt heat emanating from the dragon. The sensation of holding the dagger brought her back to the terrifying night when she first encountered the Vepar, Tobias. She had nearly died that night. What would have become of the curse if she had?

Shaking her head to clear the questions, she began her hunt for the ring. She stumbled upon it on the work table, somehow having missed it moments before. It sat on a piece of glass. Though the ring appeared as a pearl, the glass reflected flashing white and black rings as it revealed its magic.

Carefully, using another cloth, Abby wrapped the ring as well. She plucked the velvet box from the shelf and stopped by the door. The ax that Julian had retrieved from Sky Mothers stood there. The blade glinted, and Abby hesitated, remembering the story of the man-killing tree the ax had been discovered with. She took a deep breath and picked it up. It was surprisingly light. She slipped into the hallway, turning for the stairs.

"Abby?" a voice startled her, and she nearly dropped the items clutched in her hands.

Lydie stood at the hall's end, her shoulders swathed in gauze. In the light of the candelabras, Abby saw the glaze in her eyes. Lydie teetered on skinny legs, putting a hand against one wall.

"I'm not dreaming, am I?" Lydie asked.

Abby shook her head, bending down and setting the items on the dungeon floor.

"No, Lydie. It's me. I just came down to grab a few things. Let's get you back to the Healing Room."

Abby led Lydie into the Healing Room and settled her back on the bed. She covered her with a warm blanket.

Lydie blinked at her, reaching a trembling hand to Abby's cheek.

"I dreamed of Sebastian, Abby" she told her, a little smile crossing her face quickly followed by a frown. "But he was surrounded by snakes."

Lydie's eyes closed. Abby placed a lavender eye pillow on her face and returned to the hallway. She snatched the items and performed a vanishing spell before racing back up the stairs to hide them in her room.

****

"It was always you," Victor whispered, leaning so close that Sebastian could smell the rank of his breath. He had changed, grown larger, hulking even. His breath smelled of death and decay. He also looked haggard. The skin on his face and shoulders appeared burned, huge blisters shiny and sore covered his neck. His eyes had a yellowish tinge. One of his shoulders drooped, the result of Oliver's arrows.

He thought to ask the man, the once witch, what had turned him into such a monster, but Sebastian already knew. He had given in to that dark desire and it had swallowed him whole.

Sebastian twisted away, but a steel cable bit through his shirt and tore at his skin. Victor had bound him to a thick wooden rail. He grimaced and jerked his head further away from Victor's.

He had no memory of Victor capturing him, but realized with growing unease he had likely come willingly. His last memory included the rush of wind beneath his wings as he sliced through the night sky. Had Victor been calling out to him? Or was it not Victor at all, but Clyde who now spoke?

"Surrender Sebastian. You're so close. I can feel it. I feel your walls breaking down, collapsing. Let go."

Victor's words slithered into Sebastian's ears, coiled like a snake on the floor of his brain. The snake rose, sharp fangs dripping. His head grew thick, fuzzy and then as if the serpent truly lived within him, he felt it lash out and strike.

Sebastian howled and again jerked away, but a heavy steel cable cut into his chest. He hung, limp, sweating, exhausted. The pain traveled from his brain into every cell of his body. His fingertips hurt, his toes, the skin on the back of his neck. He couldn't find a single spot that didn't shriek with pain.

"Ask for it to be over," Victor continued. "Say the words and I'll set you free."

Sebastian said nothing. He clenched his teeth together to keep from crying out.

Victor stood back and watched him. His black, hungry eyes made Sebastian's skin crawl.

"I didn't take you, Sebastian," he continued, pulling back his lips to reveal sharp white teeth. His teeth seemed to be the only thing not rotting on his body. "You came to me, to Clyde, your father."

Sebastian spit at Victor's feet. "You're nothing," he roared.

Victor or Clyde moved closer, touched Sebastian's arm.

"Such a strong, healthy body," he groaned. "This is what happens when you call a witch to power," Clyde muttered touching a piece of his own singed skin. "Barely a week in this body and already it's destroyed." He shook his head as if disgusted.

Clyde occupied Victor's body, not Victor. But where was Victor during the possession? Did he cease to exist?

"You can't escape your destiny, Sebastian. No more than I could escape mine. We are bound you and I, by blood, by the dark dream that was born within us long before we came into the world. Our power lives in fulfilling that dream. You want it. I feel your desire pouring off your body, leaking from your thoughts. I can taste it." Victor's black tongue darted between his red lips.

Sebastian closed his eyes and tried to search for the root of his power. Somewhere within him that strength waited to be tapped, channeled. But how did he access it?

"You don't have to give it all up, Sebastian. Abby, Vidya, even the witches of Ula. You could protect them forever. It's the ultimate sacrifice. No one could ever hurt them. You could fear nothing. Abby could fear nothing. You could change the world. You can change the world."

The words seeped in. They slithered and danced. What did he want more than an end to the fear? An end to the constant anxiety of what would come next, what new evil would arrive at their door? He needed to say no, started to say no and then…

"How?" he croaked, surprised to hear his own voice ask the question.

Victor smiled, revealing those sharp white teeth. His eyes gleamed with triumph and Sebastian wanted to shout that he hadn't spoken that word, that it wasn't him that wanted to know, but his lips stayed sealed tight against the words he needed to speak.

"It's so easy, Sebastian. It's already within you. Open yourself to me, to Clyde."

Sebastian didn't understand. But the moment he allowed the thought, a well of black opened. It stretched forever, beyond Sebastian, into a realm where light could not penetrate. There, deep in its center, a voice called out. It was not a voice with words, but a sound that reverberated through his being. It wanted Sebastian's resonance. They could be one, Sebastian and that sound, if only he surrendered.

"Surrender," the sound seemed to pulse. "Surrender."

And he did.

****

Oliver waited downstairs and Abby walked into her bedroom, closing the door behind her. He had accompanied her to grab a few things from her house in Trager: clothes, bottles for Vidya and toiletries. Pausing at the bed, she picked up one of Sebastian's crumpled t-shirts and held it to her nose. The smell was so familiar, so perfectly Sebastian that it brought her to her knees. She sank onto the floor, stuffing the shirt into her face and soaking it with her tears. It was going on twenty-four hours since he'd rushed into the night. Abby had stayed at Ula after he left, but sleep had been impossible. She had been biding her time to step back through the mirror, not wanting to alert the other witches to her plans. Setting the t-shirt aside, she forced herself back up. She had to keep it together for Vidya.

On her bedside table, she saw the note, folded and propped against a water glass. When she opened it, Sebastian's familiar scrawl greeted her.

"Meet me at the sand dune. Please forgive me for running away. It's all going to be okay. I know what to do. Bring Vidya. Tonight 8pm."

She read it a second time. He referred to the sand dune they'd visited just weeks before during one of those perfectly normal days where they pretended that the world was not collapsing around them.

Bring Vidya the note said.

"Abby?" Oliver called from downstairs.

"I'm coming," she yelled back, quickly stuffing the note in her jeans pocket. She gathered her clothes and Vidya's bottles and met Oliver in the foyer by the mirror.

****

Abby held Vidya and sang "Somewhere over the rainbow," as she hiked through the forest that led to the sand dune. She had slipped away from Ula after dinner, offering the excuse that she and Vidya both needed to sleep. While the library was empty, she stole through the mirror into her home in Trager. She had left Clyde's artifacts safely in her and Sebastian's bedroom. Now she moved with fearful anticipation. Sebastian waited for her at the sand dune. She had already sensed him. What would she say if he wanted to run away? Take Vidya and flee from Trager, Clyde, and the curse? Could she leave Ula behind? If it meant protecting Vidya, herself and Sebastian, she thought yes, she could.

When she moved up the sandy bluff, she saw him. He faced away from her, his shoulders broad beneath a black t-shirt. As the sand crunched beneath her, Vidya let out a little cry.

Sebastian spun around. He did not smile when he saw her and Abby paused, afraid.

****

"How are you feeling, Lydie?" Elda asked, massaging aloe over Lydie's wounds.

"Better," Lydie murmured, grimacing when she bent forward and saw her hand still bandaged. "But I'm worried about Sebastian."

Elda paused, but did not reveal Sebastian's disappearance. Had someone else told Lydie?

"Why is that?" she asked.

"I dreamed he was surrounded by snakes and skin-walkers," Lydie said, her eyes huge in the firelight. "I told Abby when I saw her last night."

"You saw Abby?" Elda asked. "Down here?"

Lydie nodded.

"In the hallway. She had a bunch of stuff in her hands, and an axe, but I must have imagined that. I was pretty out of it."

Elda pursed her lips and glanced at the door.

"I will send Bridget down to check your shoulders. Okay? I need to speak with Faustine."

Elda stood and left the Healing Room, but she did not immediately go upstairs. She stopped in the room where she knew Faustine had placed the items needed to end the curse. The moment she stepped into the space, she detected Abby's presence. The young witch had been in the room. Elda looked at the glass on the table and saw the ring no longer sat on its surface.

****

Sebastian looked different. The light had gone from his eyes, and Abby took a step back, ready to turn and race back into the forest.

He held out a trembling hand, gesturing for her and she watched a single tear slip over his cheek.

"Oh, Sebastian," she choked, moving towards him, her own tears breaking free.

"Please, can I hold Vidya?" he asked.

Abby paused, feeling the tiny being pressed against her, but then she saw the sorrow in Sebastian's face and she could not resist him. Tenderly, she pulled their sleeping daughter from the baby carrier and hander her over.

"What now?" she asked, but the words had barely left her lips and Sebastian was running.

He turned and fled, exploding from the sand dune. One moment he was the man that she loved and the next he was a skin-walker. Black wings blotted out the sun as he disappeared over the lake.

****

Abby fled down the steep dune, stumbling, falling. Her outstretched arms hit the sand, and she tumbled. She tasted sand in her mouth, felt it in her hair and began to cry. The sand stuck to the wetness on her face, and she rose to her hands and knees.

"Vidya!" she screamed, choking on the word. She buried her face back in the sand, crying, not caring that it stuck to her eyelashes, slipped into her nose.

"Please, please," she whispered, not to anyone, or perhaps to that infinite someone who everyone prayed to in moments of despair. "Please, help me." She stood again and ran, continuing down the dune. Reaching the water's edge, the power surged through her and in her grief, she screamed at the tranquil lake. A spire of water exploded and rained upon her. She fought it. She wanted it to be Victor, Alva, Clyde and one more image rose at the thought of them, but she shook her head, jerked it no. Sebastian was not evil. They had not taken him from her. Sebastian had not stolen their child to give to an evil monster. He loved Vidya. He loved Vidya with the same desperate intensity that she did. He would never hurt her.

She ran down the beach, her feet sinking in the soggy ground. It was too slow. She'd never get home. She had to. She had to get to the house where Oliver and Helena and Julian would be. They would help her. But what would she tell them? How could she tell them that Sebastian had taken Vidya?

She slowed and stopped, fell to her knees and sobbed into her hands. Oh, how it hurt. Had anything ever hurt so much? As if her own heart had been ripped from her chest. She thought she could die right then. What if she never held her child again?

She thought of the diary that Dafne had left behind, of the story she told. The anguish as she walked the beach alone, all of her friends dead, her lover having betrayed her. The part of Dafne that died when she left her child with the midwife, walked out on the only hope she might have had at happiness during her lifetime.

Abby felt herself dying inside, shrinking and slipping away.

She couldn't stand up, she couldn't continue without Vidya and Sebastian.

"Abby?" the voice echoed to her across the water. She jerked her head up, searching and heard it again, further away. An echo from a world not a part of her own. It had been Sydney's voice. Sydney calling out to her. Sydney giving her strength.

She stood and ran for home.

CHAPTER 28

Oliver met Abby at the edge of the woods. Sweaty, streaked in sand and exhausted, she collapsed into his arms.

"Abby? Where's Vidya?" he whispered into the top of her head. Her curls were wet and matted. Tears streamed down her face and it took several minutes before she could speak.

"Sebastian," she choked. "He... he took her."

"He took Vidya?" he asked. He picked her up and ran for the house. Julian flung the door open before he reached it and Oliver stopped.

"Is she hurt?" Julian asked, meeting Oliver.

Abby looked wild-eyed. She jumped from Oliver's arms and charged into the house.

"Sebastian took Vidya," Oliver told him, following Abby, but she raced up the stairs and slammed her bedroom door in his face.

Abby spun in a circle, momentarily lost in her grief and fear. Vidya's purple baby blanket lay crumpled on her bed. A pair of Sebastian's worn tennis shoes sat by the bathroom door. Everything about the room looked ordinary. The occupants had just stepped out, maybe for dinner, they would return and all would be right in the world, but even as Abby allowed the crazy thought to pass her by, the truth reverberated through her like a shock wave. Sebastian had taken Vidya from her arms. He had turned into a skin-walker and carried her daughter into the sky.

Running into her closet, she crashed shoe boxes to the floor. She had tucked the concealment bag from Ula in her closet. It contained the amulet, the dagger, the ring and even the axe, but fit into a neat little shoebox. She yanked open the box she'd used and slipped it into a backpack before running to the window.

****

"What's she doing?" Julian asked, but before they could knock, they heard the window open and the sound of feet dashing across the roof.

"Shit!" Oliver yelled, running back down the stairs and hoping to intercept Abby before she leapt from the roof. She was already down and in the driver's seat of her car. Oliver reached for the door handle. She started it and squealed down the driveway.

He chased her down the driveway onto the road, losing her as she sped away.

Julian pulled next to him in the VW bus.

"Get in," he yelled.

Oliver jumped for the passenger handled and yanked as Julian slowed, but didn't stop. He plunged into the seat and pulled the door closed behind him.

"Go, go," he screamed, waving Julian forward.

****

Abby gasped, rolling over on the beach at Snake Island, struggling onto her hands and knees as another wave crashed over her. She pitched to the side and swallowed a mouthful of water. Sputtering, she stood and stumbled forward as another wave hit from behind. Her eyes blurred and her throat felt raw. The backpack had slipped off, but she pulled it back onto her shoulder.

As she left the turbulent shore, the light of the moon revealed thousands of snakes, gold and black and green, they slithered over one another, some of them sensing her and rearing up to bare their fangs. She had expected them and yet they appeared more lethal than her previous visit to the island.

She shook the amulet from the pouch around her waist and slipped it over head. Abby felt the immediate pulse of the heart close to hers. The heat seeped into her clammy skin, and she wanted to pull it away, break the connection. Fighting the urge to rip the necklace off, she turned back toward the trees. She saw him first. Sebastian walked among the snakes. They parted for him, slithering away, some of them rubbing affectionately around his ankles. His face looked drawn, his eyes were hollow pools of blue in his gaunt face. In only a day, the magnetic life force had waned. He appeared sallow and lost.

Within the necklace, Abby felt a jolt and the edges of consciousness grew blurry. Sebastian turned as if sensing her watching him. An instant of agony stole over his face. Abby saw him as he truly was, a man trapped in the heart of darkness, desperate to run to her, but rooted in place.

As her own grasp on reality faded, she watched a change in Sebastian. His features shifted, growing narrower, his eyes black holes against yellowing whites. Abby felt she too had transformed. She now watched from behind another set of eyes Kanti's.

Kanti released a cry that seemed to shake the ground beneath them. The agony of her journey erupted through that sound, and then she turned to the house in the distance and began to sing.

****

Oliver swam beneath the water, taking short sips when he surfaced, following the trail of energy that Abby had left behind. The turbulent waves thrashed above him. When he came up for air, he swallowed water instead. When he finally reached the rocky shore, he rushed forward, fighting against a tide trying to draw him back into the lake.

As he found dry ground, he spotted Abby and Sebastian. He watched their transformations in muted terror. He saw Abby stumbling from the beach, Sebastian moving through the woods, and then the two of them locked in a stare that seemed to stop time. And then, more horrifying than each moment before, they began to look different. As he stood, jaw slack, he understood that Clyde and Kanti watched each other across that stony beach. Clyde's mouth stretched wide. His grin held no humor, only a malicious satisfaction. Kanti faced the house, her lips moving, her arms raised to the sky.

Oliver shifted his gaze to the old house, recoiling as fire exploded through one of the upstairs windows.

Clyde, in Sebastian's body, howled as if he felt the fire.

Kanti bared her teeth and broke into a run, sprinting across the beach with her arms outstretched as if she intended to claw the eyes from his head.

A glimmer of Abby appeared in Kanti's face. Oliver stared as Abby reached up and ripped the amulet from her chest, flinging it away. At the same moment, Clyde's features melted away and Sebastian reappeared. He fell to his knees and held his arms out for Abby. She barreled into him, tears streaming down her face.

Oliver saw Sebastian's lips moving. He turned and pointed at the house.

"Oliver, watch out," Julian's voice barely reached him in the wind ripping across the lake.

Oliver dove to the sand, rolling to the side. He followed Julian's gaze to Alva who stood on the beach. A dozen or more skin-walkers took flight from the trees. Alva opened his arms wide and a black cavity appeared in the center of his chest. Somehow the skin-walkers flew into him, disappeared into the black abyss. Alva's human body twisted and warped. A huge skin-walker, as large as the house, stretched its leathery wings. Its wolfish face turned to face them.

Oliver looked back toward Sebastian and Abby.

Sebastian screamed, "Go," at Abby and shoved her toward the house that had started to burn.

It was all happening so fast. Oliver watched Julian's mouth fall open in horror at the sight of the enormous skin-walker taking shape. Julian did not flee, but charged full-speed at the creature, pulling a black dagger from his waist.

****

The moon seemed to fall out of the sky into the yawning mouth of the giant skin-walker. Its black eyes reflected the witches as they stood on the shore of the island watching the beast seem to consume the world.

Abby looked at the cloth in her hand, heavy. Sebastian had told her not to open it, to take it beneath the house and put it in the hand of Clyde.

"Go," he screamed, and she turned back to him. Time seemed to slow as Sebastian stood and pulled the knife that Oliver had given him from a sheath against his leg.

He ran at the monster, launching himself into the sky, plunging the dagger down.

Abby couldn't save them both. She turned and fled into the old house, holding up her hand to block the smoke and fire that lapped at her skin. She whispered an incantation and a bubble of water surrounded her head, allowing her several deep breaths before it burst. She created another bubble, diving to the side as a wall crashed down. Where basement stairs should have stood, she found a gaping black hole. She descended into the hole, trying to hold the floor above her, but it crumbled and broke beneath her weight. She dropped into the small space, the earth cool beneath her feet.

Darkness met her eyes as she searched the far corners, but then she saw it, a pulsing red light tucked in the far end, down a path she had to crawl through. She felt the tightness of the space, the dirt walls pressing in overhead and against her belly. A small cavern opened and on a marble slab she saw the emaciated body of Clyde. Skeletal, with skin stretched over his bones, she recoiled at the sight of him. She saw the bones of his teeth through his pale lips, practically gone. And next to him, nestled in a cardboard box, her pale eyelids quivering, lay Vidya. Abby surged toward her, crying out and wanting to rip the tiny filaments that ran from her beautiful child into the nearly dead thing lying next to her. As her fingers clutched the tubes, she stopped. She needed to do it right otherwise she might hurt her child, split her soul and allow some of it to travel with Clyde.

Carefully, she removed the patches stuck to Vidya's head and slid the needles from the veins in her arms and legs. She had to bite her lip to keep from beating the monster next to her in an absolute rage. She wanted to kill him, remove him from the world, but if he were not ended properly, he would travel into those he'd cursed. He might live in her Vidya forever.

Abby pulled the amulet from her pouch.

"Goodbye Kanti," she whispered placing it around his neck.

****

Oliver watched Julian attack the skin-walker. He stabbed at the giant beast, but it easily flung him aside. Julian landed on the beach where snakes slithered from the forest towards him. Oliver ran to his aid, sending blasts of energy into the earth around the snakes. They flung into the air. Oliver bent close to Julian, offering him his hand. As Julian stood they both paused watching the rocky shore near the house. A figure stood there, a dark cloak concealing his face. A pentagram, seemingly made of light, pulsed on his chest.

Before they could consider him, the skin-walker brought a huge leathery wing down on the beach. The ground shook and Oliver jumped aside as the beast's jaws snapped toward him.

Sebastian screamed and sunk his blade into the skin-walker's back. His scream tore across the island. The land shook and trees groaned as their roots pulled from the earth. One tree crashed into the burning house. The leaves erupted in flames and soon more of the forest burned. Snakes appeared in droves on the rocky shore.

"Into the water," Julian screamed as they scrambled away from the fleeing snakes.

Oliver dove beneath the surf as the waves crashed over them. The skin-walker too had backed into the lake. It shifted from side to side snapping at Sebastian who still clung to its back. Oliver pulled a dagger from the sheath at his ankle and swam down, hacking at the beast's leg.

****

As the amulet touched his skin, Clyde's eyes flickered open. Black chasms stared at her. His mouth opened, and Abby stopped, transfixed by the black churning hole within him. A spiral of darkness that seemed to descend forever stared back at her and somewhere within it, a sound emanated, called for her. She stepped closer, reaching a hand toward the darkness.

A figure appeared near Abby's elbow, pushing her gently aside. Glancing up, breaking her momentary stupor, Abby looked into light-filled blue eyes. The man, thousands of years old surely, looked at her from the folds of his crinkled skin. He nodded toward Vidya and Abby understood - she needed to take her baby and run. She lifted Vidya into her arms, leaving the backpack and moving from the crawl space, watching the figure. He lifted the cloth wrapped item Sebastian had handed Abby. She had forgotten all about it. Clyde's mouth opened wider. An ear-splitting scream erupted and Vidya started to wail. The old man opened the cloth and Abby saw a purplish stone glowing bright. The stranger placed the stone on Clyde's chest.

Abby shielded Vidya as the stone seemed to explode with light. Dark shadows swept passed Abby into the blazing vortex. It pulled and yawned, and though she felt the tug, it did not try to take her. As the light blinked out, Abby stared into the empty crawl space. She stood for a second watching the vacant slab where Clyde's body had likely lain for hundreds of years.

Overhead the house groaned, collapsing beneath the fire. Abby ran.

CHAPTER 29

Oliver poked his head above the surface, took a gulp of air, and then dove again. He pulled his arm back, blinded by the streaming black blood of the skin-walker, ready to chop again at his leg. In the murky water, he could not find the beast. He rose to the surface, fighting to see, but the skin-walker no longer towered above him. Oliver spotted Julian as he too lifted from the water.

"Where did it go?" Oliver yelled.

"It disappeared," Julian called back. "I was holding its wing and it vanished from my hand."

Oliver shook his head, incredulous. He dove beneath the surface. The black blood of the beast still streamed in rivulets, but already the turbulent water had begun to disperse it. Oliver searched for Sebastian, and then remembering Abby pushed back toward the shore. As he struggled from the surf, he started to blast the ground to remove the snakes, but they too had vanished.

****

For days they searched the lake for Sebastian. Abby plunged in and out for hours. The witches of Ula gathered on the shore of Snake Island.

With the combined stories of Abby, Oliver and Julian, they knew that a strange man with a pentacle on his chest had placed a glowing stone in Clyde's hand and moments later the evil had ended.

Julian and Oliver had told Abby they saw Sebastian pulled into the lake as he fought the skin-walker. That was the last anyone had seen of him.

Abby crawled onto the shore, panting and sat down hard on the rocks. Lydie came to her and paused. She lifted her arms overhead and a wave of heat descended over Abby, drying her instantly. Despite all of their magic, none of the witches of Ula had found a trace of Sebastian and Abby knew what they were all thinking. He had vanished with Clyde and the skin-walker.

They drove back and forth in Faustine's whaler, but found nothing. Had the skin-walker consumed him? Had he drowned?

Abby searched for a sense of him, but exhaustion muted every emotion. She could sense nothing except the trickle of cold fear that snaked down her spine. Torn between holding her child and searching for her lost love, she felt she might split in two.

Helena sat with Vidya in another boat. Vidya watched the witches traipse in and out of the tide. Seagulls swooped overhead and several settled on the boats bow to be near her.

"Abby," Faustine said, pausing beside her. "Elda has just contacted me." He tapped a finger to his temple and Abby understood that Elda had reached out to him telepathically. "The Sky Mothers called her to the cave of Elders. They have news of Sebastian."

Abby wrinkled her brow.

"But they're in Australia," Abby argued, not understanding, and then something dawned on her. The moment the old man had placed the stone in Clyde's hand, Clyde had vanished. Had the stone been the portal that Clyde and Meghan used to escape to Australia three centuries before?

"It's best if we go to Ula," Faustine told her.

****

Abby watched impassive as Kit, Liam, and Hannah stepped from the Boston whaler onto the dock at Ula. Kit whistled and nodded toward the castle.

"It's imposing, that's for sure," she said.

Oliver greeted them and he gave Kit a stiff peck on the cheek before leading them to the castle where Abby stood with Helena by her side.

Elda had Vidya in the Healing Room. She had offered to give her a bath in the giant tub.

"Hey'ya mate," Liam told Oliver slapping him on the back. Hannah smiled sadly at Abby and took her hands.

"I'm so sorry, Abby. I know how you feel."

Abby forced a smile and nodded. Of anyone, Hannah probably was the closet to knowing how she felt, but that didn't make her feel any closer to the beautiful witch. Even in moments of sincerity, Hannah's warmth never extended to her eyes. Sharp little chips of blue with no true empathy watched her curiously.

Kit, on the other hand, said nothing, but squeezed her shoulder and Abby felt a rush of kindness pour through her.

"I wish we were here under better circumstances," Liam told her, taking her hands. "I owe Sebastian my life and I want you to know that's why I did what I did. I hope you can forgive me."

Abby narrowed her eyes at him, but had no interest in offering forgiveness until she had the whole story.

They settled in the library and Liam began to talk.

"Sebastian came to me three weeks ago," Liam said.

"In Australia?" Oliver interrupted, but Abby silenced him with a stare. She wanted the truth, uninterrupted. "Sorry," he told her.

"Yes. I was at the house that Hannah and I share on the beach. He knocked on the door. You can imagine my surprise when I saw him standing there. I invited him in for a beer, thinking you guys were all visiting the Sky Mothers. Then he revealed to me that he had discovered the portal that Clyde and Meghan had used to flee Michigan three hundred years ago."

Liam looked healthy. His scrawny body had filled out. His hair had grown back in and his eyes had lost their yellow.

"He dug it out of ground near the foundation of Clyde's childhood home. Where you guys live, apparently. When he touched the rock, it transported him to Clyde's room in Australia."

Abby thought of the times Sebastian had come into the house with dirt beneath his fingernails. Why hadn't she forced the truth from him then?

"He found the portal back to Michigan in Clyde's room," Liam continued. "It was the same rock shoved deep into the cave wall. Insane to think I never touched that damn rock. A year in that hell and I had freedom at my fingertips."

Hannah wrapped an arm behind his back and hugged him close. She kissed his neck, and Abby felt an irrational urge to stride across the room and slap her as hard as she could.

"He told me about the curse, everything. He was there for two hours, filling me in on the bloodlines and the human who succumbed to the evil call every century. He told me that he couldn't stop it. It was in his blood, his bones, his brains; it was like cancer. The only way to save you was to sacrifice every last thread of the darkness. Sebastian was confident he had come closest to resisting the call, but it was taking him. The urge to allow Clyde had become a constant itch, a buzzing in his brain. He said he thought he understood what it felt like to be an addict. The problem was he'd never done the drug, but he knew it was only a matter of time. Nothing any of you did was going to change his fate, but he would not destroy you in the process. He would die first."

Abby closed her eyes and braced her hands on the armrests of her chair, but of course that couldn't stop her world from spinning.

Liam continued.

"Sebastian had already spoken with Meghan. He promised her Clyde and in exchange she bewitched the portal so that it would pull all of Clyde's dark magic back with him. Sebastian told me that Clyde continued to draw power from Meghan. He said that he was going to give in, let the darkness take him. When he had found Clyde's whereabouts and had all the items that he drew power from, he would use the portal to force all of them back to Australia. In order to find Clyde and put the portal in his hand, he had to join him."

"So, he took Vidya," Abby breathed, remembering the moment on the sand dune when Sebastian had begged to hold their daughter. Desperate to draw him back to her, Abby handed her over, and Sebastian had turned and ran, becoming a skin-walker with their baby tucked in a pouch beneath him.

Abby gritted her teeth and tried not to speak.

"I tried to talk him out of it. He cut me off and swore that he'd set Clyde upon us if I spoke a word of it to anyone. It hurt him to threaten me. I could tell, but he was desperate, Abby. He didn't believe he had any other choice. As long as he and Clyde both lived, you would be in danger, your daughter would be in danger. I agreed to help him."

"What did you do?" Abby whispered, afraid to know.

Liam looked away, the color draining from his face.

"He left me a bag, made me swear not to open it. I had to go into the dream wood into the lowest layer, the Forest of Purgatory. He distracted Meghan while I put the bag in Clyde's old room and then made my escape."

"What was in the bag?" Abby demanded.

"I don't know," Liam admitted. "I thought it was something he would need when he came back, but then yesterday…" he paused.

"Tell me!" Abby shrieked and the teacup in Hannah's hand exploded.

Hannah recoiled, but Kit had thrown up her hands and the pieces stopped their trajectory. They hovered in the air.

Liam shrank deeper into his seat.

"The whole place went up in flames," he said. "The bridge, the forest beyond it. The dream wood is gone."

Abby put her face into her hands and cried.

"It pulled him back, didn't it? Sebastian had become part of the dark magic so it pulled him back as well?"

Liam nodded.

"I think so. I was sure he would escape. He implied that after they were all drawn back, he would get out. I never thought…" Liam didn't finish his statement.

Abby stood and left the library. She walked from the castle and wound through the forest to the crumbling stone steps that led to the floating garden. As she emerged in the garden, the realization that Sebastian was gone hit her full force. Falling to her knees, she let out a terrible sob of anguish. As she lay on the ground, the flowers seemed to gather around her.

****

"An ancient saved you, Abby. Saved us all, perhaps," Elda told her.

Abby sat in the oratory on a stiff wooden stool. Sunlight beamed through the stained-glass window. The patterns of light on the stone floor were beautiful but everything of beauty made Abby ache for Sebastian.

"An ancient?" she asked, thinking of the old man who appeared beneath the Serpent House. Ancient seemed like an appropriate description.

"Yes." Elda opened a thick book with rough papyrus pages.

Abby saw a drawing of a cloaked figure with a pentacle of light on his chest.

"Until now, I've believed they were a myth of sorts in the world of witches. A way to keep the peace. When I was a young witch, the elders were always threatening us with the ancients to keep us in line, but nobody ever saw one. Eventually the practice of speaking about them went out of style."

"I don't understand," Abby said, pulling off her moonstone wedding ring and staring into the glistening surface. If she looked hard enough, maybe she could catch a glimpse of Sebastian in the iridescent stone.

"The story of the ancients was that they righted wrongs, they stepped in when the balance between light and dark was shifting. No one really knows where they come from, but it is said they are the original witches. The very first witches to ever exist, and that all the witches in the world descend from them. They hold the source of all magic within their grasp."

"Why would they help me? You've lived hundreds of years and they never showed up. Why now?" Abby asked somewhat bitterly.

Sebastian had handed her the portal. She had not known it at the time, but he intended for Abby to send him to the dream wood, but she had failed. Left to her, the curse would not have been broken, but she would still have Sebastian.

Elda nodded as if hearing her thoughts.

"I believe he appeared to prevent a great injustice," Elda offered. "Why now? Why in this instance when they have not stepped in for so many others?" Elda shrugged. "I don't know. Perhaps they saw a future in this curse too terrible to allow."

Abby considered her words. Was Sebastian's sacrifice actually the best possible outcome for them all? The ache in her heart said no. But what if she sat mourning Vidya instead of Sebastian?

"Vidya was connected to Clyde's body," Abby whispered, struggling to get the words out. "If Sebastian were only pretending to join Clyde, why would he do that? He gave him our child."

Elda blew out a breath and stood from her chair, grimacing as if her back ached from sitting.

"Faustine read about the power of three in the Egyptian text for immortality. If the spirit survived for three hundred years, the Gods would grant them a new body, a baby born within their lineage. Your Vidya would have been that for Clyde. I believe that is why Clyde was not satisfied with Victor. He intended to turn Sebastian and would stop at nothing to attain that goal. Sebastian was strong, but all the energy that Clyde had amassed over three centuries was directed at pulling him towards the darkness."

"He couldn't resist it."

"I believe so. But Sebastian may not have given Vidya to Clyde. Alva or Victor or any other Vepar on Snake Island might have grabbed the child and taken her to Clyde. We will probably never know."

Abby looked at Elda doubtfully. She wanted to believe that Sebastian had not been the one, needed to believe it.

"My heart breaks for you, Abby. I wish that Sebastian had not perished, but I understand that if an ancient had not appeared your future would have been a horror that we cannot even imagine. For that I am thankful."

Abby stood. She wasn't angry at Elda's words, but had heard enough. She needed to see her daughter and get lost in the scent of her baby's skin. Perhaps then she could begin to heal the wound in her heart.

****

"Are you sure you want to stay here, tonight?" Helena asked again as she settled Abby into her and Sebastian's bed.

Abby could smell him, feel him, though he was not there, maybe he was not anywhere.

"Yes, Helena. I'm sure. I need to be home, at least for tonight."

Helena nodded and patted Abby's arm.

"You call me if you need me, honey. I'm going to rock Vidya and put her to sleep in the nursery, give you a little break."

Abby nodded, already rolling away from Helena and burying herself in Sebastian's pillow. She was so exhausted that even grief didn't find her as she slipped into sleep.

Hours later, Abby woke to the smell of smoke. In the darkness of her bedroom, she stood, disoriented, and fell from the bed.

"Vidya?" she choked, searching the bed for her daughter.

And then she remembered Helena had put Vidya in the nursery so that Abby could sleep. The smoke that had seemed to fill the room a moment earlier was gone. Had it all been a dream?

She moved down the hallway, sleepy, on the edges of consciousness and pushed into Vidya's room. She stopped hard. Above Vidya's bed a strange image greeted her. A ball of fire, an orb of water, and a mass of rock floated in a circular motion, around and around, like a cosmic mobile. She crept closer to the bassinet. Vidya lay within it, her blue eyes wide and twinkling, and a smile playing on her lips. Her chubby little hands waved and the cycle of elements flowed with her movements. She squeezed one of her hands into a fist and the fireball shot to the curtain. It lit the fabric and they were immediately engulfed in flames.

"Oh," Abby gasped and stumbled back, shaking her head as if that might make sense of the scene before her. She threw her hands up and sent a wave of water crashing over the flames, but already they'd leaped to the carpet and the ceiling.

Abby snatched Vidya from the bassinet and ran from the room, pounding down the stairs.

"Helena!" she screamed.

The witch appeared behind her on the stairs.

"Are we being attacked?" Helena asked, also disoriented.

Abby flung open the front door and Helena followed her into the night.

"Vidya," Abby sputtered, pointing at the window. "Vidya somehow…"

Helena looked at her, bewildered, and then glanced down at Vidya, the fire reflected in her huge blue eyes.

Abby hurried to her car and tucked Vidya into her car seat with the door propped open. She returned to Helena and together they sent gusts of water billowing at the blaze. It did nothing. The house burned.

At the edge of the forest hundreds of birds had flown to the trees. They filled the branches and the ground below, the flames reflected in their black eyes.

CHAPTER 30

Two Years Later

"Vidya," Abby called to her daughter, who stood on the end of the dock staring into the placid Lake Michigan waters. She held a pink fishing pole in one hand a neon yellow net in the other.

"Mama, Bossy ate my fish," she shrieked, pointing at the eagle perched on the huge metal rod at the end of their dock.

Abby could see the remnants of a fish hanging from his taloned feet. She almost thought he smirked at her as if to say, "I am an eagle after all," but since he couldn't talk, she surely imagined it.

Beyond the dock a head broke the surface of the water. She watched his tan chest follow. In his hands, he held a long slender trout.

"Daddy!" Vidya squealed, reaching for the fish.

Oliver handed the trout to the tiny light-haired girl who waved it wildly in the air before Bossy swooped from his perch, reaching with a taloned claw. Before the eagle could snatch the fish, Abby flicked her fingers at the lake and a streak of water rose up and sprayed him. He veered and flew away, ruffling his feathers, and shedding water droplets as he rose higher.

Vidya had called Oliver *Daddy* for the first time just weeks before. When it happened, Abby had almost corrected her. The name caused a twisting, aching pull in her stomach, but she'd fought the desire to tell her daughter the truth. It was not that she intended to hide Sebastian from Vidya, only that she wanted her to be allowed to choose Oliver. He was, after all, the man raising her. Her real father, Sebastian, was merely a phantom, a man that Vidya would know through stories and photographs tucked in albums.

Oliver grabbed Vidya from the dock and lifted her high.

"Swim," she screamed. "Swimmie, swimmie."

Oliver grinned at Abby and dove under the water. With Vidya perched on his back, Oliver swam along the shore. At the edge of the beach, she climbed off and swam on her own, an awkward doggie paddle that sent plumes of water in every direction. A row of black birds flew to the water's edge, hopping along the shore beside her. The birds always hovered close to Abby's magical daughter, but since the arrival of the eagle, known to

Vidya as Bossy, the birds kept their distance. He had staked his claim over the girl and smaller birds understood the pecking order.

Oliver's blond hair had grown long, nearly to his shoulders. He shook his head like a dog and Vidya squealed, delighted. He tied it back in a ponytail and jogged to where Abby stood at the edge of the yard.

He swept her against him, his body cold and wet, and kissed her. She felt the heat sucked from her own body as his lips sought hers. She leaned into it, savoring the chill of his skin suddenly slick with goosebumps.

When he pulled back, she saw the question in his eyes.

"If you prefer she doesn't say it, we can talk to her," he said, hiding his own feelings behind his ever-present smile.

"No." Abby shook her head. "You are her daddy now."

He grinned and lifted Abby high before tossing her over his shoulder and splashing into the lake.

****

"Lydie!" Abby exclaimed, hugging the young witch who had somehow grown into a young woman since Abby last saw her. "You look gorgeous."

Lydie smiled, twirling around.

"Helena said I could choose my own costume this year so I'm going as a butterfly." She opened her arms and her gown extended to reveal flowing silk wings in black and copper.

Abby had only attended one All Hallow's Ball more than two years before. As the memory of stepping through the mirror with Sebastian rose in her mind, she returned her focus to Lydie.

"It's beautiful Lydie. How's Florida?"

Lydie grinned.

"Awesome! Aunt Cammi and I go fishing, we hike the Everglades. I'm even enrolled in school for the fall," Lydie gushed.

"Human school?"

"Human all the way, but Elda has me set up with a summer program in Italy. Witches only." She winked. The door behind Abby opened and Lydie squealed. "Oliver!"

She rushed into him, nearly toppling him over.

"Lyds!" he roared, catching her and spinning her around. "You've grown five inches since December!"

"Hardly," she laughed, punching his shoulder. "Two if I'm lucky. But I have been learning to drive."

"What? A car? Or an air boat while you hunt gators?" Oliver asked, holding out Lydie's arms so he could admire her butterfly wings.

"A car, silly. Cammi owns a Firebird."

"Oliver," Helena chastised, sweeping into the room in a frothy white gown studded with glass bubbles. "I need to invoke your stardust."

Oliver rolled his eyes.

"Stardust?" Lydie grinned.

"Why does Abby get the celestial rain and I have stardust?" Oliver asked.

Abby demonstrated by grabbing her midnight blue dress and waving the skirt toward them. A mist of warm rain fell over their heads.

"Because she is a water element, you fool. In case you forgot, you are earth. Now stand still," Helena demanded.

"Where's Vidya?" Lydie asked, looking around the library as if the toddler might be playing on the rug.

"With Grammy Becky," Abby responded, taking out her compact and flipping open the lid. Faustine had created a magic baby monitor. The mirror in Abby's compact allowed her to peer through every mirror in her mother's house. She spotted Vidya and Becky in the sitting room reading a book. Her dad stood at the bookshelf thumbing through paperbacks.

Her parents had moved into Sydney's lake house six months after Sebastian disappeared. During that time, Abby and Vidya had lived at Ula. Oliver had stepped in to help Abby and a year after Sebastian vanished, they had begun officially seeing each other. Six months later, Oliver surprised her by purchasing a house close to Sydney's. Her mother had been delighted. Abby herself had been unsure about returning to Trager, but Oliver's enthusiasm got the best of her.

Abby held out the mirror so Lydie could see Vidya.

"She's getting so big!" Lydie exclaimed, frowning. "I want to come visit soon, okay?"

"We'd love it, Lyds!" Oliver called out as Helena pulled at the pouch near his waist. "We never get to use the magic rooms seeing as how most of our friends are human."

He mimed gagging and Helena gave him a little push. He nearly toppled over, straightening himself up and holding his head high.

"Is that any way to treat a cosmic lover?" he asked, looking past Helena to Abby.

His blue eyes bore into hers and she experienced the spread of warmth and gratitude that she often felt when Oliver looked at her. Theirs was a different kind of love. Passionate in its way, but placid compared to her time with Sebastian. She tried not to compare them, but often couldn't help it.

"It's time," Faustine said, striding into the room with Elda on his arm. They were dressed in plain dark robes having chosen to forego costumes that year. Abby envied the ease of their wardrobe as she stepped to the mirror in her complicated gown.

Oliver took her hand and kissed it.

"See you on the other side," he whispered, smiling mischievously.

****

Abby danced until her feet grew sore. She laughed and drank champagne and kissed Oliver beneath a sky bewitched to reflect four moons and a million stars. Sometime after midnight, she slipped away citing a need for fresh air.

Alone on the veranda, Abby watched the distant forest far below. She examined the silhouette of dark trees, their branches thick with the dying leaves of autumn.

She had glimpsed the dead on that night as expected. Sydney's face peeking at her from the crowd of costumed witches, Dafne traipsing down a long staircase only to vanish into thin air. She had even seen Ezra, only for an instant, as she slipped behind a curtain and disappeared. But she had sought only one face that evening and not a fragment of him had appeared - Sebastian. How could he not arrive on this night - All Hallow's Eve - when the veil between the living and the dead vanished?

Two years had passed without a sight of her lost love. He no longer tormented her dreams, but this year, especially, she hoped to catch him for just a moment.

"Sebastian..." she whispered, staring at the moonstone ring she had moved to her right hand, but still never took off.

Abby sighed and pulled the navy mask from her face. She drew her thick braid over one shoulder, and allowed her eyes to linger another moment on the dark forest below.

A movement caught her eye, subtle and quick. She squinted, trying to make out the shape. It had looked like a man, tall and dark, slipping into the woods. A breath had caught in her diaphragm and she let it out. Only shadows greeted her as she searched the tree line.

She turned and walked back to the double doors, glancing back a final time. Another movement caught her eye, not on the ground, but in the sky. A dark shape rose from the shadowy woods. A skin-walker soared away from the castle, a silhouette beneath the glowing moon.

AUTHOR'S NOTE

I love characters. For me that's the heart of writing and reading. I would love to hear about your experience with my characters and what other fictional characters you love. Reading has truly shaped my life and there's nothing more amazing than connecting with other readers who share passions similar to my own. I write as J.R. Erickson, though my legal name is Jacki Riegle. I live in Northern Michigan with my excavator husband and my beautiful little boy.

Don't forget to check out the next book in the Born of Shadows Series. Visit my author website www.jrericksonauthor.com for more information about upcoming book releases.

Made in the USA
Middletown, DE
05 December 2025

24184440R00116